DEDICATION

For Akiko, Akira and Kai.

DAVID BLAKE

THE DI TANNER SERIES

"And the LORD said unto Cain, Where is Abel thy brother? And he said, I know not: Am I my brother's keeper?"
Genesis 4:9

- PROLOGUE -

Friday, August 24th, 2004

THE LIGHTEST TOUCH of a passing breeze pushed gently back against the tall bank of elegant reeds that crowded in around an old wooden pontoon. Standing on its crooked broken planks was a man, his eyes filled with tears, cold muddy water cascading down his sodden threadbare clothes. At his feet lay the bodies of two tiny children, one a boy, the other a girl, their tangled wet hair clinging to faces plump but ashen grey.

He lifted his head to the sound of a radio, drifting through the warm summer's air. It was coming from a cottage set back from the water's edge, its grey thatched roof floating above a surrounding sea of corn-yellow reeds.

With one last desperate look at the tiny bodies, resting by his feet, he tore his gaze away to step over the pontoon's narrow wooden decking.

Nudging through the dry brittle reeds, he emerged out onto a cracked, sun-baked lawn littered with plastic toys, their colours faded by the high summer's sun. With the radio growing louder, he stopped to take in the back of the cottage, searching the windows for signs of life.

The hollow screech of a chair being scraped over a hard tiled floor brought his eyes to an open window. There he could see the bleached blonde hair of a woman, reaching up to pull something down from a cupboard above.

With a juddering breath, he pulled himself up to begin picking his way over the toy-strewn lawn, up to a series of steps to a veranda, a half-open door just beyond. With his hand resting on the handle, he held his breath to push it open.

'Is that you, darling?' the woman called out, her back facing him as she busied herself with something on a kitchen counter. 'Did you see the children?'

Without responding, the man stepped silently inside.

'They're in the garden somewhere,' the woman continued. 'I've let them play out there for most of the day. It's been so hot, I could hardly keep them in.'

The man's eyes were drawn down to a small kitchen table. Lying there, next to a scarred wooden chopping board, was a kitchen knife, its blade glistening red in the slowly setting sun. Leaning over, he picked it up to spend a moment turning the blade over in his hand. As fresh tears began spilling down the sides of his face, he fixed his jaw to start edging his way forward, closing the gap between himself and where the woman stood, her hands now buried inside the steaming soapy water of a large kitchen sink.

'Maybe you could call them in for dinner?' he heard her ask, lifting out a plate to leave it dripping on the side. 'It won't be ready for another ten minutes, but it will take them that long to wash their hands.'

The man now stood directly behind her, the breath

from his nostrils gently pressing against stray hairs on top of her head. He glanced down, over her shoulder, to see her hands working furiously under turbulent pink water, soapy bubbles glistening red.

He took another half-step closer to slide an empty hand around the woman's delicate narrow waist.

'You're soaking wet!' the woman complained, nudging him back with a pointed elbow. 'What on Earth have you been doing?'

With the knife held firmly in the other hand, he lifted his arm over her head to drop down around her neck.

'Honestly, darling, I really don't have time for this.'

His mouth just inches away from her ear, he opened his mouth. 'I've been hearing them too,' he whispered, barely loud enough to be heard.

The woman froze, her hands clenched around a dented saucepan.

'The reeds,' the man continued, 'they've started talking to me too.'

He eased his head back, waiting for the woman to reply. When no words came, he leaned in again.

'I'm sorry, darling, but I don't have a choice. I have to do what they say.'

With that he gave her ear a delicate kiss before wrenching his arm back, the knife at the end opening up her throat to leave a line of crimson blood spurting out over the sink, splattering hard against the windowpane beyond.

- CHAPTER ONE -

Sunday, 8th August

WITH HIS SAILS tied down, and the end of his yacht's long wooden boom resting against the crutches at the back, John Tanner motored his way slowly up the River Thurne. It had been almost two years since he'd last gazed out over the Broads' vast open horizon, and as a full moon slid out from a cluster of clouds above, he shook his head clear of the many memories that were already beginning to creep their way into his mind.

The top of a dark canvas sail emerging out from a gathering mist ahead brought his attention back to the task at hand, that of finding a suitable mooring; somewhere far enough from other boats to give him the solitude he'd come to crave, but not too far, as his eyes were already beginning to close.

He cast his eyes over to a thick bank of reeds on his left, searching for something to tie his yacht to, but there was nothing there, nothing he could see at least. The nearest secluded public mooring he knew of was a hidden narrow dyke, just past Martham Ferry, but he wasn't sure he'd be able to stay awake that long.

He lifted his head to gaze up at the craft still drifting silently towards him. It was an old gaff-rigged sailing boat, similar to his but half the size, and no cabin to take shelter in, giving Tanner clear sight of the tall thin man he could see standing at the back, a bony hand resting over a carved wooden tiller.

As the boat steered over to the left, Tanner kept right, as were the rules of the road. It was also Tanner's responsibility to keep clear. He may have been at the helm of a forty-two-foot sailing boat, but it was currently being driven by its engine, and motor-powered vessels were always supposed to give way to those under sail.

As the boat began drifting slowly past, Tanner glanced over at the person behind the helm, lifting a hand in friendly acknowledgement.

Without turning, the man nodded back, his face hidden in part by the worn peeked sailing cap he had pulled down over his eyes, but also the shadow cast by the moon hanging low in the sky behind him.

About to look away, Tanner's attention was drawn to what was lying at the bottom of the open boat. For a briefest of moments he thought he saw something move, but when he looked again, all he could see was an old tarpaulin cover pulled over whatever it was that the man was busily transporting.

Realising he'd allowed his yacht to drift in towards the starboard-side bank, he pushed the helm away from him to correct his course, bringing the boat back into the middle of the river, its surface sparkling gently in the light of the moon. Happy with his direction, he glanced back over his shoulder, expecting to see the sail of the boat he'd just passed drift slowly away. But it was nowhere to be seen.

Unable to think where it could have gone, Tanner lifted himself up onto the balls of his feet, craning his neck as he did. Presuming its helm must have dropped his sails as soon as he'd passed to pull over into the reeds, Tanner shrugged his shoulders to return his attention to the river ahead.

Ten minutes later, Tanner zipped the collar of his salt encrusted sailing jacket up against the cold night air as he turned into the hidden dyke he'd been aiming for.

Grateful to find only a single varnished motorboat moored up there, he picked a spot on the port-side bank where the wind was coming from. Turning the boat in, he slotted the engine's lever into neutral. As the boat continued gliding forward, he pulled the tiller a little towards him before launching himself out of the cockpit, up onto the walkway, stepping lightly towards the yacht's bow at the front. There he fetched a mooring line from off the deck, giving the fender he found lying next to it a kick at the same time, leaving it to fall over the side to dangle down between the hull and the swiftly approaching grass bank. The moment the boat was close enough, he stepped onto the grass to heave at the rope, bringing his old wooden yacht further up the dyke towards a nearby mooring post. As the boat crept forward, he stooped down to quickly loop the line around it. Making it fast, he strode back towards the cockpit, just in time to pick up the line at the back to help glide it in towards him. With that line tied off as well, he stepped back on board to turn the engine off.

Waiting for it to splutter into silence, he took a quiet peaceful moment to gaze about, casting his eyes over at where the land met the sky. The wind had dropped to almost nothing. The only sound was the water, lapping gently against the hull beneath his feet. Having spent the last twenty-one months at sea, drifting aimlessly from port to port, never willing to stay anywhere for more than a few weeks, a large part of him felt as if he was home.

With a wave of exhaustion rolling over the top of him, desperate for sleep he forced himself back up to the front of the boat. There, he knelt down to prise a rectangular-shaped lip from off the deck to haul out a bulky white tarpaulin cover. Lifting it up, he slung it over the cabin roof, just behind the mast.

A shuffling noise from the public carpark behind had him turning his head to stare out through the cool moonlit night. There he could see a lanky young lad weaving his way over the grass towards the old wooden motorboat about a hundred yards ahead. The way he was walking, he'd clearly had a skinful.

With an amused smirk, Tanner returned to the job of getting the yacht's cover on, rolling it out over the boom to eventually tie off at the back, before finally allowing himself to turn in for the night.

- CHAPTER TWO -

Monday, 9th August

THE AGONISING SOUND of a horrific scream jolted Tanner awake. In the eerie silence that followed, he lifted his head from his pillow, straining his ears for further noise. But all he could hear was nothing more ominous than the distant chatter of birds, busily greeting an already risen sun.

Questioning whether or not the sound had been real, or part of one of his normal harrowing dreams, he tugged his phone out from under his pillow to check the time. It wasn't even half-past seven. Far earlier than he'd normally get up.

Knowing he'd be unlikely to get back to sleep, he rolled over to stare up at the sloping cabin roof, still thinking about what he'd heard, or at least what he thought he had. It was then that he heard something else; the muffled but all-too distinctive sound of someone crying.

Realising it had to be coming from the vintage motorboat he'd seen the night before, he threw himself out of bed to pull on the clothes he'd been wearing the previous day, a pair of torn faded jeans and a threadbare navy roll neck jumper.

Emerging out into the cockpit, he tucked his phone into his back pocket, hooked his bare feet into a pair of old crocks, opened the canvas entrance and stepped up onto the boat's side to peer up the dyke towards the motor launch. The sound was much clearer now. There was definitely someone crying on board.

Stepping down to the grass bank, he hurried over to the boat.

Arriving at its open cockpit, he peered inside to see a skinny teenage boy sitting on a bench seat, his head buried deep in his bony white hands.

'Are you OK?' Tanner asked, crouching down.

The boy stared up, his lips trembling, his eyes red with tears.

'It's – it's my d-dad,' he stuttered, turning his attention to the stairwell leading down into the cabin below. 'He's – he's been hurt.'

'Hurt?' Tanner enquired, leaning inside, trying to follow the boy's gaze. 'In what way?'

'I'm – I'm not sure.'

'Have you called an ambulance?'

The boy shook his head to clasp his shaking hands together, staring down at them as he did.

With no idea as to the extent of the man's injuries, and with the boy seemingly unable to tell him, Tanner caught his attention. 'Do you mind if I take a look?'

Seeing him nod, Tanner slipped off his crocks to step down inside the dimly lit cockpit. From there he made his way cautiously down the companionway steps, into the cabin below. With no sign of anyone, he edged his way towards the front of the boat to find a small door left slightly ajar. Levering it open with the back of his hand, he peered inside.

Lying face up on the bed directly in front of him was the body of a half-naked man, his skin as white as marble, his neck, torso, and the sheets he was lying on all drenched in dark coagulated blood.

Tanner's heart lept inside his chest as he stumbled

back into the cabin behind. Frantically searching his pockets for his phone, he took a moment to compose himself before turning to stare up at the boy.

'I'm going to call an ambulance,' he said, struggling to keep his voice level. 'What's your name?'

'Andrew,' the boy muttered. 'Andrew Longshore.'

'Is there anyone else on board, Andrew?'

As if being awoken from a trance, the young man glanced down at Tanner. 'Susie, my little sister. She's in the cabin at the back.'

Phone in hand, Tanner nudged himself to where he was being directed to. Doing his best not to touch more than he already had, he prised open the door with his elbow, only to find an empty bed with the covers thrown back.

'Is there anywhere else she could be?' he called up, turning to begin glancing about.

'What? Why?' the boy spluttered, lurching onto his feet. 'She's there. She's definitely there. She has to be!'

- CHAPTER THREE -

AFTER CALLING FOR an ambulance, Tanner did his best to help the distraught young man search the boat for his missing sister, all the while trying not to contaminate what he knew by then to be the scene of a major incident.

The moment they ran out of places to look, with still no sign, Tanner shepherded him away to his own boat with the assurance that his sister would show up soon enough, and that she was probably hiding in the garden of one of the nearby houses.

Once on board, Tanner sat him down to place a blanket over his bony narrow shoulders before setting about making him something hot to drink.

Leaving him with his hands wrapped around a steaming mug of hot chocolate, Tanner climbed out with the intention of heading over to the pub he'd seen the young lad stumble out of the night before, hoping to ask if they'd seen any sign of the missing girl. He'd only just managed to reach the edge of the pub's carpark when the blast of a siren had him glancing up to see the ambulance he'd called for, tearing down the road towards him, a police squad car directly behind.

Remaining where he was, he waited for the ambulance to come juddering to a halt and its doors to fling open before directing the emerging paramedics over towards the vintage motor launch.

As they raced away, his attention turned to the squad car, and the two uniformed police constables he could see levering themselves out.

Relieved to find neither was familiar, he shoved his hands deep into the pockets of his jeans to make his way over.

Nodding at them as he approached, the taller, better-looking of the two called out, 'Was it you who made the call?'

'It was,' Tanner confirmed, taking a moment to glance over the PC's shoulder at the cluster of houses beyond. 'There's no sign of the girl, I'm afraid. I was about to head over to the pub, to ask if anyone's seen her.'

'I don't suppose you know her name?' the same PC asked, tugging out a notebook to glance briefly at his colleague.

'Susie Longshore,' Tanner replied. 'She's only five.'

'She's definitely not hiding on board the boat?'

'Well, we couldn't find her,' Tanner replied, 'and to be honest, there aren't all that many places to look.'

The young PC took a moment to finish what he was writing before stepping over to his colleague. As Tanner watched him lean in towards him, he heard him whisper, 'You'd better start knocking on doors. Maybe start with the pub?'

A nod from the other PC saw him turning on his heel to begin jogging over towards the village, leaving the other returning his attention back to Tanner.

'We were also told you found a body?'

'I'm afraid so,' Tanner confirmed, glancing over to the boat in question. 'He's a white male,' Tanner continued, turning back. 'I'd say somewhere between thirty-five to forty-five, medium build, light brown hair, pale blue eyes.'

'Does the boat belong to you?'

Tanner shook his head. 'Mine's the old sailing one,' he replied, gesturing over at where he'd come from.

'So...how come you found the body?'

'It was the missing girl's brother who found it. I was asleep when I heard someone call out, so I came over to take a look.'

'What time was that?'

Tanner glanced down at his watch. 'About half an hour ago. I found the brother in the cockpit. He was in quite a state. He said his father had been hurt. When he wasn't able to say to what extent, I didn't think I had much of a choice but to step on board to take a look.'

'And that's when you found the body?'

Tanner nodded. 'He was in the front cabin, lying face up on top of the bedding. From the amount of blood, I'd say his carotid artery had been cut open. As there was no sign of any on either his arms or hands, I think it would be safe to assume that someone else had done it.'

The young PC raised his head from his notebook to take Tanner in.

'You seem remarkably knowledgeable about these sorts of things; if you don't mind me saying.'

'Sorry. I should have said. I'm a detective inspector, or at least I used to be.'

The constable ran a sceptical eye over Tanner's somewhat dishevelled appearance. 'May I ask which constabulary you work for?'

'As I said, I *used* to be.'

'When you were?'

For a brief moment Tanner found himself reluctant to say. 'If you must know, it was this one.'

'I see,' the young PC replied, with just the hint of a smirk. 'And your name is?' he continued, returning to his notebook.

'Tanner.'

The constable's head jolted back up to examine his face.

'Tanner...as in John Tanner?'

Taken aback by both the man's reaction and the fact that he knew his name, Tanner nodded back in cautious response.

'We were told you'd disappeared – sailing off around the world?'

Tanner gave him a sheepish smile. 'I only made it as far as the Mediterranean, I'm afraid.'

With the PC's expression turning from surprise to open scepticism, he fixed Tanner's eyes. 'I don't suppose you have some form of identification on you, by any chance?'

With an impatient sigh, Tanner began searching the pockets of his jeans. 'My formal ID's buried inside my boat somewhere,' he eventually replied. Pulling out an old leather wallet, he opened it up to prise out a discoloured plastic driver's licence. 'Will this do?'

After taking a moment to peer down at it, the PC pulled himself up straight. 'Yes, sir. That's fine. Sorry about that. It was an unusual story, that was all.'

'That's OK. I assume you're new?'

'Relatively speaking. I signed up shortly after the news about what happened to DS Ev... The constable stopped mid-sentence, glancing briefly down. 'There was a big recruitment drive going on at the time. It was either this or having to move down to London to find work. Not something I fancied, I'm afraid, not after having been brought up here.'

'I can't say I blame you,' Tanner agreed, taking a moment to gaze over at the wide open horizon.

'Anyway,' the PC continued, returning his attention back to his notebook, just as the sound of another siren could be heard drifting through the air towards them. 'Is there anything else you can tell me, about what you found?'

'Not much,' Tanner shrugged. 'There was no sign of a forced entry, but that doesn't mean much. Most people who moor up around here seem to leave their doors and windows open at night, certainly during the summer months.'

'What about the man who you said found the body?'

'He's on board my boat. Andrew Longshore. He was pretty shaken up when I found him, but that's hardly surprising. After helping to search the boat for his sister, I took him over to mine to make him something to drink. I suspect he's in shock. With that in mind, it may be wise to ask the paramedics to check him over before anyone attempts to interview him.'

'Do you think there's any chance he was responsible for what happened to his father?'

Tanner raised a surprised eyebrow at the young man. It was a good question; one he'd not normally have expected from such a youthful looking PC.

'It's possible,' he eventually replied, 'but I didn't see any blood on him. I can't see how whoever's responsible could have done so without ending up being drenched in the stuff. I'm also fairly sure I saw him returning to the boat last night, just after I moored up.'

'What time was that?'

'It must have been a little after eleven. From the way he was walking, it was fairly obvious that he'd had too much to drink.'

'Do you think his father could have already been dead when he stepped on board?'

Another good question, thought Tanner, casting his mind back to the scene.

'It's certainly a possibility. The blood was heavily

coagulated, so it had clearly happened a good few hours before the body was found. And the door to the cabin was closed. If he'd been as drunk as he looked, he probably passed out as soon as his head touched the pillow, without even realising his father had been killed. The autopsy should give you a more accurate idea as to exactly when he died.'

The sudden blast of a siren had them both glancing over towards the carpark where another squad car was turning in, closely followed by a white forensics services van and another unmarked car after that.'

'Right, well, thanks for your time,' said the PC, turning back to tuck his notebook away. 'I think that will be all for now. I'll ask one of the paramedics to pop over to your boat to take a look over the missing girl's brother, after which we'll be needing to take a statement from him. Maybe you could give him a heads-up to expect it?'

'Yes, of course.'

'Do we have your contact details?'

Tanner scratched his head. 'Well, my address is the boat.'

'And your phone number?'

'You should have that on file somewhere. It hasn't changed since I left.'

'Understood.'

'I assume you're going to want me to stick around for a while?'

'If you could. I'm sure someone from CID will be keen to have a word.'

- CHAPTER FOUR -

TANNER HAD ONLY just put the kettle on after helping Andrew Longshore step down off his boat, into the hands of an awaiting paramedic, when he heard someone knocking on his cabin roof.

'Hello, is anyone home?'

Smiling at the all-too familiar sound of the woman's voice, Tanner pulled back the canvass entrance to gaze into the tired blue eyes of his former colleague, DS Vicky Gilbert.

'Only me, I'm afraid.'

'Good morning,' she replied, giving him the briefest of glances before casting her eyes along the length of his boat. Holding out her police ID, she turned back to face him. 'Detective Inspector Gilbert, Norfolk Police. Sorry to bother you. I've been told that you were the one who found the body this morning?'

With it obvious that she hadn't recognised him, Tanner couldn't help replying with a self-amused smirk. 'I was. I just gave one of your constables a statement.'

'So he said.'

'If you don't mind me asking,' Tanner continued, struggling to keep a straight face, 'but just exactly how long have you been a DI for?'

'I'm sorry?' Vicky replied, sending Tanner a reproachful glare.

'I'm just curious to know what you had to do to get Forrester to promote you? Nothing too salacious, I hope.'

'Jesus Christ!' she suddenly exclaimed, her mouth falling open. 'John?'

Tanner glanced down at himself. 'Well, I was the last time I looked.'

'My God!' she continued, a broad grin spreading out over her lightly freckled face. 'Sorry, but I - I didn't recognise you!'

'I haven't changed *that* much, have I?'

'What, you mean apart from that beard thing growing over your face, and the fact that it doesn't look like you've had a haircut since the last time I saw you?'

'I'm not sure I have,' Tanner mused. 'I don't think I've shaved, either,' he added, running a hand through his dark, unkempt beard.

'You've lost weight as well, unlike me. I don't suppose you'd be willing to share your secret?'

'I think it's called the North Sea.'

'I suppose that's where you got the clothes from as well?' she enquired, taking in what was left of his roll neck jumper with a disapproving eye.

'M&S, actually. They have an outlet off the coast of Greenland.'

Exchanging amused smiles, Gilbert crouched down to bring her eyes level with Tanner's. 'When did you get back?'

'The day before yesterday.'

'But you were here last night?'

'I was.'

'Did you see anything?

'Only what I told the PC, that I saw the person I assumed to be the victim's son come stumbling back to the boat, somewhat the worse for wear.'

'And that was around eleven o'clock?'

'Around then.'

Tanner took a moment to glance over at all the forensic and emergency personnel, now swarming over the grass between the carpark and the vintage wooden motor yacht. 'I don't suppose there's been any sign of the girl?'

'Not yet,' Vicky replied, her eyes trailing after his.

'Well, hopefully she simply ran off, maybe after finding the body of her father.'

Vicky gazed back at Tanner with a haunted expression. 'I assume you haven't heard – about what's been happening around here recently?'

'I can't say I have. Why?'

She looked away again, back over to the other boat. 'This girl, she's not the first to go missing.'

'Shit,' Tanner replied, glancing down towards the grass. 'How many more?'

'Three so far. If we can't find this one, she'll be the fourth.'

'When did the first go missing?'

'Back in April.'

'All under the same circumstances?'

'This is the first time an adult has been killed, but apart from that, it does seem similar. They've all been taken off boats, and all late in the evening. During the previous instances, the parents were so drunk when they went to bed, they didn't even notice. I can only assume that with this one, the father must have heard what was going on and went to have a look.'

'I suppose that would explain why he was lying on top of the bedsheets, as opposed to being underneath them.'

'The Norfolk Herald's started calling whoever's been taking them The Wherryman.'

'For God's sake,' Tanner groaned, rolling his eyes. 'I suppose they've been saying he's some sort of ghostly apparition who spends the night wandering the Broads, luring children from their beds with some sort of magical flute.'

'This one supposedly sails around in an old wooden boat, with what they describe as having a torn blood-red sail.'

The remark had Tanner's mind taking him back to the boat he'd seen drifting past him the night before. That had a dark coloured sail. Whether or not it was red, he wasn't sure. Remembering that he thought he'd seen something move under the old canvas cover at the bottom, and how the boat had vanished into the mist behind him, a cold shiver ran down the length of his spine.

'Are you OK,' Vicky enquired, glancing over at him with a concerned frown.

'I was just thinking that I may have seen something similar myself.'

'When was that?'

'When I was looking for a mooring, at about half-ten last night. I saw a man sailing downriver towards me in a small gaff-rigged boat.'

'Did it have a red sail?'

'I'm not sure.'

Vicky paused for a moment. 'I don't suppose there's any chance you saw his face?'

Tanner shook his head. 'The moon was rising directly behind him. He also had a peaked sailing cap pulled down over his eyes.'

'But it was definitely a man?'

'I had the feeling it was, but I can't be certain.'

'Did you see where it went?'

'That's the odd thing. I don't wish to say anything that could play into the hands of The Norfolk Herald's story, but the boat seemed to vanish, just after it sailed past.'

'That sounds similar to what the other witnesses

have been saying.'

'How's Forrester been holding up?'

'Not well. To be honest, he hasn't been the same since Je...'

Vicky's voice trailed away.

'Since Jenny died,' Tanner replied, completing the sentence on her behalf.

Seeing the way she was now looking at him, he held her eyes to say, 'It's alright. I don't mind talking about her.'

'Sorry. I didn't know where you were with all that.'

Tanner's eyes drifted past the cluster of houses, out towards the horizon beyond. 'I must admit, it has taken me a while. Taking my boat out to sea certainly helped. You don't realise just how vast and unforgiving the oceans are until you're fighting to stay upright in the middle of one. Such situations do tend to put life into perspective.'

'Had you done anything like that before?'

Tanner shook his head. 'Not even close!'

'Did it meet your expectations?'

'I'm not sure I had any. I think, initially, I set sail thinking, maybe even hoping, that I wouldn't come back; that at some point I'd be swallowed up by the sea. I suppose the times I was tested made me realise just how precious life is. When I would eventually come out the other side of whatever storm I found myself being thrown about in, I'd be left with a feeling of overwhelming gratitude, for what I had, and the memories of those most precious to me.'

A moment of silence followed before Vicky drew in a breath to continue. 'Have you thought about what you're going to do now?'

'Not really.'

'Does Forrester know you're here?'

'I've not spoken to him, if that's what you mean.'

'You do know that he's going to ask you to come back, don't you?'

'Well, he can ask.'

Vicky held Tanner's eyes. 'What if *I* asked you?'

'Is it really that bad?' Tanner questioned, unable to ignore the look of pleading desperation he could see staring back at him.

'You've no idea,' she replied, glancing away, just as her eyes began filling with tears. 'It was bad enough before, but with these children going missing. We've never had anything like it. We're all praying that they'll turn up somewhere, unharmed, but I don't think anyone believes that's likely. Not anymore.'

'Why do you say it was bad enough before?'

Vicky glanced back at him, pausing as she did.

'After what happened to Jenny,' she eventually continued, 'we had the nation's media bearing down on us for ages, them and Professional Standards. Forrester ended up taking the full brunt of the fallout. He told them that it was his fault Roy Carter had been allowed to walk without being charged. He also took the blame for Jenny not wearing a stab vest.'

'But – none of that's true!'

'No, it isn't, but that's what he told them. Deep down I suspect he blamed himself. After all, he does have overall responsibility for us. To be honest, I also think he was trying to protect you. Headquarters were looking for someone to feed to the press. Forrester made the decision that it should be him.'

'But he's still there, right? They didn't fire him?'

'I was told he offered his resignation. Thankfully, they declined to accept.'

Tanner raised a curious eyebrow. 'Did they say why?'

'I suspect it just came down to a lack of staff. Having lost both a DS and a DI within just a few days of each other, I'm not sure they felt it wise to lose a DCI as well.'

'And how about you?'

A brief smile flickered over her face. 'I must admit, I did think about going. I even had the conversation with Forrester. That's when he offered me the promotion. I thought about it for a while, eventually deciding to accept. I suppose at the end of the day, I couldn't see what else I could do. Besides, any other job would have seemed incredibly dull in comparison.'

'What about Sally?'

'Yes, well, she wanted to leave, but they somehow managed to persuade her to stay, but only on the basis that her role would be predominantly office based.'

'And Cooper?'

'Oh, *he's* still here alright,' she replied, not sounding particularly happy about it. 'Forrester's made him the senior investigating officer for the missing children. This as well, probably.'

'Aren't you two getting along?'

'Not really. He became insanely arrogant after you left. We all get the feeling he's eyeing up Forrester's job.'

'Not seriously?'

'He's ambitious enough. I know that much. But Forrester would have to leave first, of course.'

'Then I suppose we'd better hope he doesn't!' Tanner replied, just as he heard the kettle begin to whistle. 'Anyway, can I make you a coffee?'

'Go on then.'

'Still milk two sugars?'

'I'm down to one now; well, I am since seeing how much weight you've managed to lose.'

Ducking down inside the cockpit, he turned off the

gas to hear the burbling sound of a boat's engine, drifting steadily up the dyke towards them. A moment later, Vicky called out, 'Look's like there's a Broads Ranger coming up the channel.'

- CHAPTER FIVE -

POURING OUT THE water, Tanner listened as the approaching boat's engine began to slow, just as a woman's voice called over to them.

'What's going on?'

Curious to see who it was, Tanner grabbed the mugs to step nimbly up onto the side of his yacht. Staring over the top of his cabin roof, he saw a long white wooden patrol boat motoring up the dyke towards them with a surprisingly attractive Broads Ranger standing behind the wheel, a dull red life jacket hanging down over her light-blue office shirt.

'A body's been found,' Vicky called back, 'and a young girl's gone missing.'

'But – that's Martin's boat!' the Broads Ranger declared, hooking a wayward lock of greying blonde hair away from a pair of striking emerald green eyes.

'I take it you know the owner?'

'Martin Longshore,' the woman replied, frantically steering her patrol boat towards the empty mooring between Tanner's yacht and the motor launch ahead. 'Please don't tell me it's him!'

Vicky glanced over at Tanner, shadows of anxiety hanging down from her face.

With the patrol boat rapidly approaching the bank, Tanner ditched the mugs on the ground to spring forward, just in time to nudge its bow away from the moorings edge with his foot.

Leaning over the railings, he fetched up the rope found coiled on the walkway to begin dragging it back, leaving Vicky to catch the stern line thrown to her by the woman behind the wheel.

As the boat came to a gradual halt, Vicky waited for the ranger to turn off the engine before catching her eye to finally offer her a response.

'I'm afraid we think it is.'

'What about his son?' the ranger asked, stepping down off the patrol boat to take the mooring line Vicky was holding out for her.

'He's a bit shaken up, but he's OK,' she replied, digging out her formal ID. 'DI Gilbert, Norfolk Police. May I ask your name?'

'Christine Halliday,' the woman replied, crouching down to loop the rope around a short post jutting up from the grass beside her foot.

Replacing her ID, Vicky pulled out a small black notebook. 'How do you know the owner?'

'He's my colleague. Another Broads Ranger. I was on my way to pick him up for work.'

Pushing herself up to her feet, the woman gazed over at the vintage motor cruiser to watch a couple of police constables peg out an area around the boat with Police Do Not Cross tape. 'Are you sure it's him?'

'We found his wallet on board, which had his ID inside. His son also confirmed it. It's possible he was mistaken, but it doesn't seem very likely.'

'Christ! I can't believe it. I only saw him yesterday.'

'Which was when, may I ask?'

'When I dropped him off here, after work.'

'Where did you go afterwards?'

'I stopped off at Potter Heigham for some shopping, then headed for home.'

'Were you there all night?'

'Until I left to come here.'

'And can anyone vouch for you?'

The ranger shook her head. 'Just me, I'm afraid.'

Seeing her glance discreetly over at Tanner, standing patiently to one side, Vicky took the opportunity to introduce them. 'This is John Tanner, a former colleague of mine.'

The woman gave Tanner a curious look. 'A *former* colleague?'

'I've been away for a while,' Tanner replied, stepping forward.

'Not at her majesty's pleasure, I hope?'

'Nothing like that, no!' he grimaced. 'I've just been taking some time off.'

'He's been at sea,' Vicky explained, turning to look over at him. 'How long's it been now? Two years?'

'Something like that.'

The ranger apologised with a regretful frown. 'Sorry. It's just that, well, you look as if you've recently escaped from a maximum security prison and have spent the last few months on the run.'

Tanner glanced self-consciously down at his clothes, and not for the first time that day. He'd hardly given a single thought to what he'd been wearing for months, probably not since he'd left, but was quickly becoming aware that he'd better find something else to put on, although he wasn't sure exactly what. Apart from his old suit he had folded up somewhere, all his clothes were in a similar state to the ones he was currently dressed in.

'How long have you known Martin?' Vicky asked, steering the conversation back to more urgent matters.

'Three, maybe four years?'

'Can you tell us anything about him?'

'Not much. Quiet. Good with people, which was probably why he made such a good Broads Ranger. I never knew him once to shout at anyone, not even drunk teenagers.'

'Did he have any friends, outside of work?'

'None that I knew of.'

'Hobbies?'

'I suppose he was quite into his photography.'

'Was he a member of a club?'

'I doubt it. I think he used it more as an excuse to spend time on his own than as a way to be social.'

'How about a partner?'

'A wife, at least he did. She ran off with some guy a while back. I think she lives in London now.'

'Did he live on board the boat?'

'Only during the warmer months. The rest of the time they'd all stay with his father. He owns one of the pubs downriver at Potter Heigham. The Anchor Inn. He lets Martin live in one of the flats above with his children, in exchange for him helping out behind the bar at the weekends.'

'Do you know his father's name?' Vicky asked, busily scribbling notes.

'Thomas.'

'Does Martin have any other family members who live around here?'

'Not as far as I know.'

'OK, then I suppose I'm going to have to head down there to let him know what's happened,' Vicky replied, her tone flat with sullen despondency.

Tanner's heart went out to her. He knew from bitter experience that informing a parent that their child had been found dead was by far the worst part of the job. 'Can't Cooper go instead?'

'No, it's fine. He'd only moan.' She paused for a moment to look down at the ground, before casting her eyes into his. 'I don't suppose there's any chance you could come with me?' she asked, quiet desperation ringing out in her voice. 'It's been hard enough breaking the news to three sets of parents that their children have gone missing and that we don't have a single idea as to where they are. I'm not sure I'm up for the task of telling an old man his son is dead and that his granddaughter has gone missing as well.'

'I suppose it wouldn't do any harm,' he replied, offering her a smile of gentle reassurance, 'but only as a friend, mind. As I said before, I'm nowhere near ready to come back.'

'If you need to get down to the Anchor Inn, I can always give you a lift,' the ranger offered, evidently having been listening in on their conversation. 'If it really is Martin you've found, then I suppose I'm going to have to head back that way anyway.'

'It's probably best if we drive,' Vicky replied, running her eyes over the patrol boat, 'but thanks anyway.'

'It will be quicker by boat, especially with them digging up the road at Martham, that and all the tourists, of course.'

Vicky glanced over at Tanner to see him shrug back a response.

'Would you be able to give us a lift back?' Vicky asked, returning her attention to the ranger.

'Of course, no problem. I only wish there was more I could do.'

- CHAPTER SIX -

RETURNING TO HIS yacht, Tanner left Vicky to inform Cooper of their intended plan; to head down river to let the victim's father know what had happened. With the few minutes he had to spare he quickly washed his face, cleaned his teeth, and ran a dusty old brush through both his beard and dark shoulder length hair. Replacing his threadbare roll neck jumper for his salt-encrusted sailing jacket, the one Jenny had bought him all those years before, he re-emerged to down his now lukewarm coffee before joining Vicky and the Broads Ranger, waiting for him beside the patrol boat with a rope in each hand.

'All set?' the ranger asked, giving him the once over with a more approving eye.

'Yes, sorry about that. I had to get out of that old jumper of mine.'

'That was a jumper, was it?'

'Well, it was when I first bought it. I think recently it had become more of an offshore fishing net.'

Taking the mooring line she was holding out for him, his eyes were drawn to a thin faded white scar running down the left side of her forehead, crossing the end of her eyebrow to stop just short of her eye.

Catching him staring at it, the woman whipped her head around to step up to the patrol boat, calling out to Vicky at the front to prepare to cast off.

Half an hour later they were nudging up against the purpose-built moorings at Potter Heigham, with the locally infamous, precariously low medieval bridge just up ahead.

'I'll stay around here,' Christine called out, holding the boat against the hard wooden side for Tanner and Vicky to step safely off. 'Just give me a shout when you're ready to go back.'

Offering her their thanks, Vicky nudged the boat's bow back out into the river before turning to lead Tanner over a well-kept grassed bank to the Anchor Inn beyond.

'Thanks for doing this,' she said quietly over to him, as they made their way up towards the entrance.

'As the ranger said,' Tanner replied, 'I'm happy to help. Have you thought about how you're going to introduce me?'

'I just thought I'd say that you're my colleague; and leave it at that.'

'Sounds fine, but if anyone does ask, I'm going to have to say that I'm not there in any official capacity.'

'Understood.'

Reaching the pub's black-stained solid wooden door, Tanner stepped forward to heave it open. After standing back to let Vicky in first, he followed her into a cosy bar with a low oak-beamed ceiling and dark mustard-coloured walls, one that bristled with tourists of all shapes and sizes.

Forced to elbow their way up to the bar, Vicky caught the eye of a thick-set middle-aged woman who seemed to be trying to serve two customers at the same time.

'Is Mr Thomas Longshore about?'

'I'm not sure?' the woman replied, heaving down on a pump with one hand whilst the other reached up

33

for a packet of peanuts, hooked into a wall-mounted display. 'Hold on,' she added, filling the glass to the brim before exchanging both it and the peanuts for the ten pound note a customer was holding out.

Spinning around to head over towards the till, she leaned over to a door to bellow out, 'Tom! There's someone here to see you!'

As the woman opened the till to delve around inside for some change, a large well-built man with a shaved grey head and brown weather-worn skin emerged.

Catching his attention as he approached, Vicky placed her ID on the bar, leaving him to cast a wary eye down at it.

'Is there somewhere quiet we can talk?' she asked, glancing around to tuck it discreetly away.

Narrowing his eyes at first her, then Tanner, he let out a world-weary sigh to guide them towards the end of the bar, through a narrow dimly-lit corridor, out into what appeared to be the loading bay at the back of the pub that was littered with empty boxes, orange plastic crates and rows of stainless-steel beer kegs.

'OK, so, how can I help?' he asked, folding his tree-trunk like arms over his wide barrel-like chest.

'Detective Inspector Gilbert,' Vicky replied. 'This is my colleague, John Tanner. I take it you are Thomas Longshore?'

'I am. I'm also exceptionally busy at the moment, as I'm sure you can tell.'

Vicky paused for the briefest of moments to take in a breath. 'Mr Longshore, with regret, we have some distressing news regarding your son, Martin. His daughter as well, I'm afraid.'

Longshore's jaw visibly tightened as his eyes shifted over to Tanner.

Vicky swallowed. 'The body of a man who we

believe to be your son was found on board his boat this morning.'

The pub owner's eyes returned to focus on hers.

'The girl we've been told is your granddaughter has been reported missing as well,' Vicky continued, holding his gaze.

'Little Susie?' he questioned. 'Are you sure?'

Vicky replied with a solemn nod.

He continued to stare at her for another moment, before taking a half-step back to start shaking his head. 'No, I'm sorry. You must have been looking at the wrong boat. Martin's fine. He was here helping me behind the bar on Saturday. And Susie's starting school in September. It's all she's been talking about.'

Breaking eye contact, Vicky pulled out her notebook. 'The boat's called Medusa, moored up along the dyke just past Martham Ferry.'

As the words slipped out of her mouth, the colour began draining from Longshore's face.

'My son,' he eventually muttered, his voice nothing more than a broken whisper. 'How did he...?'

'At the moment, we're proceeding on the basis that he must have interrupted, or maybe even challenged whoever it was who boarded the boat to take your granddaughter.'

With Longshore now staring vacantly down at the ground, they watched him bite down hard on a trembling lip.

'But we're still at the very earliest stage of our investigation,' Vicky added, glancing over at Tanner. 'We should know more in a few days' time.'

A moment of silence followed, before he eventually lifted his head.

'Will I be able to see him?' he asked, his eyes filling with tears. 'I need to be sure.'

'It would help if you were able to make a formal

identification.'

Longshore nodded, his heading sinking once again.

Vicky glanced briefly over at Tanner as she drew in a fortifying breath. 'Due to the nature of your son's passing,' she continued, turning back, 'I'm afraid I have to ask you something which on the surface will seem both inappropriate and unnecessary.'

'You want to know where I was at the time of his death,' Longshore responded, anger flickering at the corners of his eyes.

'We need to ask everyone who knew him, I'm afraid.'

'I suppose you'd better tell me when that was then, hadn't you.'

'Yesterday evening, between nine and twelve.'

'I was here,' he replied, staring up at the outside of the pub, as if it was the wall of an impenetrable prison. 'I'm always here.'

'Would anyone be able to vouch for you?'

'Andrea, the barmaid.'

'Anyone else?

'No. My wife passed-away last year.'

'I'm sorry to hear that.'

Longshore didn't respond. He just kept staring up at the wall, as if willing it to collapse.

'Before we go,' Vicky continued, 'we'll also need to arrange a time for us to take a DNA sample, as well as your fingerprints.'

'I don't think that will be necessary,' the man replied, returning to stare back at her. 'As you'll find out soon enough, I've done time. You should have all that personal identity stuff filed away on a computer somewhere.'

- CHAPTER SEVEN -

'T HAT MUST BE the *worst* part of the job,' stated Vicky, bursting out of the noisy pub into the stark brightness of the day.

'I'm not sure that anyone finds it particularly easy,' Tanner agreed, catching up to her.

'Anyway, I can hardly complain,' she continued. 'God knows what it must be like to be told something like that. Oh, and thank you as well,' she added, glancing over at him.

'I wasn't aware I did anything.'

'You were there. That was enough.'

As they began making their way down the grass verge towards the edge of the river, they looked out to see Christine, standing behind the wheel of her patrol boat whilst having what looked to be a serious chat with a man hunched over a fishing rod.

Catching her attention, they watched as she began motoring back towards them.

'So, what've you got planned for the rest of the day?' Vicky asked, in a more relaxed, conversational tone.

'Not much,' Tanner replied. 'Have a shower. Go shopping.'

'Shave that beard off and get a haircut?' Vicky added, with a half-supressed smirk.

'I don't look that bad, do I?'

Vicky turned to take Tanner in. 'I suppose that

depends on the look you're going for.'

'I was hoping for something along the lines of a man who's just stepped off a boat, having spent the last two years at sea.'

'I see,' Vicky responded, resting a finger against her chin. 'The problem is,' she continued, 'I think that would only work for the brief few seconds when you're actually stepping off the boat. After that, I suspect most people would just assume you were some homeless drug-addict.'

Tanner ran a thoughtful hand through his beard. 'I suppose I could get a trim.'

'Then maybe you could pop into the office to say hello?'

'Ah, I see where you're going with this now.'

'They're all going to know you're back, so you may as well.'

'Maybe tomorrow,' Tanner replied, turning to watch as the patrol boat approached. 'I do have one or two things I need to do first, one of which is my car.'

'Do you still have it?'

'I left it in storage, well, someone's garage. Assuming it's still there, I'm going to have to get it taxed and MOT'd before I can use it, that's if it even starts.'

'OK, well, if you need a lift anywhere, you've got my number.'

'I should be alright. With any luck, I'll just have to charge the battery and pump the tyres up, although whether it passes its MOT or not is another matter.'

- CHAPTER EIGHT -

T ANNER EMERGED FROM the local garage; shoulders slumped as his head stared down at the pavement. Having managed to get the battery of his somewhat dated jet-black Jaguar XJS charged and the engine started, he'd driven it in for what he'd hoped would have been a quick and uneventful MOT. His intention had then been to sell it to raise some much needed cash, but the moment he'd set off, it was obvious it wasn't right. For a start, the engine was misfiring. There was also a gaping hole in what he'd discovered to be a heavily corroded exhaust, and he could feel the rear offside wheel bearings were shot. On top of that, the rubber on all four of the tyres was rotting and the electrics were playing up. He didn't need to hear the mechanics troubled assessment to know that it was going to cost him a small fortune to repair, money he simply didn't have.

He hadn't told Vicky, but the main reason he'd come back to the UK was the same one most long-term travellers did. What little money he'd left with had virtually gone. If he'd have been able to sell the car, he could have spent another few months at sea, before eventually being forced to do something as drastic as finding a job. But after the garage's depressing mechanical assessment, it sounded like having the car fixed would cost him more than he'd make selling it.

With him now being forced to consider the only other option available, that of finding gainful employment, Tanner's mind turned to something he felt like he'd spent half his life thinking about; what he could do for work, or more to the point, what he'd *like* to do. He'd known for a long time that he'd only joined the Force because of his father, who'd spent his entire working life with the Metropolitan Police and from all accounts, happily so. At the time, it had only been natural for Tanner to follow in his footsteps. The problem had been that he'd never really enjoyed it. He simply wasn't the type who liked being told what to do all the time. Unfortunately for him, it hadn't taken him long to discover that once he'd signed up and had a few years of police service under his belt, career opportunities outside of the Force were few and far between. This meant that the obvious answer to his current predicament was the one he wanted the least; the one that came with unwanted memories attached, most of which he felt he'd only just managed to forget. But if he'd be able to come to some sort of an agreement with Forrester, maybe to work on a short-term contract, it should give him enough to pay for the car and to put something aside for him to disappear back out into the vast oceans once again.

With no idea what Forrester would say, Tanner's mind turned to more practical short-term matters, that of how to get to Wroxham Police Station in order to have that discussion. It was too far to walk, he'd no idea which bus he should take and calling for a cab was a luxury he couldn't afford. He briefly flirted with the idea of asking Vicky for a lift, rejecting it a moment later. The thought of being cooped-up inside an unfamiliar car, forced to make what he'd come to consider to be pointless small-talk, or worse still, have to discuss what had happened all those years ago, something he'd not talked to anyone about, at least not since it had happened, was a situation he was keen to avoid.

As he began the slow journey back to his boat by foot, it didn't take long for the answer to become clear. It may not have been a long-term solution to his lack of a car, but it would at least allow him to get around under his own steam, albeit rather slowly.

- CHAPTER NINE -

Tuesday, 10th August

EARLY THE FOLLOWING morning, having scrubbed himself clean inside a nearby public shower block, giving his beard a much needed trim at the same time, Tanner tugged on some freshly laundered clothes to take advantage of what was forecast to be a stiff westerly breeze. Having called ahead the day before, his plan was to simply sail over to Wroxham, a journey he expected to take roughly four hours, aiming to meet DCI Forrester in his office just before lunch.

After a pleasant, uneventful trip, Tanner eventually found himself drifting around a bend in the river to see Wroxham bridge spanning the River Bure ahead. Spying a large flotilla of hire boats waiting to go under, Tanner was fortunate enough to find an empty, and more importantly free of charge, public mooring to his left.

With his yacht tied safely to the bank, it didn't take him long to walk into town, over the bridge and up Stalham Road, eventually reaching the police station on the left about twenty minutes later.

Noting a collection of news vans parked up on the curbs outside, he straddled the low wall to make his way over the carpark, heading for the station's main entrance.

Doing his best to supress what felt like a million memories, each clamouring desperately for his attention, he heaved open the door to step inside the station's reception. After glancing briefly over at a few disparate-looking people slumped on the plastic chairs attached to the far wall, he turned to find the all-too familiar head of Sergeant Taylor, hunched over a keyboard behind the front desk, as if he'd not moved since his departure.

'Good morning,' Tanner chirped, offering the top of the man's head an affable smile.

'How can I help?' Taylor asked, glancing up with a wearisome expression.

With the realisation that he'd also not recognised him, Tanner cleared his throat. 'I've, er... I've an appointment to see DCI Forrester?'

'News to me,' Taylor grumbled, leaning forward to pick up his phone.

With a number dialled, he waited a moment. 'I've someone at the front desk to see you, sir.'

Covering the mouthpiece, he returned his attention back to the man standing in front of him. 'What was your name again?'

'I know it's been a while, but it's Tanner. *John* Tanner?'

Taylor continued to present him with an unwelcoming blank stare for another few moments before the clouds of unfamiliarity finally began to part.

'Tanner?' he questioned, an uncertain grin spreading out over his face. 'Jesus Christ! Vicky said you'd changed but...my God!'

Feeling suddenly rather awkward, Tanner glanced around at the door leading through to the offices behind him. 'May I go through?'

'Of course, yes, sorry,' Taylor spluttered, bringing

the phone back to his ear. 'Anyway, good to see you again. I'll let Forrester know you're here.'

- CHAPTER TEN -

CREEPING HIS WAY through the doors, Tanner stopped to stare about. With no sign of Vicky, and thankfully nobody else he could recognise, Tanner crept his way inside the large open-planned area.

Reaching Forrester's private office, he rapped his knuckles on the door to nudge it gently open.

'Ah, Tanner!' Forrester exclaimed, pushing himself up from his desk.

Tanner stared over at him, his mouth hanging open. Vicky had mentioned that his former DCI had experienced a challenging couple of years, but she'd neglected to say anything about the effect it had had on his physical appearance. Maybe it had happened over time and she'd simply not noticed, but for Tanner the difference was striking. Not only had he lost a vast amount of weight, so much so that great folds of skin clung awkwardly to his face, but his eyes were dull and lifeless, made worse by the dark bags he could see hanging underneath each.

'Afternoon, sir,' Tanner replied, finding himself instinctively coming to attention.

'No need for any of that,' Forrester chided, sitting back down in his chair. 'It's not as if I'm your boss anymore.'

'No, of course,' Tanner continued, relaxing his stance to take the seat he was being offered. 'Force of habit.'

'I've been told you've only just arrived.'

'I sailed into Great Yarmouth the day before yesterday.'

'Well, it's certainly good to have you back in one piece. To be honest, when you first told me of your intentions, I was a little worried that we'd never see you again.'

Tanner crossed one leg over the other in a bid to relax. 'I had what would probably best be described as a trial by fire, being that I could hardly sail at the time, but I think it was what I needed.'

'And how's that old XJS of yours doing?'

'Well, I've still got it.'

'I must admit, I was half-expecting to see you pull up in it.'

'It would have been nice,' Tanner muttered. 'Unfortunately, I had to take it into the garage.'

'Nothing serious, I hope?'

'The mechanic advised me to have it put down.'

'Ah.'

'But I'm going to see if I can keep it going, for a little longer, at least.'

'Does that mean you're planning on sticking around for a while?'

'I think that depends.'

'On anything in particular?'

'On whether you feel there's a need for me.'

Forrester leaned back in his chair to study Tanner's face. 'Are you saying you'd like to come back?'

'I was actually wondering if it would be possible for me to return on a short-term contract, before agreeing to anything more permanent?'

'Well, I'd have to run it by headquarters, but I don't see why not. I assume you've heard about what's been going on around here recently?'

'If you mean about what The Norfolk Herald's been calling The Wherryman, then I'm afraid I have. Vicky told me yesterday.'

'She mentioned she'd seen you. I also read that you were the one who found the body on board that boat.'

'To be precise, the victim's son found the body. I only went on board when I heard him call out.'

'But you did see it, though?' Forrester questioned, his gaze turning to face his monitor. 'Martin Longshore, wasn't it?'

'I did.'

'Any thoughts?'

'Only that he was lying on top of the bedsheets, not underneath, making me think that it was likely he'd overheard whoever it was who'd boarded his boat to take his daughter, and went to take a look.'

'Did you have any thoughts about the method by which he was killed?'

'To be honest, I didn't pay as much attention as I would have done had I been there in a professional capacity.'

Forrester continued reading from the monitor. 'Dr Johnstone's post-mortem report came in this morning. It says he was killed by a knife being passed up into his brain from underneath his jaw.'

Tanner found himself shifting uncomfortably in his chair, another distant memory stabbing at the back of his mind.

'I must admit,' Forrester continued, re-facing Tanner, 'the conclusion he came to at the end was somewhat unexpected.'

'I assume he said that he thought it looked like a professional job?'

Forrester gave Tanner a surprised look. 'That's exactly what he said! Do you know something I don't?'

'Only that it was a method of assassination used by criminal organisations down in London. One in particular.'

Forrester sat back in his chair, an anxious frown rippling over his forehead.

'Dare I ask which one?'

'The Camden Crime Syndicate.'

'Shit,' Forrester cursed, leaning forward to rest his elbows on top of the desk.

'But it must be a coincidence,' Tanner continued. 'I mean, what possible reason could they have for feeling it necessary to execute a Broads Ranger stuck on a boat in the middle of the Broads, taking his five-year-old daughter at the same time?'

'From that I assume you've not heard about this either.'

'Not heard about what?'

'The head of the so-called Camden Crime Syndicate, Frank Julius Clayton, moved up here about a year ago.'

Tanner stopped to stare over at him.

'You're not being serious?'

'I'm afraid I am. Superintendent Whitaker had a visit from the National Crime Agency to warn him. There was so much concern, we decided to both go round to see him in person, endeavouring to find out what his motives were for having made the move.'

'And what did he say?'

'He told us he'd done so to retire. According to him, his parents used to bring him here every year for a boating holiday. Subsequently, the place holds what I believe he said was a "special place in his heart".'

Tanner replied with a spurious frown. 'I didn't know he had one.'

'I'm not sure he does. We weren't convinced he

was telling the truth, either.'

'Well, it's possible, I suppose. From what I understand, it's a popular theme. He must certainly be of age.'

'I think we both know that people like him never retire, especially not when they bring half their organisation with them.'

'Is that what he did?'

Forrester nodded. 'Even his son moved up.'

'So, he hasn't then.'

'As I said, it did seem unlikely. However, saying that, since we heard the news, we've not heard a peep out of either him or his son, until now that is.'

'You're thinking that the Broads Ranger may have either seen or found out something he wasn't supposed to, ending up dead?'

'More so now you've told me about how they used to execute people.'

Tanner thought for a moment. 'I think there's something else you should know as well.'

'I don't like the sound of that.'

'It's about his son.'

'Go on.'

'Nothing was ever proven, but shortly before I left the Met, Gary Clayton was implicated in a charge of paedophilia.'

- CHAPTER ELEVEN -

WITHOUT SAYING ANYTHING in response, Forrester leaned forward to pick up his phone, craning his neck to stare out through his office partition window as he did. After waiting for a few seconds, Tanner heard him say, 'Vicky its Forrester. Can you come in for a moment?'

Replacing the phone back into his cradle, he rested his elbows on his desk to take Tanner in.

'Do you know Frank Clayton?'

'Not personally.'

'You've never met him before?'

'Not to my knowledge.'

'How about his son, Gary?'

Tanner shook his head.

'And the victim, Martin Longshore?'

Realising Forrester was trying to find out if Tanner had any personal connection to either the murder victim or who he must have been considering to be two of the most likely suspects, Tanner replied, 'Again, no.'

Forrester was about to ask him something else when there was a knock at the door, immediately followed by the voice of Vicky Gilbert.

'You wanted to see me, sir?'

Tanner turned to see her head appearing through the gap to stare first at Forrester, then over at him.

'Oh, hi John. I didn't see you come in.'

'Close the door,' Forrester ordered, the briskness of his manner making it clear that he was in no mood for social pleasantries. 'And take a seat.'

Waiting for her to do so, Forrester continued.

'We've just been discussing the idea of John coming back to work with us, initially on a short-term contract.'

A brief smile flickered over Vicky's face.

'I assume that would be OK with you?' Forrester continued.

'I think he'd be most welcome, sir, especially with everything that's been going on recently.'

'Would you be happy for him to tag along with you?'

'More than happy, sir,' she replied, sending Tanner a welcoming smile.

'I don't suppose you have any idea how Cooper would react?'

Vicky shrugged. 'As long as he remains the SIO, I can't see why he'd have a problem. He already knows John's back, so he's probably half-expecting it.'

'OK, I'd better have a word with him at some point. In the meantime, Tanner's brought something to my attention which I think may have a bearing.'

Vicky raised a curious eyebrow over at Tanner.

'Do you remember what Johnstone said at the end of his post-mortem report?' Forrester continued.

'That he thought it looked like a professional job?'

'Well, Tanner's just told me that it was a popular method of assassination used down in London, in particular by the Camden Crime Syndicate.'

'You mean, Frank Clayton's old outfit?'

Forrester nodded. 'He's also mentioned that there were some rather nasty rumours circulating about Frank's son, Gary; that he may have had an unnatural interest in children.'

'You think it could have been Gary Clayton who boarded the boat, with the intention of taking his daughter, killing Martin Longshore when he tried to stop him?'

Without answering, Forrester leaned back in his chair. 'Do you know if Cooper has had a chance to go through the forensics report?'

'He gave it to me.'

Tanner caught Forrester rolling his eyes.

'Anything?' the DCI continued.

'The boat was pretty clean. The only prints and DNA they found have been identified as belonging to either Martin or his children. There were two outstanding sets, one of which we've just identified as belonging to Martin's father, Thomas.'

'He's the guy who owns the Anchor Inn?'

'Who we spoke to yesterday,' Vicky confirmed.

'We?' Forrester repeated. 'I thought you went on your own?'

'Oh...sorry, sir,' Vicky spluttered, her neck and ears flushing. 'I neglected to mention that I took John with me, but not in an official capacity.'

Realising she'd been caught lying to her boss, Tanner jumped to her defence. 'I offered to go with her,' he lied, 'for moral support.'

'And Cooper was tied up at the crime scene,' Vicky added.

'I suppose it's never easy relaying the news to a family member that a loved one has passed away. Anyway, I assume that neither of you would consider him a suspect?'

'For a man to murder his son whilst taking his own granddaughter,' mused Tanner, 'he'd certainly need an unusually strong motive.'

'I take it you haven't found one?' Forrester asked, directing the question towards Vicky.

'Not yet, sir, no. He'd done time for GBH, but admitted as much when we met him. And everyone we've spoken to so far has said he had a good relationship with his son. There's certainly nothing to give us reason that he would want to take his life. Certainly not using the method by which he was killed.'

'So, at the moment, the only suspect we have is Frank Clayton's son?'

'I'd describe him more as a *possible* suspect, sir,' Vicky continued, 'being that we don't have any evidence against him.'

'Of course, but I think we have enough to justify you and Tanner having a discreet word with him, preferably without having to involve his father in the process. From what I've heard, Frank Clayton really isn't someone we want to cross.'

Tanner caught Forrester's eye. 'I assume that means you're happy with what we discussed earlier?'

'As I said, I'll have to clear it with head office, but I can't see it being a problem. With yet another child going missing, they're all too aware of the urgency of the situation, that and our normal staffing problems.'

'And Cooper?' Vicky queried.

'Don't worry, I'll have a chat to him after you've gone.'

Vicky pushed herself up from her chair, smiling at Tanner as she did. 'So, looks like it's you and me.'

'When you find Gary Clayton,' Forrester continued, catching her attention, 'don't forget to ask him about the other children; in particular, where he was at the time they went missing. And on your way out, maybe you could ask young Townsend to start running a background check on him?'

'Townsend as in *PC* Townsend?' Vicky questioned, glancing back.

Forrester opened a file on his desk. 'At the moment he is. He finished his CID training course with flying colours, and after receiving an application from him this morning, I've decided to accept.'

- CHAPTER TWELVE -

CLIMBING INTO THE passenger seat of Vicky's car, Tanner waited for her to start the engine before asking her something he'd been curious about since Forrester had brought it up.

'You'd better fill me in on what the Clayton family has been doing since moving up here.'

'Nothing to write home about,' Vicky replied, with casual dismissiveness.

'So Forrester said, but I can't believe they haven't been up to something.'

Vicky swivelled herself around to reverse out of her parking space. 'All I know is that he went up to see Frank Clayton with Superintendent Whitaker, which is when he told them he'd retired.'

'And nothing's happened since?'

'Not that we've heard.'

'So, what have they been doing all this time? Don't tell me they all took up fishing!'

'Oh, they've kept themselves busy enough,' Vicky continued, driving towards the road ahead, 'just nothing criminal. Soon after they arrived, they bought out the old Brooks Boat Hire business, rebranded it Broadwater Boats and started offering boating holidays.'

'And...?'

'They've since become the largest boat hire firm on the Broads.'

'I meant, is that really all they've been up to?'

Vicky shrugged. 'As I said, that's all we know about. From what we know, Frank seems to spend the bulk of his time managing the main boatyard.'

'And where's that?'

'Brayden Marsh, over near Dunford; that small town near the coast, where that massive old windmill is.'

With Tanner none the wiser, Vicky added, 'Just up from Horsey Mere.'

Hearing the words, a deluge of unwanted recollections began pouring down into his mind. 'Christ!' he shuddered. 'I've not heard that name in a while.'

Desperate to move the subject away from a place that held so many unwanted memories, he fought to focus his mind on the here and now. 'What about his son, Gary?'

'He looks after a smaller boatyard in Coltishall, which is where we're going now.'

A few minutes later, the road opened up to reveal a sparkling river, meandering its way past a large village green towards a cluster of houses beyond.

Turning left into a gravel-lined carpark, they stepped out of the car to make their way down to the water's edge, where they could see a row of identical hire boats lined up along the bank.

'I think that's him,' said Vicky, pointing ahead.

Standing next to a narrow pontoon was a small middle-aged man, thinning black hair swept back over his head, who seemed to be doing nothing more arduous than watching a skinny youth wrestle with one of the hire boat's mooring lines.

'Mr Clayton?' Vicky called out, leading the way down towards the river.

The man turned his head to stare over, a pair of dull blue eyes staring out from a lumpy grey face.

Coming to a standstill in front of him, Vicky held out her ID. 'DI Gilbert, Norfolk Police.'

The man took a moment to study it, before looking up at Tanner.

'Who's your friend with the beard?'

'DI Tanner,' Vicky replied, glancing briefly around to offer him a nod of professional acknowledgement. 'I take it you are Mr *Gary* Clayton?' she continued, turning back.

'Depends who wants to know,' he replied, glancing down at a phone held in his chubby white hand. 'I'm also expecting a call, so if you could make this quick.'

'We were just wondering if you'd heard about what happened to that Broads Ranger, Martin Longshore, a couple of nights ago?'

'No, why? Did he get caught doing more than four miles an hour down the River Thurne?'

'He was murdered on board his boat.'

Gary shrugged.

'His five-year-old daughter was taken at the same time.'

'And what's any of this got to do with me?'

'We were simply wondering if you'd heard about it?'

'I can't say I have, although in fairness, I've never taken much of an interest in the local news. It's normally just so insanely dull.'

'How about the Norfolk Herald?'

'Ah, now that's completely different. Always good for a laugh.'

'So, can I assume you've heard about the person they've been referring to as The Wherryman?'

'You mean, the ghostly apparition who's been seen drifting about in a boat with a blood-red sail, nabbing children when their parents are off down the pub? As I said, great stuff!'

'May I ask where you were on Sunday night, between the hours of nine o'clock and twelve?'

'Watching the football, why, where were you?'

Referring to her notes, Vicky continued. 'How about during the evenings of Friday, the twenty-third of April and Saturday, the fifteenth of May?'

'No doubt doing something very similar.'

'Don't you wish to check your diary?'

'Not really.'

'OK, then would anyone be able to vouch for you?'

'I sincerely hope you have some actual evidence for me having been in the immediate vicinity of wherever it was you seem to be desperately hoping I was? Otherwise, this falls firmly into the category of unjustified police harassment.'

'We're simply asking the question, Mr Clayton. We're in no way accusing you of having done anything.'

He took Vicky in for a moment before accessing his phone. 'When were the dates again?'

'The first one was Friday, the twenty-third of April.'

A triumphant smile spread over his face. 'Ha! I *was* watching the football! After that I went out for a curry with my mates. I'm sure they're all be more than happy to vouch for me, as would the guy who owns the restaurant.'

'Which restaurant was this?'

'The one just up the road. I've no idea what it's called, but there's only one up there.'

'And on Saturday, the fifteenth of May?'

'The same thing. Sunday as well.'

'At the same restaurant?'

'It's the only one here.'

With Vicky busy taking notes, Tanner took the opportunity to enter the conversation. 'I suppose you had more choice as to where to socialise when you lived down in London?'

'Ah, the beardy man speaks!' Gary exclaimed, leering over at him.

'The Broads must make quite a change from the nation's capital?'

'And how would a country bumpkin like you know anything about that, may I ask?'

'Because I spent twenty years working for the Met. Subsequently, I know all about you and your father, and what you went around calling the Camden Crime Syndicate.'

He gave Tanner a condescending smile. 'Well, good for you.'

'What I fail to understand,' Tanner continued, 'is why you decided to move all the way up here? I mean, it can't be good for business, at least not *your* business?'

'The old man wanted to retire,' Gary shrugged.

'Fair enough, but that doesn't explain why he decided to drag you up with him, along with half his organisation?'

'OK, he didn't want to retire, as such. More to lead a life where he wasn't being hounded by you lot all the time. So he decided to move up here to start a boat hire firm.'

'What about you?'

'He wanted me to help out.'

'And you agreed?'

'Why wouldn't I? I think you'd be surprised just how much money there is to be made hiring boats out to stupid tourists.'

'You're right, I would be. And what about all your other slightly more dubious business interests?'

The man tucked his phone away to fold his arms. 'You know, I've never understood why everyone always seemed to assume we were nothing but a bunch of gun-toting gangsters. I admit that some of my dad's business practices may have seemed a little heavy-handed at times, especially when he first started out, but that was just how things were done back then.'

'You're not seriously trying to tell me that your businesses have always been completely legitimate?'

'Well, I can't speak for my dad, but since I've been involved, our business has been focussed purely on property development and investment.'

'And now boat hire,' Tanner laughed.

'We don't need to be in London to manage our portfolio, and my dad wanted to spend the remainder of his days living here. He says it reminds him of the family holidays he had when he was a kid.'

'How about you?'

'I'm happy enough. I mean, it's not as if I'm short of a bob or two.'

'And what do you do when you're not endeavouring to expand your boat hire empire. Are you still using the illegitimate children of your drugged-up prostitutes to make child porn?'

Gary squared himself up to Tanner, the tips of his ears flushing with colour. 'You're treading on dangerously thin ice there, Mr Beardy Man.'

'The name's Tanner, Mr Clayton, and as I said before, I know all about you and your father's former life in London. And if you seriously expect us to believe that all you did was to manage a property development company, then you're even more stupid than you look.'

- CHAPTER THIRTEEN -

WITH TANNER CONFIDENT they'd have his prints and DNA on file, they left Clayton junior overseeing his boat hire business to make their way back to the carpark.

'What did you think?' asked Vicky, tugging open the driver's side door.

'To be honest, I'm fairly sure I've never heard quite so much crap in all my life. The idea of Frank Clayton, someone who at one point was considered to be the most dangerous man in London, has moved up to Norfolk for no other reason than to enjoy a quiet life running a holiday boat hire business, is the most ridiculous thing I think I've ever heard. And the suggestion that all they did in London was to manage a property development firm is frankly even more unbelievable.'

'What about what he said about his whereabouts for the other night. I must admit, I thought he seemed genuinely surprised to find that he actually did have an alibi.'

'That was probably because he'd had enough practice pretending he does. From my experience the old, "I was watching football with my mates before we all went out for a curry," is pretty much the standard line most London criminals use when in need of one, at least it was when I was down there. I'm surprised they don't have it tattooed on their forehead.'

'OK, so what's next?'

Tanner glanced back over his shoulder, down to the river, where they could see Gary Clayton busily talking to someone on his phone.

'I wouldn't mind having a chat with his father, to see what he has to say for himself.'

'I think we'd need to clear that with Forrester first, and I doubt he'd agree. We've little enough on his son, let alone the father. How about we have a chat with the owner of the restaurant, to see if Gary was there on the dates in question?'

Tanner gave her an ambivalent shrug. 'I don't mind, but I doubt there'll be much point. The owner wouldn't dare say anything that would contradict what Gary's told us. If that's become his restaurant of choice, he'd have threatened to burn it down with the owner and family trapped inside, just to get free food and an alibi whenever it was needed. What we really need is to find something that ties either Gary, or one of his known associates, to one of the boats the children were taken from. Can you remember if there were any fingerprints or DNA samples that were unaccounted for?'

'Loads. With the exception of Martin Longshore's, they were all hire boats.'

'Has anyone checked to see if any belong to Gary Clayton?'

'Er...I think you'd have to ask Cooper, but somehow I doubt it. I'm fairly sure he wasn't even on our radar until your meeting with Forrester.'

'OK, then I suggest we head back to the office to find out.'

- CHAPTER FOURTEEN -

ARRIVING BACK AT the office, after saying a quick hello to everyone, most of whom he knew, others he didn't, Tanner spent what was left of the day stuck behind his old desk, doing his best not to think about the person who used to sit next to him.

Come five o'clock he was desperate to escape, back out into the clean fresh Norfolk air. As neither himself nor Vicky had been able to find a single shred of evidence to suggest that Gary Clayton had been anywhere near the boats the children had been taken from, telling Forrester as much, he made his excuses and left for the day to enjoy a relaxing stroll back to his boat.

After stopping off for some food, he spent a few pleasant moments leaned up against the railings of the pedestrian bridge, enjoying the peaceful serenity provided by watching the boats coming and going, and a regatta of swans that were drifting around the hardstanding next to a busy riverside restaurant, craning their necks up towards those seated outside, hoping for an easy meal.

Drinking in the clean fresh air, he followed the river along with his eyes to where it disappeared around the corner, before pushing himself away from the powder blue metal barrier to continue with his journey.

Once he'd boarded his boat about ten minutes later, he'd only just put the shopping away when he heard a rare but familiar sound, demanding his attention from somewhere inside the coat he'd left draped over the table. A feeling of nauseous anxiety churned over in his stomach as he realised what it was; something he'd happily not heard in months, possibly even years. It was the sound of his mobile phone ringing.

Taking in a fortifying breath, he reached over to pull it out.

'Tanner speaking,' he replied, his voice brittle and tense.

'John, it's Vicky.'

'Yes, Vicky, how can I help?'

'Forrester asked me to give you a call. A man's body has been found at Brayden Marsh, near to where Frank Clayton lives.'

- CHAPTER FIFTEEN -

GRABBING HIS COAT, Tanner jumped down from his boat, heading back to the main road to find Vicky waiting for him in her car.

After a quick three-point turn, they headed north, crossing the River Ant via Wayford Bridge, then west towards Stalham. There they joined a series of country lanes that led them over the muddy swamps that made up Brayden Marsh to eventually emerge out at Waxham Cut, a narrow channel of water that meandered sedately through the reeds, hugging the edge of Norfolk's East Coast.

Parking up alongside a cluster of emergency vehicles, Tanner stepped out to stare over the roof towards an imposing windmill he could see on the horizon, seagulls drifting between its large white lattice blades.

Closing the door, his attention was caught by a small patrol boat, busily ferrying equipment over to the other side of the channel. There he could see a group of white overall clad forensic officers, gathered around something lying at the end of a large fallow field that stretched away towards open farmland beyond.

'Where does Frank Clayton live?' he asked, making his way around the car.

'It's a large farmhouse about half a mile further down,' Vicky replied, pointing into the distance. 'You can just about see the roof from here.'

'And his boatyard?'

'A little beyond that.'

Nodding, Tanner followed Vicky as she led him down to the water's edge, just as the patrol boat came up alongside, the familiar face of a woman appearing from behind its varnished wooden wheelhouse.

'Oh, hello again,' he said, catching her eye. 'Christine, isn't it?'

'I was the last time I looked,' came her glib response, taking a moment to glance down at herself.

Quietly amused by the fact that it was exactly the sort of thing he'd have said, Tanner found himself smiling over at her. 'You must have had a busy day.'

'Looks like I still am,' she replied, returning the smile as she pulled up alongside to throw him a line. 'I don't suppose there's been any news on little Susie?'

Tanner caught the rope with one hand to heave back on it.

'Still nothing, I'm afraid.'

'And Martin?'

'We're making progress,' came his somewhat curt response.

Reluctant to start a discussion about the investigation with someone who was effectively only a civilian, he diverted the conversation away. 'Can you take us over?'

'Of course. Hop in.'

Holding the boat steady for Vicky to climb on board, Tanner pushed it away with his foot before stepping on it himself.

Crouched down on the boat's side, one hand held onto the top of the wheelhouse, Tanner watched Christine spin the wheel to bring the nose back out into the narrow cut.

'I don't suppose anyone has said who the body is?'

'Not that I've heard,' the ranger replied. 'Certainly nobody I've seen before.'

'You've seen it?' he questioned, surprised to hear that she'd been allowed close enough to know.

'I was one of the first on the scene.'

Tanner cast a curious eye over at her. 'What were you doing, all the way up here?'

'I had a call from Bill.'

'Bill?'

She took a hand off the wheel to point over the narrow stretch of water.

Turning to follow where he was being directed, Tanner saw a large square-jawed man with thick grey stubble covering his head, being given the once-over by a paramedic.

'Bill Thornton. He's a local reed cutter. He found the body just as he was packing up for the day.'

'So he called *you*?' Tanner asked, confused incredulity rippling over his forehead.

As the ranger's boat reached the other side, Vicky jumped out to grab hold of a mooring line, leaving Tanner alone with the Broads Ranger.

'I used to be a clinical psychologist,' she eventually replied, shutting off the engine to glance up at him.

Finding himself momentarily captivated by her stunning emerald eyes, sparkling gently in the summer evening's sun, Tanner shook his head clear. 'Sorry, I'm still not with you.'

'Bill Thornton used to be one of my clients.'

'And you were the first person he thought to call?'

Christine shrugged. 'It's fairly normal for a close bond to form during counselling sessions, especially when they're held over a long period of time.'

'As was the case between you and Mr Thornton?'

'I met him for an hour every week for over fifteen years. I'm not sure who else he'd call. He doesn't have any family, at least not anymore, and he's always struggled with human relationships.'

'Haven't we all,' Tanner laughed. 'I don't suppose you know if anyone has spoken to him yet?'

'Not that I'm aware of.'

'OK, then I'd better have a word, at some point at least. I assume that would be alright?'

She stared over towards where the large man stood staring vacantly down at the ground. 'He's quite shaken up. Maybe if I was there when you did?'

Tanner thought for a moment. 'How long do you think you'll be around for?'

'I've been told that a couple of police boats should be here any minute,' she replied, glancing down at her watch. 'To be honest, I was hoping I'd be able to head home when they got here.'

'Then I suppose we'd better have a quick word with him before they do.'

- CHAPTER SIXTEEN -

HELPING TO SECURE the boat to the grass bank, Tanner allowed Christine to lead them over to where they could see her former patient, now crouched down on a bed of freshly cut reeds, his eyes fixed on the windmill Tanner had seen when they'd first arrived.

'Hello Bill,' she called out, hooking her arms into the straps of her life jacket.

The man remained motionless, as if he'd not heard.

'I've some people from the police who'd like to have a quick word.'

Still nothing.

'Would that be OK?' she continued, as they came to a gradual halt beside him.

Keeping his gaze fixed on the windmill, they saw his hand reach out for a thick curved piece of wood that had been lying hidden amongst the reeds to his side. As he rose to his feet, he turned to face them, revealing a mammoth old-fashioned scythe, clutched in both of his wide slab-like hands.

'Why do they want to speak to me?' he asked, staring over at them, the slowly setting sun glinting off the scythe's smooth curved steel blade.

'I think it's because of what you found when you called me.'

'But – it wasn't me. I didn't hurt him.'

'Nobody's saying you did, Bill.'

Tanner saw him lift up the blade for it to hover about an inch above the ground.

'Then what do they want to talk to me about?'

Christine glanced over at Tanner.

Taking that as his cue to speak, Tanner took a tentative step forward. 'We were just wondering if you saw anything that might be of help to us?'

'Just him,' the man replied, his gaze drifting over to where the body lay.

'You didn't see anyone else?'

'Nobody.'

'May I ask what you were doing here?'

'I've been cutting back the reeds for Mr Clayton.'

'Mr *Frank* Clayton?' Tanner questioned, glancing around to see Vicky taking notes.

'That's right.'

'Have you done any work for him before?'

'A little.'

'How did he find out about you?'

'No idea.'

'Bill is well known in the area,' interjected Christine. 'You're the last of the traditional reed-cutters, aren't you, Bill?'

'One of 'em,' the man replied, lifting his scythe a little higher to feel its weight in his hands. 'Most use machines these days.'

'But not you?' Tanner enquired, endeavouring to help him relax.

The man looked down at his scythe. 'They just don't feel right. Not natural.'

'The machines make a hell of a racket as well,' Christine added, 'and the council's under increasing pressure to reduce noise pollution, especially during the tourist season. You've been kept busy, haven't you, Bill?'

'Busy enough.'

'When you found the body, Mr Thornton,' Tanner continued, 'did you move it at all?'

'I didn't do anything!' the man fired back.

'We know, but when you saw it, do you think you may have touched it, by accident?'

Instead of answering, his eyes glazed over as he turned his head to gaze back towards the windmill.

Tanner leaned his head in towards Christine. 'At some stage, we're going to need to take his fingerprints along with a sample of his DNA.'

'But why?' she demanded; her voice harsh but low. 'He didn't have anything to do with this.'

'I'm sure he didn't, but if he did happen to touch the body when he found it, we'll need to know who it was so we can eliminate him from our enquiries.'

The ranger thought for a moment.

'I assume he'd have to come down to the station?'

'We can send forensics over to his house; if he prefers. It won't take long.'

'OK, I'll ask him a little later; if that's alright.'

'We'll need yours as well, I'm afraid.'

Christine shot him a glance.

'For the same reason,' Tanner added, in an apologetic tone.

'Then I may as well come to the station with him.'

'That would be appreciated, thank you.'

Tanner glanced over towards where the body lay before catching Vicky's eye. 'Right. I suppose we'd better go take a look; before they begin carting it away.'

- CHAPTER SEVENTEEN -

PICKING THEIR WAY over the freshly cut reeds, onto a series of rectangular aluminium platforms, Tanner and Vicky stopped beside the crumpled body of a stick-thin man, dressed in what was left of a dark grey suit. Standing on the other side were two people, one of whom was DI Cooper. The other was someone Tanner hadn't seen in a very long time.

Nodding over at Cooper, Tanner purposefully caught the eye of the man he'd recognised; their local medical examiner, Dr Johnstone.

'Good evening Doctor. Not a bad day for it.'

Johnstone stared over to look Tanner up and down. 'As I live and breathe; if it isn't our very own ocean-going seafarer, Captain John Tanner!'

'I'm back to being Detective Inspector,' Tanner replied, offering him a stoic smile, 'for now, at least.'

'Looks like you've arrived at the right time, what with everything that's been going on around here recently.'

'Any idea who he is?' Tanner continued, glancing down.

'There's no ID,' commented Cooper. 'At least nothing we've found so far.'

'I assume he didn't drown; unless he hauled himself up here after having done so.'

'Johnstone says it looks like another professional

job.'

Tanner caught the medical examiner's eye. 'The same method as before?'

'The wound is certainly similar, but there are a couple of notable differences.'

'Which are?'

'The entry wound is in the same place, piercing the brain from underneath the lower mandible, but I'd say that the blade used was slightly narrower. I've also found numerous injuries, which suggest he'd been beaten and cut before eventually being killed. He had his hands and feet tied at some point as well, and there are no marks on his hands, suggesting he'd been unable to fight off his assailant. Furthermore, there's significant bruising around his neck. At this stage I'd hazard a guess that he'd been approached from behind, choked until passing out before being tied up, beaten, cut, and eventually killed.'

'But not here, though?'

Johnstone shook his head.

'Someone dragged him up the grass bank,' said Cooper, bringing Tanner's attention down to the ground.

'One person or two?'

'Looks like one.'

'Someone quite strong, then.'

'There are also two indentations along the edge of the bank where we think a couple of rhond hooks had been embedded, presumably to moor the boat up that must have brought him here.'

'So, it's possible that one or more people could have remained on board?'

'It's possible,' Cooper shrugged.

'Time of death?'

Johnstone turned to look back down at the body. 'I'd say somewhere between six and nine this morning.'

The distant rumble of an approaching vehicle had them all looking up.

In the distance, careering over the churned up field, came some form of over-sized SUV, its sides splattered with mud.

'Looks like we've got company,' Johnstone observed. 'At least you have,' he added, smiling at Tanner before ducking away.

'You'd better go and see who it is,' Cooper ordered, catching Vicky's eye. 'Just make sure they don't go traipsing all over the crime scene.'

'Yes, *sir,*' Vicky muttered, under her breath, rolling her eyes at Tanner as she did.

- CHAPTER EIGHTEEN -

TANNER FOLLOWED VICKY around the body, onto the ploughed-up field, just as the vehicle they'd seen approaching came juddering to a halt.

With the sound of dogs barking from the back, the driver's side door was kicked open to reveal the sun bronzed leathery face of an old man, a pair of dark brown eyes staring down at them from underneath a threadbare tweed flat cap.

'What the hell's going on here?' he shouted, his face wincing in pain as he clambered down from the high driver's seat.

'Detective Inspector Gilbert, Norfolk Police,' Vicky replied, holding up her ID. 'I'm afraid a body's been found.'

'I don't give a shit if it's the Holy Grail,' the man continued, marching up to them. 'This is my land you're trespassing on.'

Ignoring his little outburst, Vicky replaced her ID for her notebook. 'May I take your name?'

'No, you may not. Now, sod off, before I set the dogs on you.'

'I'm afraid this has become a major crime scene, which means that we have every legal right to remain on your land for the duration of our investigation.'

He glared down at Vicky for a moment longer, before turning his head to stare over her shoulder, over towards where the body lay.

'Who is it anyway? Some stupid drunk tourist, no doubt.'

'That's something we'd like to ask you,' said Tanner, catching the old man's eye, 'being that it would appear he's been deliberately dumped on your land.'

Without responding, he turned to drill his eyes down into the scruffy-looking inspector's.

'You are Frank Clayton,' Tanner continued, 'former London resident, head of the notorious Camden Crime Syndicate?'

'And you are?'

'Detective Inspector Tanner. Maybe you'd be willing to help us identify the body? The way in which he's been killed should be of particular interest.'

With a dismissive snort, the man stepped between them, heading for where the body lay.

'If you could make sure to use the platforms provided,' Tanner added, as he and Vicky followed after him. 'And of course to not touch anything. I'd hate for you to do anything that could incriminate yourself.'

With another grunt, the giant heavy-set man stepped onto the first platform.

As he positioned himself in such a way that he could stare down at the body, Tanner couldn't help but notice the colour drain from his face.

'Is he a friend of yours?' asked Tanner, with a curious expression.

'I've never seen him before in my life,' came Frank's jaded response, his eyes leaving the face to continue along the length of the body, all the way down to the water's edge.

'Are you sure about that?'

'Quite sure, thank you,' he replied, turning to give

Tanner a contrived smile before returning to the edge of the field to start stomping his way back to his vehicle, his head firmly fixed on the ploughed earth beneath his muddy Wellington boot-clad feet.

'Before you go, Mr Clayton,' Tanner called out, as both Vicky and he hurried after, 'if you wouldn't mind, we'd like to ask you a few questions?'

'I've already told you; I don't know the man.'

'That's as maybe, but we still need to know where you were at the time of his death?'

Frank stopped where he was to let out an audible sigh. 'Whenever it was, I wasn't here, murdering someone on my own estate,' he eventually replied, turning around to take them both in.

'That's good to know, but he wasn't killed here.'

'Wherever it was, I wasn't there either.'

'It would be more useful for us to know where you were, instead of where you weren't, Mr Clayton.'

'Then I suppose you'd better tell me when then, hadn't you.'

'Between six and nine this morning.'

Frank laughed. 'That's an easy one. I was in bed, asleep.'

'Would anyone be able to vouch for you?'

'You can ask my dogs if you like. They sleep at the end of my bed. Shall I get them out for you? I'm sure they wouldn't mind answering a few questions.'

'That's alright,' Tanner replied, his voice becoming edged with anxiety, 'but thanks anyway.'

'It's really no bother,' Frank grinned, turning to continue marching his way over to his cumbersome four-by-four. 'They don't bite – *much*.'

'It really won't be necessary, Mr Clayton,' Tanner called out, watching as the old man strode his way to the back of the vehicle, where the muffled sound of frantic barking could still be heard.

'As I said, it's no bother,' Frank repeated, turning to face him as he reached up to place a hand on the door's handle. 'I was going to take them for a walk anyway.'

'Shit,' Tanner muttered, glancing first at Vicky, then over at all the people behind them. 'I don't like where this is going.'

'Why?' Vicky questioned. 'They're only dogs.'

Tanner gave her a look of ominous dread, as first one, then two massive Rottweilers lept out from the back to immediately begin straining at their leashes, growling at the two detectives with savage intent, glistening white fangs stark against their black angular heads.

'What did you want to ask them again?' Frank called out, a cruel smile playing over his lips as the dogs began dragging him over towards them. 'They're all ears; and teeth, of course.'

As Tanner and Vicky began inching themselves back, the call of alarm went up amongst those attending the crime scene.

Seeing two uniformed police constables begin pelting their way over the chewed-up earth towards them from the corner of his eye, each one whipping out an extendable truncheon, Tanner kept his attention on the two dogs, peeling off his old sailing jacket as he did.

'I assume you know that you're legally responsible for the actions of your little pets.'

'It's not my fault if they just happen to slip their leashes to end up gouging open your throats. However, I will take full responsibility for having neglected to feed them this morning. I had them gnawing on a couple of cow bones instead, just to keep their teeth nice and sharp.'

'As their owner,' Tanner continued, wrapping the

jacket around his forearm, 'if you allow your dog to injure someone, deliberately or otherwise, you can face up to six months in prison.'

'Is that all?'

'And if your dogs were to kill someone, you'd be looking at a fourteen-year stretch.'

'Unless, of course, they're helping to keep trespassers off what is privately owned land,' Frank replied, as the dogs became increasingly desperate to be let lose.

'Even in that scenario, they'd still be classed as dangerous animals. Subsequently, they'd be put down, so if you don't want to lose them permanently, I'd strongly recommend that you put them back inside that over-sized truck of yours.'

Tanner could almost see him weighing up his options as the two police constables began closing in, batons at the ready.

'Alright, you win, but I'll be keeping an eye on you from my house. And I want you off my land the minute you're finished up with whoever that is. Furthermore, if I see any of you venturing beyond this point, then I *will* be setting them loose.'

- CHAPTER NINETEEN -

'TWAT,' MUTTERED TANNER as they stood watching Frank Clayton reverse his cumbersome four-by-four, before plunging forward to begin careering its way back over the field.

'I don't suppose there's any chance he had something to do with it?' questioned Vicky, in a contrived, optimistic tone.

'I'm not sure.'

'I suppose he'd have to have been pretty stupid to kill someone to then go and leave his body in what is effectively his back garden.'

'Possibly, although it could be that he left it here for that very reason,' Tanner mused, 'knowing it would allay suspicion. It could have also been the reason why he hired the reed cutter, knowing it was likely he'd find him.'

Tanner turned back to look at the body, just in time to see two forensics officers lift it carefully onto a stretcher, under Dr Johnstone's watchful eye.

'I'm fairly sure there was something he was lying about, though,' continued Tanner.

'Which was?'

'Not knowing the dead man's identity. He went as white as a sheet when he saw his face. I think our first priority must be to find out who he is, and if there's any connection between him and our new friend, Mr Frank Clayton.'

Their conversation was interrupted by the sight of Cooper, making his way over the field towards them.

'Was that anyone we know?' he called out.

'Not sure who the dogs were,' Vicky replied, 'but the man was Frank Clayton. According to him, this is his land.'

'Did he know who the body was?'

'He *said* he didn't, but Tanner thinks otherwise.'

'And why, may I ask, would you think someone would feel it necessary to lie about something like that?'

'I've no idea,' Tanner replied, 'but I think we should make it a priority to find out if there's a connection between the body and our friend with the dogs.'

'Well, that's certainly an interesting perspective,' Cooper responded, with a condescending sneer. 'Personally, I'd have thought it should be to find out who killed him, but what do I know.'

Tanner grinned back in silence.

'Anyway,' Cooper continued, glancing down at his watch. 'I just came over to say that Forrester has asked me to head this one up as well, so I'm going back to the office to brief him before making my way home. Vicky, if you could stay here until Johnstone's finished, then you may as well go yourself.'

'Thanks Cooper, that's really kind of you.'

'No problem!'

Cooper turned to look Tanner up and down. 'As for you, as you're only a temp, you may as well go now.'

'I'm happy to stick around; if that's OK?'

'Doesn't bother me,' Cooper shrugged. 'You can spend the night here, if you like. To be honest, it looks like you did anyway.'

'Egocentric little prick,' Vicky muttered, as they watched him walk away.

'You know, personally, I rather like him,' Tanner replied.

'Please tell me you're joking?'

'Why, what's not to like? He's clearly highly intelligent; and has a tremendous sense of humour. I think Forrester made an excellent choice making him the SIO.'

'Rather him than me. Anyway, he's right in that you may as well go home. There's not much to do here except stand around, waiting for Johnstone to finish.'

Tanner gave her a sheepish look. 'I was – er – actually hoping for a lift?'

'Christ, sorry, I'd forgotten you don't have a car. And I can't even give you a ride back. I've got to take my mum to hospital.'

'Nothing serious, I hope?'

'Just a check-up, but it's the other way.'

'OK, don't worry.'

'Maybe one of the PCs can give you a lift?'

As she said that, they heard Christine calling out to them as she made her way over.

'One of the police boats has finally arrived, so I was about to head off. Is that OK?'

'Of course,' Vicky replied, 'and thanks again for your help.'

'No problem at all.'

Turning with a smile, Tanner called after her, 'I don't suppose I could ask which way you're heading?'

'Towards Potter Heigham. Why? Do you need a lift?'

'My car's stuck in the garage, but don't worry. I'm moored all the way over at Wroxham now.'

'I must admit, that is a little far, by river at least, but if you're happy to come with me to Potter Heigham, I can drive you to Wroxham from there. Whereabouts have you moored?'

'Just this side of the bridge, but I couldn't possibly impose on you to such an extent.'

'Don't worry, you wouldn't be. It's on my way.'

'But – I thought you said you were going to Potter Heigham?'

'Only to drop off the boat. From the sounds of it, my house is probably only about a hundred yards away from where you've moored.'

- CHAPTER TWENTY -

NUDGING THE PATROL boat off the bank, Tanner swung himself down to join Christine inside the wheelhouse.

'Thanks again for doing this,' he remarked, watching her ease the throttle forward.

'As I said, it's on my way home, so it really isn't a problem.'

An awkward silence followed, marred only by the burbling sound of the engine and the breeze brushing gently against the tall banks of surrounding reeds.

It was Christine who was first to speak.

'I hear you used to live down in London?'

Tanner nodded. 'I moved up here about four years ago.'

'And you've spent the last two years sailing around the world?'

'I think it would be more accurate to say that I spent the last two years *thinking* about sailing around the world. In reality, I only made it as far as the Mediterranean.'

'But still. There can't be many people who've gone quite so far.'

'Perhaps.'

'I must admit, it's always been a bit of a dream of mine.'

'What, to go to the Mediterranean?'

Christine offered him a the narrowest of smiles before turning her attention back to the waterway ahead.

'I was thinking more about something along the lines of what you did.'

'Oh, that!' Tanner replied, taking the opportunity to study the side of her face and the scar, half hidden under her greying blonde hair. 'Can you sail?'

'Just about. Well, I know the basics, at least, but not nearly enough to do what you did.'

'It's not as difficult as you might think. The hardest part is finding the reason.'

She turned her head to try and catch his eye. 'And what was yours?'

Tanner stared out towards the flat open horizon. Having hardly talked to a soul about what had happened all those months before, he really wasn't sure he was ready to start now.

'Something happened at work,' he eventually replied. 'How about you? What made you decide to give up clinical psychology to become a Broads Ranger, of all things?'

At first there was no response, her attention focussed on steering a straight and steady course.

'I was involved in an accident,' she eventually replied, the words sounding stilted, as if she'd had to force herself to say them.

When it became clear she wasn't going to say any more, Tanner decided to try and delve a little deeper. 'Is that how you got the scar; if you don't mind me asking?'

Christine instinctively took a hand off the wheel to tug a lock of hair over that side of her face.

Replacing the hand, she sucked in a breath.

'We were driving down to London, my husband and I, to see my parents. Our baby was in the back seat. A lorry came off the road in front of us.'

Tanner glanced into her eyes to see tears creeping into their corners.

'I'm sorry,' she apologised, her voice strained with emotion.

Tanner kicked himself. It was obvious that there would have been a story behind her scar, one that he had no right enquiring about.

'I'm the one who should apologise,' he began, looking away. 'I had no right to go prying into your life like that.'

'It's OK. It happened over five years ago now. Besides, as hard as it is, I know I need to keep talking about it. It doesn't do anyone any good to keep something like that buried inside.'

With the sneaking suspicion that the comment had been made more for his benefit than hers, Tanner turned his attention back to the horizon. He knew she was right, he *should* talk about it, but it didn't make it any easier.

More silence followed, leaving Tanner looking for something to say that would help steer the subject away from his past.

'I don't suppose the name Frank Clayton means anything to you?'

'It doesn't ring a bell.'

'Your colleague, Martin Longshore; you never heard him mention it?'

'I can't remember him doing so.'

'What about the name of his son, Gary?'

'Again, not that I can recall. May I ask why?'

'They own the Broadwater boat hire business.'

'Oh, right. I know the company, of course. You can hardly move around here without seeing one of their boats, but I didn't know who owned it.'

'Frank Clayton was the man in the four-by-four

earlier.'

'You mean, the one with the dogs?'

Tanner nodded. 'He owns the land the body was found on.'

'Do you think there's any connection?'

'I'm not sure, at least, not yet. Frank moved up from London about a year ago, with the promise that he was going to retire.'

'Retire from what?'

Tanner paused to considered just exactly how much he should be telling her. After all, she was the work colleague of one of the victims. As unlikely as it may have seemed, that made her a possible suspect.

'He's the head of what became known as the Camden Crime Syndicate,' he eventually continued, 'something that grew to become one of London's most powerful criminal organisations.'

'And now he's living here?' she asked, glancing over at him with a look of concern.

'It gets worse, I'm afraid. The method used to kill your colleague, Martin, it's very similar to how they used to eliminate people down in London.'

'You mean, you think this Frank Clayton guy killed Martin?'

'Either him or his son.'

'But – for what possible reason?'

'I can think of two so far; the first being the rumours that surrounded Gary when I was stationed down there.'

'Which were?'

'He was said to have an unnatural interest in children.'

'You think he took little Susie as well?'

'And her father tried to stop him.'

Tanner drew in a breath before continuing.

'The other possible reason is a little less obvious.'

'Go on.'

'That Martin discovered something about the Clayton's business, that they weren't too keen to be made public.'

'But surely, if he had found out something, he'd have gone to the police.'

Tanner raised a sagacious eyebrow. 'Maybe he thought he might be able to make some money from it, not realising just exactly who he was going up against. That's why I was wondering if he'd mentioned anything about them to you.'

'As I said, not a word, and we'd been working together for years. If he did know something about what they were up to, I can't imagine he wouldn't have said something about it, even if it was to simply ask if I knew who they were.'

Her comment made Tanner turn to stare over at her.

'What's wrong?' she asked, meeting his gaze.

'Oh, nothing,' he replied. 'I was just wondering if you have any friends or family in the area?'

'Er...friends, yes, but not family. Why?'

'Do you think any of them would be able to put you up for a few nights?'

'I could ask, I suppose, but I'm not sure why I'd need to. I mean, I'm not exactly homeless.'

'I was just thinking that it may be sensible if you did, at least until we know a little more about what's going on.'

'Honestly, Martin didn't mention anything to me about Frank Clayton, or his son.'

'I'm not saying he did, I'm just concerned that there may be people out there who aren't too keen to take that chance.'

Christine thought for a moment. 'I suppose I can ask, but I really don't think it's necessary.'

'Probably not, but I'd be happier if you did. Look, I may as well give you my number,' he added, digging out his wallet to prise out one of his old business cards. 'Just in case you need me.'

Taking it from him, Christine glanced briefly down at it before tucking it into the back pocket of her worn navy-blue trousers.

As the water began to open up in front of them, she looked up to say, 'Looks like we're coming up to Horsey Mere.'

- CHAPTER TWENTY ONE -

HEARING THE NAME for the second time that day, an unsettling shudder rattled along the length of Tanner's spine. Lifting his head, he stared out towards the single Hawthorn tree, standing as it had done all those years before, pitch black against a slowly setting sun.

As if his gaze had been captured by a malevolent spell, he continued to stare as a series of haunting images began flooding down into his mind; teenage girls left hanging by their necks, a lady being burnt alive on top of a car, and a beautiful young woman lying underneath the yellowing light of a streetlamp, staring at a hand dripping with blood.

Tanner forced himself to look away, tears stinging at the corners of his eyes. He knew this would happen; that his return would summon the unwanted memories he'd worked so hard to supress, like long-dead spirits, clawing their way out from the depths of hell. Worse were the all-consuming feelings of loss, guilt, and regret, that seemed to pile their way in behind. It was only then, with the silhouette of the tree burnt into the back of his retina, that he knew he should never have come back. But what choice did he have? To remain in exile from a place he loved, for fear of confronting the grief he'd done his best to forget?

The sound of Christine's voice dragged him back into the world of the living.

'You know, you still haven't told me what happened; to make you want to leave?'

With the realisation that not only was he only a few hundred yards from where the remains of Elizabeth Craddock had been found, the chance discovery that had triggered the series of tragic events leading to the death of his fiancée, and the unborn child growing inside her, but that he was also alone in a boat with someone who used to be a psychologist, someone who'd had her own share of personal tragedy, a smile of anguished wry amusement tugged at the corners of his mouth.

'Was it something I said?' the ranger asked, glancing over.

'Not at all. It's being here with you. It feels like fate's trying to play some sort of particularly unfunny joke on me.'

'Do you believe in fate?'

'That's a bit like asking if someone believes in God.'

'OK, so...do you believe in God?'

'Ah, I get it now,' Tanner replied, narrowing his eyes at her. 'You're attempting to offer me psychological counselling.'

'Forgive me,' she apologised, her tone both honest and sincere. 'It's a habit that's proved difficult to break.'

'Don't worry. I'd have to admit, I'm probably in need of it.'

As they made their way slowly over Horsey Mere, a moment of silence passed before Christine eventually endeavoured to continue with the conversation.

'Have you talked to anyone about what happened?'

'You mean, a psychologist?'

'Anyone, really.'

'Probably not.'

'How would you feel about talking to me?'

'You mean, in a professional capacity?'

'As a friend.'

'Is that what we are, now?' Tanner questioned, catching her eye.

'Do you consider us to be?' she asked back in response.

'Er...I'm sorry, but I think you're doing it again.'

Christine laughed. 'I must apologise, but in my defence, you're proving to be remarkably adept at deflection.'

'Deflection?'

'It's a technique people use to avoid talking about something.'

'And that's what you think I'm doing?'

She scowled over at him, as if he was a troublesome pupil. 'Well, you've just done it again, so I think that's a definite yes.'

Tanner allowed his head to fall down towards the floor with a bashful smirk, before lifting it again to gaze out over towards the Broads' wide open horizon.

'I suppose it just means that I'm not ready to talk about it,' came his eventual response.

'Am I right in thinking that this happened two years ago?'

'Around about then.'

'And since then you've spent the vast majority of time on your own, inside a boat, at the mercy of the world's oceans, and you *still* don't feel ready to talk about it?'

Tanner offered her a bashful smile.

'I must admit, it was easier at sea, being that the

only person I had to talk to was myself.'

'And did you?'

'What, talk to myself?'

'Well, it would have been better than not talking to anyone at all.'

Tanner offered her an indifferent shrug.

'I can't say that I did, but only because I couldn't see much point in telling myself what had happened; I mean, I already knew. It would have been a bit like reading a book for the second time, hoping for a different ending. It was also easy enough not to; with me or anyone else. After all, it wasn't as if I was surrounded by constant reminders, not like I am now.'

Tanner glanced over his shoulder, back to the Hawthorn tree to watch it creep slowly into the distance behind them.

'So, why don't you tell me what happened?' Christine asked, offering him a reassuring smile.

'I lost someone,' came Tanner's eventual response.

When it became obvious that he wasn't going to say anything else, Christine prised a little more.

'A friend or a relative?'

'She was my fiancée. She was also my work colleague.'

'Can you tell me her name?'

'Jenny,' Tanner replied, his voice cracking with emotion. 'Jenny Evans. We were about to be married when...when she was injured. She was trying to defend me against someone with a knife. Neither of us knew it, but she was pregnant at the time. Initially I thought we'd only lose the baby, but she passed away a couple of days later.'

The wheelhouse fell into a sombre silence.

'I think the hardest part was that I never had the chance to say goodbye.'

'I am truly sorry,' Christine eventually said, her words filled with heartfelt sympathy.

'There's no need to be, I can assure you,' Tanner replied, his jaw tightening. 'At the end of the day, the whole thing was my fault. None of it should have happened.'

'Under such circumstances, I think it's perfectly normal to lay the blame at your own feet.'

'Oh, in this particular situation, it was, of that I can assure you. I knew how dangerous the person was. I should have never let her within ten feet of the guy. It was also my fault he was allowed back onto the streets. He'd been arrested the day before. All I had to do was to charge him for something – *anything* – but I was stupid enough to let him walk straight out the door.'

With her eyes remaining focussed on the water ahead, Christine took in a breath.

'I too blamed myself. I was arguing with Mark, my husband. By doing so, I was distracting his attention from the road. I can't even remember what the argument was about. I was eventually able to accept that my actions were only partly responsible for what happened that day. I wasn't the one driving the lorry that overturned in front of us. I certainly wasn't the person driving the car too close behind. I think, in your case, you weren't the one holding the knife, and as difficult as it may be to accept, it was your fiancée's choice to come to your defence, just as you, no doubt, would have come to hers.'

Tanner didn't reply, but instead allowed his mind to contemplate Christine's words, whilst they continued on with their journey towards Hickling Broad and the River Thurne beyond.

- CHAPTER TWENTY TWO -

ABOUT HALF AN hour later, they were motoring their way towards the medieval bridge at Potter Heigham.

'The rangers' boats are kept moored up on the other side of the bridge,' Christine began, easing back on the throttle, 'and the tide's turned, so if you could help guide me through, I'd be grateful.'

With the patrol boat being swept along towards the bridge's infamously low archway at an ever increasing speed, Tanner was about to lever himself out of the wheelhouse, ready to head for the boat's bow, when he heard what he first thought was his phone, ringing inside his jacket.

Stopping to pull it out, he glanced over at Christine to see her doing the exact same thing.

As they both stared down at their equally dated smartphones, the realisation that not only did they have the same model, but that their ringtones were also identical, had them smiling over at each other.

'I think it's mine,' Christine eventually said, glancing down, 'but it will have to wait. Time and tide.'

Throwing it onto the window ledge, she grabbed at the steering wheel, just as the river caught the boat's stern, swinging it around behind them.

As she fought to bring the nose of the boat back in line with the centre of the arch, Tanner did the same thing with his phone before launching himself out onto the boat's side, jumping forward to fetch up a loose fender from off the deck.

Reaching the bow, he was just in time to drop the fender down between the stone arch wall and the boat's side before the two collided. With only a need for a gentle nudge, he ducked his head as they glided underneath, drifting swiftly through the cool damp air that seemed to cling to the ancient brick-lined walls.

Safely out the other side, he stood tall as Christine steered them over to where he could see three more patrol boats, each identical in shape and size, tied up to a wooden jetty.

As they approached, he stepped lightly off the bow to make short work of securing the lines, whilst Christine shut the engine off to begin collecting her personal belongings.

Jumping down to join him, she cast her eyes over at his handiwork.

'That was quick! I was about to give you a hand.'

'Years of practice,' Tanner replied, standing with a smile. 'Well, two to be precise. Did you get my phone?'

'I did. Hold on,' she replied, delving inside the backpack she had slung over her shoulder, just as a shrill scream cut through the late evening air.

Turning to stare over towards the river, they saw an enormous plastic hire boat, surging up the waterway, a red-faced teenage girl in fits of hysterics as she attempted to climb over the windscreen onto its cabin roof.

'They're not seriously going to try and go under the bridge, are they?' queried Tanner, taking the phone being handed to him.

'That probably depends on how drunk they are,'

Christine replied, closing the top of the rucksack to swing it back over her shoulder.

'But – they're not going to fit. Hadn't you better warn them?'

Christine glanced down at her watch. 'Well, I would, of course, but I'm officially off duty.'

'Not seriously?'

Shaking her head to mutter something to herself about stupid drunk teenagers, she was about to step back on board her patrol boat when they heard the hire boat's engine let out an agonising wail, just as water seemed to begin boiling at its stern.

'I think they've just worked out the problem,' she replied, watching with an amused smile as the girl who'd been attempting to climb onto the coach roof was sent flying forward, rolling down onto the walkway in fits of giggles, as the young man they could see behind the wheel fought to bring the boat to a rather dramatic halt.

'Are they going to be OK?' Tanner enquired, with a look of parental concern, watching the helm wrestle with the steering wheel in an effort to bring the boat around.

'Oh, I'm sure they'll be fine. Shall we get you home? My car's just up the way here.'

- CHAPTER TWENTY THREE -

B ACK AT HIS yacht, with some hot food inside him, Tanner settled down to watch the sun drift slowly beneath the horizon to send rich hues of orange and red blazing over Norfolk's wide open sky.

As his mind settled down to consider the events of the day, he'd only just finished mixing himself a glass of rum and coke when he heard his phone ring from somewhere inside the cabin.

'Shit,' he cursed. There were only two people it could have realistically been, and they both worked for the Norfolk constabulary.

Finding it buried inside his coat, he fished it out to answer.

'Hello?'

'Who's this?' came the petulant sound of a man's voice from the other end.

'It's, er, John. John Tanner?'

'Is Christine there?'

'Christine?' Tanner repeated, finding himself glancing around the cabin, as if she might have been hiding on board. 'I don't think so, why? Is she supposed to be?'

'This is her phone, isn't it?' the caller enquired, his voice sounding increasingly irritated.

Tanner pulled the phone away from his ear to stare down at it. The phone wasn't his. He must have taken the wrong one, when they'd been distracted by the hire boat with the teenagers on board.

Thinking back to when it must have happened, Tanner returned his attention to the caller.

'Sorry, I seem to have picked up Christine's phone by accident. Can I tell her who called?'

'Please ask her to call Simon, and as soon as possible,' the caller demanded.

'Yes, of course, does she have your...' Tanner began, only to find the line had gone dead.

'Hello?' he continued, pulling the phone away from his ear once again, checking to see if the battery had died.

But it hadn't.

'Jealous boyfriend?' Tanner thought, raising a self-amused eyebrow.

Deciding he'd better warn her that trouble may be heading her way, as well as the fact that he seemed to have her phone, Tanner dialled his own number.

'Christine?' he enquired, hearing the voice of a woman answer.

'Yes? Who is it?'

'Sorry to bother you. It's John, er, Tanner? You gave me a lift home earlier.'

'Oh, hi John. I didn't know you had my number.'

'I'm afraid it looks like I've gone one better than that.'

'I'm sorry, I'm not with you.'

'I've got your phone as well.'

'Oops,' came her eventual response. 'I must have given you the wrong one when we were mooring up. I must admit, you're the only person I know who's got one quite as old as mine.'

'Yes, well, as long as it works, I've never been too bothered. Listen, I'd better warn you that a man just called.'

'A man?'

'And he didn't sound very happy, especially when he heard my voice.'

'Did he have a name?'

'I think it was Simon.'

'Oh, him!'

'I assume he's a boyfriend of yours?'

'God no! He's my brother.'

'Ah, right, I see.'

'I hope he wasn't rude to you? I'm afraid he's never been much of a charmer.'

'A little, perhaps, but nothing to worry about. He asked me to tell you to call him. It sounded urgent.'

'I doubt it. He probably just wants to borrow some money. That's the only reason he normally calls. Anyway, I suppose you need your phone back. Shall I drop it round?'

'Don't worry, I'll come to you.'

'But – you don't have a car.'

'Didn't you say you lived down the road.'

'Yes, but...'

'Then I'd be happy to walk. Besides, I can't say I've got all that much else to do.'

- CHAPTER TWENTY FOUR -

WITHIN TEN MINUTES of leaving, Tanner found himself following the directions provided by Google Maps that were continuing to lead him down an increasingly dark and inhospitable country lane. He was looking for number thirty-two; but had yet to find it. He wasn't even sure he was close, as none of the houses seemed to have been numbered, at least none that he could see.

Beginning to wish he'd brought a torch, he was just about to give up to ask one of the residents for directions, when he finally found a house with a number. It was twenty-nine. If they'd been numbered logically, with all the houses being down one side of the lane, Christine's should have been three further up.

Counting them as he continued, he peered down the driveway at the house that logically speaking should have been hers. But, once again, there was no sign of a house number, and the only sign of life was a single light coming from one of the rooms inside.

Deciding that he may as well knock on the door to ask, he began crunching his way over the gravel-lined drive when the light suddenly went out.

With the feeling that whoever was in had just gone to bed, meaning that he was probably trespassing on private land, he stopped where he was, stranded in the middle of what must have been a stranger's drive.

'It must be the wrong house,' he said, quietly to himself, wondering if there was some old woman peering at him through one of the net curtains, a phone clutched in a frail bony hand as she tried to remember how to call the police.

That's when he noticed the car, hidden in the pitch black shadow of an over-hanging Willow tree. It was an old yellow MX-5, just like Christine's.

Unsure if it was possible for there to be two houses along the same narrow country lane with the exact same car parked in their driveways, Tanner crunched his way over to take a closer look.

Cupping a hand over his eyes, he peered inside to see a red life jacket tucked into the narrow gap behind the front passenger seat.

Now certain that it was her car, and therefore her house as well, with a sudden sense of unease, he crept his way over to the front door.

It was already open.

'Shit,' he cursed, quietly to himself.

Wasting no more time, he inched it open with his foot to poke his head into the darkness beyond.

'Hello? Christine?' he called out, edging his way inside. 'It's DI Tanner, Norfolk Police.'

The muffled sound of a chair, scraping against a tiled floor from the back of the house, had him surging inside.

Keeping his body low, his eyes desperate to penetrate the blackness, he crept down the shadowy corridor at the end of which was a half-open door. Crouching down, he eased it slowly open to see the shadowy outline of a kitchen. Nudging it open just a little more allowed him to see a person he instinctively knew to be Christine, sitting in a chair behind the kitchen table, her eyes wide with terror, gaffer tape flattened over her mouth.

Lifting a finger to his lips, he saw her eyes dart down towards her feet, before bringing them back up to continue staring at him.

Tanner lowered his stance to stare down at what she was directing him towards.

A moment later, a dense black shadow burst out from under the table to charge straight for him.

Stumbling back in surprise, he made a desperate grab for the person's coat, only to end up being slammed hard against the wall, dizzying white pain spreading out over one side of his face. By the time he'd rolled himself onto his knees to stare hopelessly down the corridor, the intruder had gone, the front door left swinging on its hinges.

Remembering Christine, he pushed himself up from the floor. With a hand held against his eye, he staggered his way into the kitchen, skirting the table to find her tied down to the chair.

'Are you OK?' he asked, peeling the gaffer tape gently from her mouth to begin fumbling with the rope.

Nodding, she caught her breath.

'He was – he was going to t-torture me,' she stuttered, using her chin to point down at the table. 'The bastard was about to t-torture me.'

The second her hands were free, she leapt up from the chair to push herself away from what Tanner was now staring at; a row of stainless steel knives, each slightly different in shape and size, all tucked neatly into the individual pockets of a pristine black leather tool roll.

'Jesus Christ!' Tanner exclaimed, unable to take

his eyes off it. 'What did he want?'

'He didn't say.'

'He didn't tell you what he wanted?'

Christine shook her head, her own eyes still fixed on the lethal looking polished steel knives, glinting in the light from a distant moon. 'He didn't say anything,' she eventually continued. 'Not a single word.'

- CHAPTER TWENTY FIVE -

LESS THAN TEN minutes after calling the incident in, the sound of a car's wheels crunching over the gravel driveway had Tanner heading out of the kitchen.

Surprised to find the hallway unlit by swirling blue lights, he tugged the door open with his elbow to peer cautiously outside. It was only when he saw the driver step out that he realised who it was.

'Cooper!' he exclaimed, glancing down at his watch. 'You made good time.'

Seeming to ignore the remark, the young DI closed the door to cast a dubious eye over at Tanner.

'May I ask what you're doing here?'

'I was returning something to Christine, I mean Ms Halliday, the victim.'

'I see. So, you know her *personally*, do you?'

'Not in the way you're thinking,' Tanner replied, in a defensive tone. 'We just happened to get our phones mixed up, when she was giving me a lift home, so I came over to bring hers back.'

'And how did you get here?' Cooper continued, casting his eyes around the drive. 'Someone said your car was in the garage?'

'If you must know, I'm moored up down the road. It's about a ten minute walk.'

Seeing him lift his head to stare over his shoulder, Tanner turned to see Christine's lightly tanned face, peering out from behind the front door.

'Don't worry,' said Tanner, smiling over at her, 'it's a colleague from work.'

'Detective Inspector Cooper,' the man in question replied, barging past Tanner to hold out his ID. 'We met briefly, earlier this evening.'

'Of course, sorry,' she apologised, pulling the door open for him. 'I wasn't sure.'

'I understand someone broke into your house?'

'They did more than that,' Tanner interjected. 'They tied her to a chair, threatening to torture her.'

'And did they?' Cooper asked, directing the question to Christine.

'Well, no,' she began, shaking her head, 'but he was about to.'

'Can you show me where this happened?'

'Of course, through here.'

Leading them through to the back of the house, she gave the kitchen table a wide berth.

'He was about to start using those on me,' she said, pulling the cardigan she was wearing around her shoulders to stare nervously down at the knives.

Following where he was being directed to look, Cooper pulled out his notebook.

'I think you'd better tell me what happened?'

'As I told John,' she replied, flicking a smile over at him, 'I was by the sink, doing the dishes, when I thought I heard a noise out in the hall. The next thing I knew, someone grabbed me from behind, stuck some tape over my mouth and tied me to the chair, forcing me to watch as he rolled *those* out in front of me.'

'At what point did DI Tanner come into the picture?'

'The man stopped when we heard someone outside.'

'And then?'

'He turned out the light and hid under the table.'

'Any idea how he got in?'

'The front door was open when I arrived,' Tanner replied.

'Did either of you see his face?'

They both shook their heads.

'He was wearing a balaclava,' Christine added.

'Gloves?'

'I'm – I'm not sure. I think so.'

'Do you have any idea what he wanted?'

'I think it was fairly obvious what he wanted,' Tanner replied.

'Then I suppose you'd better enlighten me.'

Tanner drew in a breath. 'Assuming Martin Longshore was killed because he found out the real reason why the Clayton family moved up to Norfolk, I'd have thought the fact that Christine had worked alongside him for over two years would mean they'd be just a little bit keen to find out if he'd told her anything.'

'Sorry, I must have missed something. Since when was Martin Longshore killed by the Claytons?'

'Since Dr Johnstone concluded that the method used to murder him was the same they used to eliminate people down in London.'

'I see. And I suppose they used to abduct their victims' children as well, did they?'

'If the girl happened to witness her father being killed, they'd have had no choice but to take her with them.'

'Right, although, on the other hand,' Cooper continued, 'the fact that she was abducted could just as likely mean he was killed because he tried to stop whoever it was from taking her. More so, given the fact that she was the fourth child to go missing in as many months.'

'And with Gary Clayton's interest in young children, both scenarios could easily lead to the same person.'

'I wasn't aware Gary Clayton was a convicted paedophile.'

'Gary Clayton isn't a convicted anything,' Tanner sneered.

'OK, so, what makes you think he has an unnatural interest in children?'

'It was what he was said to be involved in, down in London.'

Cooper nodded his head, rolling his eyes at the same time. 'Oh, you mean *rumours*.'

'If you like.'

'Well, unlike some people I could mention, I like my investigations to rely on facts. And as you now work underneath me, I'd appreciate it if you could do the same.'

'Forgive me,' said Tanner, his tone thick with sarcastic condescension. 'What *was* I thinking.'

Ignoring the remark, and the way in which it had been said, Cooper returned his attention back to Christine.

'Did the intruder say what he wanted?'

'Well, no, but whatever it was, it wasn't good.'

'He didn't ask you anything specific?'

'He didn't ask me anything at all.'

'What did he say, exactly?'

'As I told John, he didn't talk.'

'Not one word?'

Christine shook her head.

'So, if you didn't see his face, and you didn't hear his voice, how do you know it was a man?'

Christine exchanged a confused glance between the two men. 'I – I suppose I just assumed it was.'

Cooper raised a patronising eyebrow.

'I must admit,' Tanner began, 'I had the feeling it was too. He was certainly strong enough.'

'And what makes you say that?'

'He knocked me over on the way out, pushing past as if I wasn't there.'

Cooper cast an eye over at Tanner's slim narrow frame.

'No offence, Tanner, but I don't think that means the intruder was particularly strong. My grandmother could have probably done the same, and she's nearly ninety.'

Tanner smiled quietly back at him in response. It was obviously a comment used to highlight how much weight he'd lost, albeit in a derogatory fashion, but it didn't impact him in the slightest. During his absence, Cooper had done the exact opposite, his former sprightly frame having been replaced by a double-chin and a middle-aged beer-gut.

'Anyway,' Cooper continued, his eyes still focussed on Tanner, 'I assume you haven't touched anything, since you came in?'

'Not that I'm aware of, but I'd certainly be interested to find out who'd been taking such good care of those knives. If it *was* Gary Clayton, and any of those blades match the injuries found on either Martin Longshore or the body we found at Brayden Marsh, then there'll be no question as to who was responsible; for the missing children as well.'

'Then I suppose we'll have to wait and see what forensics has to say about them,' Cooper replied, just as the sound of another car could be heard pulling into the driveway outside.

'I'd better see who it is,' Cooper muttered, turning

to make his way out.

With Tanner knowing that a unit of forensics officers would soon be arriving en masse, he offered Christine an empathetic smile.

'Do you have anywhere you can stay tonight?'

'Why? Can't I stay here?'

'I don't think that would be a good idea. Besides, I doubt you'd get much sleep. Not with forensics traipsing all over the place.'

Christine wrapped her arms around her shoulders to stare down at the floor. 'I've got nowhere else to stay.'

'You said something about having friends in the local area?'

'Well, yes, but I can't just turn up on their door. Not at this hour.'

'It's probably too late to find you a hotel as well,' Tanner mused, turning an idea over in his head. 'I suppose you could stay on board my boat; if you like?'

The moment he said it, he wished he hadn't. It was far too small to share with someone else. If she accepted, he'd have to offer her the cabin, meaning he'd be stuck out on one of the cockpit's hard wooden bench seats. But that was far from the only reason he was regretting having made the offer. The last person to stay on board with him had been Jenny. Just the idea of offering the Broads Ranger what he still thought of as being his fiancée's home felt like betrayal, made immeasurably worse by the feelings he knew he was having towards her.

Wishing he could take the offer back, he spluttered out, 'Although, to be honest, I doubt it would be very comfortable.'

Christine lifted her head to send Tanner a look of fragile desperation. 'Would you mind – I mean

– would there even be enough room?'

Realising he'd managed to talk his way into a corner, one he wasn't even sure he wanted to get out of, he heard himself saying, 'If you don't mind the mess.'

'But – doesn't it only have one cabin?'

'Well, yes, but don't worry, I'll be happy enough sleeping out in the cockpit.'

- CHAPTER TWENTY SIX -

Wednesday, 11th August

'HOW'RE YOU FEELING?' asked Tanner, seeing Christine's tangled mop of greying blonde hair emerge out through the cabin doors.

'Better, thank you,' she replied, squinting against the morning's sun being reflected up into her eyes by the surrounding water.

Tanner crouched down to attend to a whistling kettle.

'Did you sleep OK?'

Easing herself through the doors, she nudged past him to slide herself into the narrow gap between the mahogany bench seat and the collapsible cockpit table.

'Surprisingly well, all things considered.'

Tanner glanced over his shoulder to catch her pulling a self-conscious lock of hair over the thin white line that ran vertically down the side of her forehead.

'Have you ever slept on board a boat before?'

Realising she'd been caught in the act of trying to conceal her scar, she sent him over a coy smile.

'I think I did when I was very young, but my memory is a little hazy.'

'I still remember my first time,' Tanner said,

before realising the alternative interpretation his words could have had. 'I meant, sleeping on board a boat, of course.'

Christine snorted quietly to herself. 'What, you mean to tell me that you're not a virgin?'

'Coffee?' Tanner replied, feeling his face flush slightly with embarrassment.

'I could murder a cup, thank you!'

An uncomfortable silence followed as Tanner pulled out a couple of mugs from under the bench seat next to the stove.

'So, how come you ended up living on board a boat?' asked Christine, reaching over for a cushion to place behind her back. 'I assume there must be some sort of a story behind it.'

'Not really. A friend of the family offered me his boat when I first moved up, which I ended up buying off him a few months later.'

'And that's this one, is it?'

'Er, no. The first was smaller.'

'Even smaller than this?'

'It's difficult to imagine, I know,' Tanner replied, kneeling awkwardly on the cockpit floor to place some instant coffee into the base of each of the mugs.

'And what happened to that?'

'A psychotic priest set fire to it, shortly after locking me inside, with a mud-weight tied around my waist,' he replied, in a matter of fact tone of voice.

'Not seriously?'

Tanner stood up to turn slowly around, a steaming mug clasped at the end of each hand. 'I'm afraid so.'

'How'd you get out?' she asked, accepting the one being offered.

'Jenny; the girl I told you about. She broke down the doors to drag me over the side.'

The mention of Tanner's former fiancée had

Christine falling silent.

'Fortunately, it was insured,' Tanner continued, 'and we were able to buy this one together shortly afterwards.'

'I take it that means she used to live here, with you?'

Tanner nodded whilst taking a tentative sip from his cup.

'I'm sorry,' whispered Christine, looking at him over the top of her mug.

'About what?'

'I didn't think. I should have realised she used to live here before asking if I could stay on board.'

'I thought I was the one who asked you?'

'Well, yes, but; even so. I should never have accepted.'

'It's fine, honestly.'

Christine rested her elbows on the table, staring over her mug at the man sitting opposite her. 'The boat must hold a lot of memories for you.'

Tanner eyes drifted away, glazing over as they did.

'I proposed to her here,' he eventually replied. 'She was sitting just about where you are.'

'Right, that's it!' she announced, with a nervous laugh. 'I'll finish this coffee and be off.'

'I really don't mind you being here, honestly.'

'Really?' she questioned, sending him a frown weighted with heavy scepticism.

'OK, if I'm to be completely honest, when I first suggested the idea I wasn't sure. But it's been surprisingly good to have someone staying on board.'

'That's kind of you to say, but I'll be out of your hair just as soon as I can get my house back.'

'I'm afraid that may not be for a few days.'

'Then I'll check myself into a Travelodge.'

Hearing the name, the haunting memory of Nadira Matar being taken from outside the hotel she'd been staying at with her mother, before being strung-up by the neck at Horsey Mere, led Tanner to blurt out, 'Look, why don't you stay here for a little longer, at least until we have a better idea as to who was in your house?'

'I really don't want to impose.'

'You wouldn't be, I promise. Besides, I don't think it will be for long. If we can link any of the knives the intruder left at your house to the Clayton family, they'll soon have other things to worry about than what they think Martin Longshore may or may not have told you.'

'OK, then at least let me pay you something towards the rent.'

'What, to stay here?' Tanner laughed.

Christine thought for a moment. 'Then I'll just have to provide you with a free taxi service, until you can get your car back.'

'Which reminds me,' Tanner replied, digging out his phone to scroll down the screen, looking for his garage's phone number.

- CHAPTER TWENTY SEVEN -

WITH NO REPLY, Tanner left the garage a message, asking them to call him with an update as soon as they could. He then made them both a coffee before getting ready for work, accepting a lift with Christine into the police station.

Despite being slightly early, he was surprised to find that the office was already buzzing with activity, as Forrester and Cooper prepared themselves for an office wide briefing.

Delighted to find himself in the audience, instead of heading up the meeting as he used to, Tanner dashed to the kitchen to make himself another coffee before propping himself up against the edge of his desk, all set to listen to what had to be said.

A moment later, Forrester's booming voice came echoing off the walls, bringing the various predominantly vacuous conversations to a hurried close.

'If I could have everyone's attention, please.'

Tanner looked on as the DCI cast his eyes around the room, waiting with the expectation of total silence.

'As a number of you are probably only just finding out, two incidents took place yesterday evening, both of which we believe to be directly linked to Martin Longshore's murder, as well as the abduction of his daughter: possibly the other children as well. We also think there could be a connection to the Clayton family. I'll leave DI Cooper to go over the details with you in a minute. Before he does, and I know this is a little late in the day, but I'd like to invite you to join me in welcoming back to the fold our very own John Tanner.'

With everyone turning to look around at him, Tanner cursed quietly to himself, as a smattering of applause limped slowly around the room.

'For those of you who don't know,' Forrester continued, 'John first joined us about four years ago as a DI from London. His presence here was key to helping us solve a number of high profile murder investigations. Since then, he's spent the last year or so taking some much deserved time off, but with everything that's been going on here over the last few months, especially recently, he's been kind enough to offer his services to us once again. I've no doubt you'll all make him feel very much at home.

'Now, moving on, here's DI Cooper with a more substantial update to yesterday evening's events.'

With a nod of acknowledgement, Cooper stepped forward to take Forrester's place.

'At half-past nine yesterday evening, the body of a man was found near Brayden Marsh, on the banks of a narrow channel just north of the River Thurne.'

Cooper gestured up at the whiteboard behind him. There, nestled in amongst numerous other photographs, was the bloated bruised face of the man Tanner recognised from the evening before.

'He has yet to be formally identified, but at the moment we believe he's the person who was reported missing by his wife last night, Mr Nigel Harrison. At the time of his passing, he was a partner for a small law firm in Norwich. Of more particular interest, we've since discovered that until just over a year ago, he worked for Hocks Templeton, a much larger firm based in Canary Wharf, whose services were regularly used by the already mentioned Clayton family.

'Although we've yet to receive a full report from our medical examiner, his preliminary findings lead us to believe that he was tortured before being killed, after which his body was transported by river to where it was left.

'The reason we believe the man's murder *may* have had something to do with the Clayton family are two-fold. Firstly, the manner of his death. He was killed by a long sharp object, probably a knife, being inserted into his brain from underneath his jaw. As you may recall, this was the same method used to kill Martin Longshore and, according to DI Tanner, was the preferred method used by the so-called Camden Crime Syndicate.

'The second reason is the person who owns the land the body was dumped on, the presumed head of the same criminal organisation, Mr Frank Clayton.'

A series of whispered remarks circled the room.

'However,' Cooper continued, bringing everyone's attention back to the front of the room, 'although it does look like there could be a connection to the Clayton family, there's no evidence as yet to suggest that they had anything to do with it. In fact, the opposite is more likely to be true.'

Tanner found himself raising an incredulous hand.

'If we could keep questions to the end, please,' Cooper responded, glancing over.

'Sorry,' Tanner continued, ignoring the request,

'but I was just wondering how you were able to work that one out?'

'I'm not having this discussion with you now, Tanner, thank you.'

'But I think everyone would be very interested to know why you think the Clayton family aren't involved, despite having just gone and listed the many reasons for them looking like they are.'

'Because of the location of the body,' Cooper stated, folding his arms. 'I'm fairly sure that everyone here would agree Frank Clayton would have to have been a bloody idiot to have arranged for someone to be killed, only to have the body left lying on his land.'

'OK, on that particular point, I'd have to agree with you,' Tanner continued. 'Frank Clayton isn't stupid, *unlike some people I could mention*,' he muttered, under his breath, 'which may be exactly why he asked for the body to be left there, knowing it would naturally divert suspicion away from himself.'

'Er, I think that's a little unlikely, don't you?'

'Then there's the method by which he was killed.'

'Which I've already mentioned. But just because it was considered to have been a preferred method used by the Clayton family when they were in London, it doesn't mean that they're the only people in the history of mankind to have done so, and it certainly doesn't mean that they were responsible in this instance.'

'It doesn't mean they didn't, though,' Tanner muttered, just loud enough for everyone to hear.

'Not without evidence to back it up!' Cooper stated, with an ever-reddening face.

Forrester cleared his throat from the side of the room to glare over at Tanner. 'Maybe if this discussion could be had *after* the briefing?'

With an apologetic smile, Tanner folded his arms

to lean back against the desk behind him.

Taking a breath, Cooper continued. 'The second incident occurred about three hours later, when someone broke into the home of Ms Christine Halliday, a Broads Ranger and former colleague of the first victim, Mr Martin Longshore. What that person's intentions were aren't known, exactly, as they were interrupted by the surprising appearance of none other than DI Tanner.'

Cooper grinned over at him. 'Perhaps you'd be able to explain to everyone what you were doing there, exactly?'

With a burning sense of embarrassed indignation, Tanner unfolded his arms to bury his hands deep into the pockets of his jeans.

'As per my statement, I was returning Ms Halliday's phone.'

'At half-past ten at night?'

'I'm fairly sure I don't have to explain myself to you, Cooper.'

The sound of Forrester clearing his throat again had the SIO moving the subject along. 'After breaking in, the intruder proceeded to tie Ms. Halliday to a chair, at which point DI Tanner entered the property, leaving the front door wide open as he did, so allowing the intruder to escape out through it.'

Tanner shook his head to offer the floor a sanguine smile.

'I believe the intruder also left a set of knives at the scene,' interjected Forrester, this time directing his attention towards his SIO.

'The intruder *did* leave a set of knives at the scene,' Cooper confirmed, 'however, as they looked as if they'd only just been taken out of a dishwasher, I doubt if they're going to tell us much.'

'But they have been sent over to forensics?'

'First thing this morning, sir, but with the intruder reported as having been wearing gloves, I don't think we should hold out too much hope that they'll provide any useful evidence. So far, the only prints we've found at the property belong to either the owner, or our very own DI Tanner.'

'But there still remains the possibility that some of the knives could match those used on our two victims,' Forrester continued, stepping forward.

'They could, sir, yes, but without being able to find either prints or DNA, we'd still be none the wiser as to who they belong to. We don't even know if the intruder was a man or a woman, being that they were wearing a black ski mask, and according to Ms Halliday, didn't say a word during the entire event.'

'But surely,' Tanner urged, finding himself unable to remain quiet, 'doesn't the fact that Ms Halliday *was* targeted give us reason enough to consider either the Claytons, or at least one of their known associates, to be a prime suspect, even if we don't yet have the necessary evidence to prove it?'

'Why?' Cooper retorted. 'Because the victims were killed in a similar manner to how you say the Claytons would take care of people down in London?'

'You've also neglected to mention anything about Martin Longshore's daughter being taken, and the rumours surrounding Gary Clayton's unnatural interest in children.'

'As I've told you before, Tanner, we don't run our investigations based on idle speculation, or at least *I* don't.'

Tanner was happy enough to let that one go, and once again directed a smile down at the carpet.

'However,' Cooper continued, 'I would like to

thank you for reminding us about what has to remain our primary focus, that of finding those missing children. Does anyone have anything to report since our meeting yesterday morning? Vicky?'

The DI looked up with a start. 'I'm, er, afraid we still haven't made much progress. Door-to-door enquiries haven't led to anything. Extending our investigation to include sex offenders throughout East Anglia only unearthed one person who'd ever owned a sailing boat, and that was a yacht he keeps down at Lowestoft. We're still working our way through owners of cabinless boats and dinghies that fit the witnesses' descriptions within the Broads area, but there are literally hundreds, and it's going to take time.'

'There also remains the unfortunate possibility that the boat he's using isn't registered with the Broads Authority,' came an unfamiliar voice.

Glancing up to find the person who'd spoken, Tanner recognised Mark Townsend, the young PC he'd met when he'd first arrived, now dressed in a smart suit and tie.

'Has there been any progress identifying more of the prints found on the boats the children were taken from?' questioned Cooper.

'No, sir, but as you know, they were all hire boats.'

'What about the one Martin Longshore lived on?'

'We only had two that were unknown, one set we've since been able to identify.'

'And who did that belong to?'

'Er...DI Tanner, sir.'

Cooper rolled his eyes, leaving Tanner raising his hand whilst doing his best to supress a self-amused smirk.

'Has a press conference been held yet?'

'Only for the first three missing children,' Cooper responded.

Tanner continued to hold his hand in the air. 'But not for the murder of Martin Longshore and the disappearance of his daughter?'

'Not as yet, no.'

'May I ask why not?'

'Because we feel the investigation has already generated quite enough media attention, or hadn't you noticed the vans clogging up the road outside?'

'But surely, when it comes to a missing child, you can never have too much media attention.'

'As you should know better than most, in the case of a murder investigation, you most definitely can, or have you forgotten what happened to DI Burgess, when the press made up their own mind who the murderer was, leading to an innocent man being beaten to death?'

'If it was just a murder enquiry then I'd have to agree with you, but this isn't, though, is it!'

'And if it was the first incident of a child going missing, then I'd have to agree with you as well, but this is the fourth, and all we got back from the previous ones were numerous people saying that the only thing they saw was an old fashioned sailing boat, leading to an ever-increasing number of stories about a ghostly apparition that's since been called "The Wherryman", who sails around the Broads, looking for unguarded children to steal away into the darkness of the night.'

'Then wouldn't it be a good idea to remind them all of the facts, whilst making an urgent call for more witnesses?'

'Anyway,' said Cooper, glancing around the room

with a dismissive wave of his hand. 'I don't need to remind you all of the urgency of the situation. You all know your jobs. The sooner we find Susie Longshore and the other missing children, the sooner we find our murderer. That's it for now; and remember to keep me posted.'

- CHAPTER TWENTY EIGHT -

THE MOMENT THE briefing concluded the room burst into activity, as everyone hurried back to their desks.

Unsure what he should be doing, Tanner scanned the room, searching for Vicky. Instead he found Forrester, shoving his way through the crowd towards him, his face flush with anger.

'If I could have a quick word in my office,' he growled, coming to a the briefest of standstills before spinning on his heel to head back the way he'd come.

Knowing full well what it would be about, Tanner followed after, entering the DCI's office to find Cooper hovering nervously by the side of the desk.

With the door closed, Forrester directed them each to take a seat.

'Now, would either of you mind telling me what *that* was all about?' he asked, finding his own to begin glowering over at them.

'Sorry sir,' Cooper began, offering him a look of angelic innocence, 'I'm not with you.'

'That was supposed to be a briefing to discuss the investigation into no less than two murders and four missing children, not an opportunity for the two of you to belittle each other in front of the entire office.'

'It's not my fault,' Cooper huffed, glancing around at Tanner. 'The man is constantly trying to undermine my authority.'

'How can he be constantly trying to undermine your authority?' Forrester questioned. 'He's only been here two days!'

'I meant; since he got here, sir.'

'And as for you, Tanner, an office-wide briefing is *not* the time to openly question the direction of an investigation.'

'I apologise,' Tanner offered, 'but there were things being said that I found myself unable to ignore, like, for example, that the Claytons aren't being considered the prime suspects for the murders and child abductions, sir.'

'That's probably because there's not one shred of physical evidence to suggest that they are,' Cooper stated, his attention remaining focussed on Forrester.

'You mean, apart from the fact that the method used to kill both murder victims is exactly the same as the one used by them down in London.'

'Which in itself has never been proven. If it had, they'd both be serving life in prison. Besides, Johnstone says the weapons used were different.'

Tanner shook his head with unhidden incredulity. 'Why do people like you always assume an assailant would only ever use the same weapon? Such moronic rhetoric is about as stupid as saying a mechanic would only use one screwdriver. I think the knives left at Ms. Halliday's house prove that.'

'But what it doesn't prove is who owned them.'

'How the hell do you know?' Tanner demanded, his voice rising as his eyes bored into the side of Cooper's face. 'You only sent them to forensics this morning.'

'Because you only had to look at them to know they won't find anything.'

Tanner sat back in his chair, his eyes remaining fixed on Cooper. 'This is hilarious. You've just spent the last twenty minutes having a go at me for making judgements based on lack of evidence, and yet here you are, jumping to conclusions, before anyone's even had a chance to see if there's any actually there!'

'All right, you two,' Forrester began, raising his voice to equal that of the two DIs, 'that's enough!'

'And whilst I'm here,' Tanner continued, happy to ignore his DCI, 'what's the deal with not holding a press conference?'

Cooper finally turned to look at Tanner. 'Because, as I said during the briefing, both Forrester and I've agreed that we've already had quite enough attention from the press.'

'And as *I* said,' Tanner began, leaning forward, 'you can *never* have enough attention from the press, not when you're dealing with missing children.'

'Unless, of course, the media decides to do nothing in response but continue to circulate the same ridiculous stories about ghostly apparitions and shimmering sailing boats.'

'I'm sorry, but Cooper's right on this one,' said Forrester, catching Tanner's eye. 'We've held three press conferences already, immediately following each of the child abductions, and all they did was to generate increasingly far-fetched stories about the so-called Wherryman.'

'You're telling me that you haven't had a single useful lead from any of them?'

'I suppose that depends on what you term useful. Excluding the usual inundation of crank calls, all we heard from anyone was something very similar to what you told Vicky, that of a small boat with a dark red sail being seen in the immediate vicinity, which then proceeded to vanish into thin air.'

'I said it *seemed* to vanish. I never said it actually did. It was far more likely that he simply steered into the reeds to take his sail down.'

'Which is why we've spent the last few months tirelessly tracking down every registered sex offender in East Anglia who's known to own a sailing boat, whilst also endeavouring to speak to every person living in the Broads who's registered as having one. Then there were all the house-to-house enquiries. And it's not as if we didn't circulate Susie Longshore's picture to the press, along with the normal plea for anyone to come forward with information.'

'But sending out a press release is hardly a substitute for holding a news conference, is it? You *have* to maximise media attention by every and any means possible. For all we know, someone who knows something vital to finding the missing children is sitting at home, too frightened to come forward, waiting for another nudge before doing so. Or maybe they've just moved into the area, and don't know how important what they've either seen or heard actually is.'

A sullen silence fell over the office as Forrester leaned back in his chair to steeple his fingers together.

'I think Tanner may have a point,' he eventually muttered, his words being met by Cooper letting out an exasperated sigh.

'But I thought we agreed that it would do more harm than good?'

'Maybe it will, maybe it won't,' Forrester continued, pushing himself forward to reach for his mouse, 'but with nothing transpiring from either the sex offenders register, the endless door-to-door enquiries, or our seemingly fruitless search for the person who owns the boat, I think we're going to have to give it another try.'

'In the meantime,' Tanner continued, taking advantage of the discussion swinging in his favour, 'I'd like to speak to some of the staff employed by the law firm our most recent victim worked for.'

Forrester caught Cooper's eye. 'I assume that's alright with you?'

'I was going to suggest he went there anyway,' he replied, with a huff of indifference.

'And I was hoping to take DI Gilbert with me?'

Forrester raised a questioning eyebrow at Cooper.

'I'm sorry, but there's no way I can spare her,' came his dismissive response.

'How about the new boy, DC Townsend?'

'I can't spare him either. Not if I've now got to organise another bloody press conference.'

Forrester glanced over at Tanner. 'You'll be alright on your own, won't you?'

'Of course, sir. I'll just have to take the train.'

'You still don't have a car?'

'Not yet, but I'm sure it won't be much longer.'

'OK, well, if it's not ready by the end of the day, you'll have to sort something else out for yourself, but not a Jag, mind. Our budget is stretched quite thin enough as it is.'

- CHAPTER TWENTY NINE -

T AKING THE TRAIN from Wroxham to Norwich, Tanner made his way over the bridge located just outside the station to begin searching for the address. Finding himself being led towards a large modern office block, one which seemed to be shared by a number of small local businesses, he heaved open one of the doors to step inside.

'May I help you?' asked an attractive young lady, glancing up from behind an elegant oval-shaped reception desk.

'Hi, yes. I'm looking to speak with someone from Allen & Atkinson, about Nigel Harrison?'

'And you are?' she asked, picking up a phone.

'Detective Inspector Tanner, Norfolk Police.'

Raising a curious eyebrow, the lady turned her head to speak quietly into the mouthpiece.

'Hi, Patricia. I have someone from Norfolk Police down at reception, asking about Nigel.'

There was a pause as she took a moment to give Tanner a reassuring smile.

'OK, I'll send him up.'

Following the directions given, Tanner soon emerged from a lift to be met by a small, stern, pale-faced woman dressed in a smart black suit.

'Detective Inspector Tanner?' she questioned,

her eyes taking in his somewhat dishevelled appearance.

Tanner nodded with a smile.

'I'm Patricia, Mr Harrison's PA. I understand you're from Norfolk Police?'

'That's correct,' he said, holding out his ID.

Glancing down at it with a raised eyebrow, she looked up to continue. 'Do you have any news? All we know is what his wife told us this morning; that he didn't come back from work last night.'

Tanner glanced briefly down the corridor he found himself standing in to see some people wandering down towards them. 'Is there somewhere quieter we can talk?'

'Sorry, yes, of course. If you follow me.'

Doing so, Tanner was led into a spacious office with a desk on one side and a couple of slim black leather sofas tucked away on the other. Hearing the door being closed, he stepped over to the desk, behind which was a large window offering panoramic views of Norwich, and the bridge he'd walked over earlier.

'Is this Mr Harrison's office?'

'It is.'

'And yours is?'

'The one next door,' she replied, gesturing behind.

'You said his wife told you Mr Harrison hadn't come home last night,' he began, fishing out his notebook to glance down at the desk.

'His wife phoned this morning, asking if anyone had seen him.'

'And what did you tell her?'

'That I hadn't. Not since he left work yesterday.'

'When was that?'

'At around five o'clock.'

'Was that when he'd normally leave?'

The lady shrugged. 'It was perhaps a little earlier

than normal.'

'Did he say why he was leaving early?'

'No, and I didn't ask,' she replied, with a disapproving look.

'And did anything happen before he did? Anything unusual?'

'Nothing obvious. I put a call through to him. A few minutes later, he put his head around my door to say that he'd see me tomorrow.'

'I don't suppose you have any idea who the call was from?'

'I put dozens of calls through to Mr Harrison every day.'

'I take it that means you don't?'

'I'm afraid I can't remember,' the lady confirmed, glancing briefly away. 'Even if I could, I'm not at liberty to discuss Mr Harrison's private business with you.'

'Of course, but you could at least tell me the name of the person who called him?'

'If I could remember, then I'd be more than happy to, but unfortunately, in this particular instance, I can't.'

Tanner cast his eyes over the top of the desk, taking note of the various files and documents piled high around its edges. 'Late yesterday evening, a body was found lying on a ploughed-up field in the north east corner of the Norfolk Broads.' He paused to catch the woman's eye. 'It had been stabbed and beaten to the point where it's unlikely that even his wife will be able to recognise him. The man was then executed by having a knife pushed up into his brain from underneath his jaw.'

The woman's already pale face became as white as a sheet.

'At this moment in time we believe the man was your boss, Mr Nigel Harrison. If that turns out to be true, then this is a murder investigation, and the person who called him before he suddenly announced his early departure could well be the person who tortured and killed him. Now, bearing all that in mind, and the fact that a seeming unwillingness to help us with our enquiries could be viewed by a court as obstruction of justice, I'd like to ask you again if you can remember the caller's name?'

Tanner saw her swallow before opening her mouth.

'It was one of his clients. Mr Clayton. Mr Gary Clayton.'

A thin smile played out under Tanner's beard.

'Were you able to overhear the conversation?'

'It's not my job to eavesdrop, inspector.'

'I'm sure it isn't, but if your office is right next door, you must occasionally find yourself overhearing what's being discussed, whether you want to or not?'

The woman took a moment before answering. 'It sounded like the caller wanted to arrange a meeting.'

'Did you hear what the meeting would be about?'

The woman shook her head.

'How about where?'

'Only that he wanted to meet.'

Tanner thought for a moment, his eyes returning to the desk, searching for some sort of a clue as to where it could have taken place.

'Would you describe Mr Harrison as being heavy handed?' he asked, crouching down to stare over the surface of a notepad left open beside the keyboard.

'Sorry, but – how do you mean?'

'I don't suppose you have a pencil I could borrow?' he asked, somewhat absently.

'Er...there's one on the desk,' she replied, her tone

133

uncertain as she gestured down.

Seeing her pointing at a black mesh pen holder, he plucked out a pencil to begin rubbing gently over the pad's surface.

A rap at the door had him glancing up to see an immaculately dressed grey-haired old man cast a curious pair of piercing blue eyes first at Tanner, then at the PA.

'Good afternoon, Patricia. Sorry to bother you. I heard someone from the police was here, asking about Nigel?'

Her eyes led his over towards Tanner, who took a moment to finish what he'd been doing before using the same pencil to jot something down in his little-used notebook.

'Mr Atkinson, this is Detective Inspector Tanner, from Norfolk Police.'

The man looked Tanner up and down. 'May I see some identification?'

'Of course,' Tanner replied, tucking the pencil behind his ear to pull out his ID.

Stepping forward to examine it, the man lifted his head to stare down his nose at the scruffy-looking policeman.

'OK, thank you, but I therefore assume that you know you're not allowed to conduct a search of this office, or anywhere else for that matter, without being in possession of a valid search warrant?'

'I wasn't aware that I *was* conducting a search; Mr Atkinson, wasn't it?' said Tanner, returning to his notes.

'Then may I ask what you were doing just now; when I came in?'

'I was endeavouring to find out where your colleague, Mr Harrison, went after work yesterday, which we feel is of particular importance, being that his body was found just a few hours later.'

'His *body?*'

'And with that in mind,' Tanner continued, 'would you mind me asking what you were doing yesterday evening between the hours of six and nine?'

'Me?'

'I take it you did work with him?'

'Of course, but...'

'Then we'll need a statement from you as to where you were at the time of his death, along with your fingerprints and a DNA sample. You too, I'm afraid, Mrs...'

'Ms Fitton,' the PA replied, her eyes drifting between the police detective and the grey-haired old man.

'We'll of course be requiring statements from everyone who works here, but in the meantime,' Tanner continued, focussing his attention on Atkinson, 'I don't suppose the name Gary Clayton rings any bells?'

'Gary Clayton?' Atkinson repeated.

'According to Ms Fitton, she put a call through to Mr Harrison just before he left work somewhat earlier than usual. Apparently, the caller was looking to arrange a meeting.'

'I don't know anyone by that name.'

'How about Frank Clayton?'

'Again, no.'

'I see. May I ask how long Mr Harrison has been working here?'

'About a year, why?'

'I assume you were directly involved in his employment, being that you're a managing partner.'

'I interviewed him myself; if that's what you mean.'

'Did you ask him *why* he wanted to move up to Norfolk?'

'He said it was for personal reasons.'

'You do know who he worked for, before he just happened to wake up one morning with the idea of moving up here?'

'I'd have to look it up, but I'm seriously struggling to see the relevance.'

'Don't worry, I have it here,' Tanner continued, turning a page of his notebook. 'It was a law firm called Hocks Templeton. Had you heard of them, before offering Mr Harrison the position?'

'Only by name.'

'Not by reputation?'

'I'm sorry?'

'You didn't know that their main client was the Camden Crime Syndicate, a criminal organisation owned by the Clayton family, who just happened to move up to Norfolk at around the same time Mr Harrison did?'

'I've no idea where you're going with this.'

'Was that why you were so keen to take Mr Harrison on, hoping, or maybe even knowing he'd bring that client with him?'

'Are you insinuating that we employed Mr Harrison for the single purpose of gaining one of his clients?'

'Knowing how much business that one client would be likely to bring in through the door, then yes, Mr Atkinson, that's exactly what I'm insinuating.'

- CHAPTER THIRTY -

BEFORE HE'D EVEN made it out of the building's lobby, Tanner was clawing out his phone to put a call through to the station.

'Forrester, it's Tanner. Just phoning to say that I'm on my way back to Wroxham.'

'Were you able to speak to anyone at the law firm?'

'Nigel Harrison's PA. The senior partner as well, a Mr Philip Atkinson.'

'Do you think either could have had any involvement?'

'I doubt if his PA did, but I wouldn't rule out the senior partner. One thing I did find out.'

'What was that?'

'Gary Clayton is one of their clients. I can only assume that means his father is as well. I wouldn't be surprised if they employed Harrison purely on the basis that he'd bring the Clayton family's business with him, especially as he moved up at about the same time. But that wasn't what was most interesting.'

'Go on.'

'According to his PA, Gary was the last person to speak to Harrison, before he announced he was leaving early to meet him.'

There was a momentary pause before Forrester's voice came back over the line. 'I don't suppose she had any idea as to where they were planning on meeting?'

'She said she didn't, but I managed to find an address anyway.'

'Dare I ask how?'

'One had been left on a notepad.'

'In plain sight, I hope?' Forrester queried; his voice filled with questionable doubt.

'Just about,' Tanner replied, before moving the subject along. 'It's the location that's of most interest.'

'Which was?'

'The Broadwater boatyard, in Coltishall. The one Gary Clayton is supposed to be in charge of.'

The line fell silent.

'So anyway,' Tanner continued, as he began marching his way back towards the station, 'I'd like to apply for a search warrant, to take a look around. If they did meet there, then there's every possibility that that's where Harrison was both tortured and killed.'

'Naturally, but do we have any other evidence that would support the application?'

'Other than the fact that Gary Clayton is Nigel Harrison's client, that he's also in charge of the boatyard in question, and that we have a witness who says he phoned him up to arrange to meet him there?'

'Look, Tanner, you know the magistrate is going to demand a lot more than that before granting a search warrant, like some physical evidence that the victim was murdered there, or something to prove that Gary Clayton had a hand in what happened.'

'I admit, it would be nice, but without being able to search the place, I'm not sure how that's going to happen?'

'Then at least something to prove he went there

at the time in question, and I don't mean because you just happened to see the address of the boatyard written on a notepad in his office whilst interviewing a potential suspect.'

It was Tanner's turn to fall momentarily silent. 'Have we heard anything else from forensics?'

'They promised to have something back by end of play today.'

'Nothing on that roll of knives left at Ms. Halliday's house?'

'I left a note with Cooper, but I suspect he's been too busy organising the press conference to chase them.'

'So, you are holding one, then?'

'At five o'clock this evening.'

Tanner checked his watch. 'OK. I should be back in time.'

'Oh, there's er...no need to hurry back. Cooper and I can handle it.'

'Of course,' Tanner replied, his tone flat with rejected despondency. From the way Forrester had said it, it was abundantly clear that he didn't want him taking part.

'Any more news of that car of yours?' the DCI asked, in a somewhat obvious attempt to change the subject.

'I'll need to chase the garage again,' Tanner replied, having only just remembered.

'OK, but don't forget what I said earlier. If it's not ready by end of play today, you'll need to get something else sorted out for yourself.'

Ending the call, Tanner shuddered. The idea of being forced to drive around in some cheap ugly Korean hire car, instead of his gleaming black Jaguar XJS, had him scrabbling around for the garage's number. The fact that he'd not heard from them all day, despite having left them a message in the morning, couldn't have been good. If it was done, and had passed its MOT, they'd have called to demand payment. Hopefully, they'd just been too busy.

'Hello, it's John Tanner. I'm calling about the XJS?'

'Oh, yes. Sorry, Mr Tanner, I meant to return your call this afternoon.'

'Has there been any news?' he asked, feeling like an expectant father.

'I'm afraid not. We're still waiting on parts.'

'Oh, right. Any idea when they'll arrive?' he continued, resisting the urge to ask what the parts were, or more importantly, how much they'd cost.

'Dunno. Could be tomorrow, could be the day after. Not many places stock old Jag parts these days.'

'But they have been ordered, though?'

'I think so. It's just that it will take a while for them to arrive. Don't worry, Mr Tanner, I'll give you a call just as soon as they have.'

'Great, thanks,' Tanner replied, doing his best to sound like he meant it.

- CHAPTER THIRTY ONE -

ARRIVING BACK AT Wroxham station about forty-five minutes later, knowing the press conference would be in full swing, Tanner found himself a coffee and something to eat before wandering up Stalham Road.

Nearing the police station, he arrived in time to see Forrester and Cooper heading back inside the building, leaving the dozen or so reporters and cameramen crowded outside shouting a series of questions after them, most of which seemed to be in reference to the so-called Wherryman, and if there had been any more ghostly sightings.

Tanner waited a moment for them to start packing up, before straddling the low wall to make his way discreetly over the carpark.

Ducking in through the main doors, he found Vicky standing in the middle of the reception area, having what appeared to be a light-hearted chat with the newest member of CID, the handsome young Detective Constable Mark Townsend.

'How'd it go?' Tanner asked, catching her eye.

'Not great. They kept asking why we still hadn't been able to find any of the missing children, before harping on about the bloody Wherryman. I don't think Forrester enjoyed it very much, either; not if the look on his face was anything to go by.'

'Have there been any developments in my

absence?'

'Forensics came back to us, just before the press conference started.'

'And?'

'Gary Clayton's DNA was found on the lawyer's body, the one dumped on his father's land.'

Tanner turned to hurry over towards the double doors that led through the main office, a broad grin spreading out over his face.

'How d'you get on in Norwich?' Vicky called out, taking off after him.

'Nigel Harrison's PA told me that he had a call from someone, asking to meet,' Tanner replied, his hand resting on one of the door handles, 'a few minutes before deciding to leave early for the day.'

'Did she tell you who it was?'

'The same person you just said matches the DNA evidence found.'

- CHAPTER THIRTY TWO -

WITHOUT BOTHERING TO knock, Tanner burst into Forrester's office to find him with his elbows planted firmly on his desk; Cooper sitting opposite.

'Vicky told me they found Gary Clayton's DNA on the body,' he stated, his eyes predominately focussed on the DCI.

'Come in, Tanner, why don't you,' Forrester muttered, his tone drenched in sarcasm.

'Sorry, sir. I came straight in when I heard the news. I assume you're going to arrest him?'

'We've decided to wait,' Cooper said, a conceited smile spreading out over his face, 'to see if anything comes in from the press conference.'

'But...' Tanner began, struggling to believe what he was hearing, '...didn't Forrester tell you what I found out from Nigel Harrison's PA?'

'That she thought Gary Clayton *may* have called him before he left work?'

'She didn't *think* it was Gary Clayton, she said it *was* Gary Clayton!'

Cooper shrugged. 'Even if it was, it doesn't prove anything.'

'Not on its own, perhaps, but when you combine it with the fact that he was calling him to arrange a meeting, that the address I discovered written on a notepad next to his phone was that of his boatyard, and now the physical evidence of his DNA being found on Harrison's body, it's virtually an open and shut case, surely.'

'Er, I think to say it's an open and shut case is being a little over-dramatic, don't you think?' Cooper scoffed, flicking a smile over at Forrester. 'Besides, even if it was Gary Clayton who'd called him, and his PA thinks it was to arrange a meeting, that could have been for anytime. And the fact that he did is also hardly a great surprise, being that you found out he's one of their clients.'

'And what about the DNA evidence?'

'It was found on the victim, not at the scene. All it proves is that the two had been in contact with each other at some point, which again is of no great surprise, when taking into account what I've already said.'

Tanner sent Forrester an imploring look.

'I'm sorry, Tanner. He's right, I'm afraid.'

'But it must be enough at least to apply for a search warrant, to have a look around his boatyard.'

'With that I completely agree,' said Cooper, offering Tanner a calculating smile. 'But before we do, I think you're going to have to clarify just exactly how it was that you came by the address you said you found.'

'As I told Forrester, it was written on a notepad.'

'That you just happened to see when interviewing his PA.'

'That's right.'

'It's funny, but we had a call from the senior partner of Harrison's law firm. A Mr Atkinson,' Cooper continued, fishing out his notebook. 'He said there was nothing written on Harrison's notepad, at least there wasn't until you scribbled over the top of it with one of their pencils.'

'At which point I just happened to see it,' Tanner replied, unable to stop the corners of his mouth from curling up.

Forrester slammed his fist down on his desk. 'For God's sake, Tanner, this isn't a game!'

'I never said it was,' he replied, still smirking.

'It's not funny, either!'

'I think that's a matter of opinion.'

'I take it you do still wish to continue working here?'

At that precise moment in time, all Tanner really wanted to do was to climb back on board his boat to set sail for the Mediterranean, but with still hardly a penny to his name, and his car stuck in a garage having work done which he couldn't even afford, he didn't have much choice but to straighten his face and apologise.

'I'm sorry, sir, but I didn't conduct an unauthorised search of Harrison's office, and I certainly didn't take anything. I simply noticed that an impression had been left on the notepad, so I ran a pencil over the top of it to reveal what it said.'

'That's hardly "in plain sight", though, is it.'

'I'm not a lawyer, or anything, but I think it could be argued either way.'

'Yes, well, unfortunately, Tanner, they *are* lawyers. And they're saying that it wasn't in plain sight, being that you had to run a pencil over it in order to see it.'

'To read it, maybe, but I could already see the impression.'

'Can you please stop arguing with me, Tanner.'

'I'm not arguing with you, sir. I'm simply endeavouring to state my case.'

'But nobody gives a shit!' Forrester bellowed, his face going from red to puce. 'All I know is that we can't use the information you uncovered, being that you found it without having first acquired the necessary search warrant.'

'Then it's a good job we don't need to use it as evidence in a court of law.'

'But we did need it to present to the local magistrate as evidence to be granted access to Gary Clayton's boatyard.'

'Then I suggest we don't tell them how we obtained it.'

'The law firm you lifted the evidence from has filed for an injunction, preventing us from being able to use it.'

'That's funny. You'd think they'd be bending over backwards to help us find out who killed one of their employees, not the exact opposite, which only goes one step further to prove that it is the Claytons who are behind all this. There's no other explanation for their new law firm to be doing all that they possibly can to prevent us from finding out who killed one of their employees.'

'You could well be right,' Forrester continued, 'but it doesn't help our current situation, does it! Without being able to include the address of the boatyard you found, there's no way we'll be granted a search warrant to gain access.'

'Then we'll just have to find more evidence, won't we!'

'We wouldn't need to if you hadn't lifted that address from out of Harrison's office, with one of their senior partners watching you do so, would we,' accused Cooper, glaring over at Tanner.

'Excuse me, but how was I to know that they'd object to us trying to do all that we could to find out who'd tortured and killed one of their own employees?'

'For the very reason you've only just highlighted;

that they represent the very person you seem hell-bent on blaming for not only the murders, but the child abductions as well.'

Doing his best to ignore him, Tanner turned to look at Forrester.

'What about those knives that were left at Ms. Halliday's house?'

'Yes, well, unfortunately...' Forrester began, steering his eyes over towards Cooper, 'when I made the effort to chase them up myself, they said they'd never received them.'

'What?' Tanner demanded, joining Forrester in staring over at Cooper.

'There's no point looking at me!' Cooper exclaimed. 'It's forensics' job to make sure everything's been bagged and collated properly.'

'But it *is* your job to make sure they have, being that you're the senior investigating officer!' berated Forrester.

'What was I supposed to do? Spend half the night standing over them with a clipboard?'

The room fell into a resentful silence as Forrester pushed himself away from the desk to make his way over to the window, hands clasped firmly behind his back.

Feeling someone had to say something, Tanner cleared his throat. 'Look, why don't I head over to the boatyard in Coltishall, to ask if anyone working there saw Nigel Harrison yesterday evening?'

'I didn't think you had a car?' jibed Cooper.

'Then why don't you go?'

'I've got better things to do than hang around a boatyard asking the staff if anyone just happened to see their boss murdering his own lawyer, for no apparent reason, before loading the body onto a boat to spend the next four hours driving it all the way to

Brayden Marsh for the sole purpose of dumping it in what is effectively his dad's back garden, thank you very much.'

'Will you two shut-up!' bellowed Forrester, spinning around to glare at them.

'I'm sorry sir, but it was just one of the dumbest ideas I've ever heard in my entire life.'

'At least it *was* an idea, which is certainly more than you've been able to come up with.'

With Cooper fixing his eyes on the carpet, evidently sulking, Tanner took in a breath. 'I still think it's worth a shot. All we need is to find some sort of evidence that Nigel Harrison did meet Gary there, or failing that, something to prove that he at least went there after work last night.'

Forrester glanced down at his watch. 'Well, look, there's no point going now. The place will be closed for the day. I suggest you head down there first thing tomorrow. I assume you *will* have a car by then?'

'The garage is waiting on parts.'

'Then it looks like you're going to have to hire one, doesn't it!'

- CHAPTER THIRTY THREE -

LEAVING COOPER IN the office with their DCI, Tanner made his way back to his desk to find Vicky about to go into the kitchen.

'How's Forrester?' she asked, glancing around. 'We heard him shouting.'

'Mostly at me,' Tanner laughed.

'About anything in particular?'

'Nothing really. Cooper was winding me up.'

'Oh, well, I shouldn't worry. He's been winding us all up recently.'

'To be honest, I just don't understand,' Tanner continued, glancing about. 'It's almost as if he's deliberately going out of his way to prove that the Claytons didn't have anything to do with what's been going on.'

'Maybe they don't.'

'Not you as well?'

Vicky shrugged. 'I can understand why they may have wanted Martin Longshore dead, especially if he was stupid enough to have been trying to blackmail them. And if what you say is true about Gary Clayton having an unnatural interest in children, it's possible that he's the one whose been taking them, but none of that explains why he'd want to torture and kill his own lawyer.'

'When you say it like that, I must admit, it doesn't seem very likely. But he did phone Nigel Harrison up to arrange a meeting, just before he left early for the day, and the address I found on his desk only makes it appear more likely that he had a hand, even if he lacks any form of motive.'

'Where was that?'

'Sorry, I thought I mentioned it earlier. It was the boatshed at Coltishall, the one he's supposed to be in charge of. That's what all the arguing was about. I was trying to get Forrester to agree to apply for a search warrant, to have a look around the place, but he's not convinced it would be granted.'

'You think that's where Nigel Harrison may have been murdered?'

'If Gary Clayton was behind it, then I think it would make sense. Don't forget, he was tortured before he was killed. To do so, he would have needed somewhere completely private, where he could guarantee he wouldn't be seen.'

'But would Gary really have killed someone inside his own boatshed?'

'You're forgetting that people like the Clayton's consider themselves to be above the law. It probably didn't even cross his mind that evidence found there would link him directly to the crime. He probably just thought it was the most obvious place.'

'So, what are you going to do now?'

'Forrester told me to head over there in the morning, to see if anyone saw anything.'

'Is that very likely?'

'Not really. I suppose it's possible that someone working there may have seen Harrison arrive, maybe at the same time they were leaving. Anyway, for now I'm just going to head back to my boat,' he added, his voice both tired and despondent.

Vicky lifted her head to hold Tanner's eyes. 'If you fancy some company, we could always go out for a drink?'

'Er, thanks for the offer,' Tanner replied, suddenly feeling a little awkward, 'but I have Christine staying with me for a few days.'

'Who's Christine?' Vicky questioned, her face tightening.

'You know, the Broads Ranger?'

'Oh, right.'

Beginning to wonder if she'd just asked him out, a sense of guilt for declining had him blurting out a more detailed explanation. 'She stayed over last night, after her house was broken into. I slept out in the cockpit. I told her she could stay for a few days, just until we find out who it was.'

'Make's sense, I suppose. I just thought you could do with the company. Anyway, I better get back to work, before Cooper sees me chatting.'

'Another time?'

'Of course,' she replied, with a crooked smile, spinning away to leave Tanner wondering if she had asked him out or not.

- CHAPTER THIRTY FOUR -

LATER THAT EVENING, after a relaxing walk back from the police station, Tanner reached the river where his boat was moored to see Christine, propped up against its white tarpaulin cover, her attention directed down at her phone.

'Ahoy there!' he called out, as he made his way along the grass bank.

'Evening, Captain,' she replied, glancing up with a smile.

'I hope you haven't been waiting long?'

'Not at all.'

Stopping in front of her, he cast a casual eye over the boat. 'You should have gone inside.'

'I didn't know if it was still OK for me to stay.'

'Of course. As I said this morning, it's good to have the company. So anyway, how was your day?'

'Oh, you know. About average. Yours?'

'Oh, you know. About average,' he repeated, leaving them both grinning at each other. 'Can you give me a hand with the cover?'

'Absolutely!' she replied, tucking her phone away. 'I don't suppose there's been any news on the missing children?' she continued, helping him unclip it from the deck.

'Not yet,' came Tanner's honest reply, 'but a press conference was held earlier, so hopefully something will come from that.'

'What about the person who broke into my house?'

'I have my suspicions, but I can't help think that the investigation is being hindered by the very person who's supposed to be in charge.'

'Anyone I know?'

'You met him yesterday. DI Cooper. The young-ish man with the short dark hair.'

'A bit plump around the middle?'

'That's the one. He was promoted when I was away and has somehow talked himself into being the SIO.'

'SIO?'

'Senior Investigating Officer, but I can't help but feel that he's in over his head. I'm fairly sure my boss thinks so as well.'

'So, Cooper isn't your boss?'

'Er, no. He's just in charge of the investigation, or at least he's supposed to be.'

'And you think he's trying to de-rail it?'

'I'm not sure. It's probably that we just disagree with certain aspects.'

'Such as...?'

'Well, for example, I was hoping to apply for a search warrant to take a look around the Broadwater boatshed over at Coltishall, but he doesn't think there's any point.'

'What would you be hoping to find?'

Tanner took a moment to remind himself that the woman he'd found himself sharing his boat with was still officially a suspect for the murder of Martin Longshore. But when he remembered that the only reason she had been was because she used to work alongside him, and that she herself had been a target, most likely by the very same person who murdered her colleague, he found himself feeling happy enough to allow the conversation to continue.

'Remember the body you found, up near Brayden

Marsh?'

'I believe it was my old patient who found him; but go on.'

'We found out that he was a lawyer by the name of Nigel Harrison, and that up until about a year ago he worked for a large legal company based in London, known to be used by the Clayton family. So anyway, I paid a visit to his new firm today, over in Norwich. I'm fairly sure he brought the Claytons with him, probably as part of the package they offered him.'

'What makes you think that?'

'I found out that none other than Frank Clayton's son, Gary, phoned him up, just before he left work, the evening he was murdered. Nigel Harrison's PA said he was calling to arrange a meeting. He left soon after, but not before writing an address down on a notepad.'

'I take it that was the boatshed over at Coltishall?'

Tanner nodded.

'So, why can't you get a search warrant to take a look around?'

'Because I didn't have one when I found the address.'

'I'm not with you. Why would you have needed a search warrant?'

'To be honest, at the time, I didn't think I did, but only because the thought hadn't crossed my mind that the law firm Harrison worked for may not want me to find out who'd actually killed him.'

'Because that person could have been a client of theirs.'

'Exactly!' Tanner exclaimed, smiling over at her. 'You know, someone should give you Cooper's role. I reckon you'd do a better job of it.'

'I'm quite happy being a Broads Ranger, thank you very much.'

'Anyway, by the time I'd got back to the office, they'd already taken out an injunction to prevent us from using it.'

'But doesn't the fact that they went to the effort of preventing you from using it make it all the more likely that the Claytons *are* involved, being that their new law firm are willing to defend them over the murder of one of their own, the very person who gave them the client in the first place?'

Tanner took a moment to take Christine in. 'Are you sure nobody's ever told you that you're in the wrong profession?'

Christine sent him a reproachful frown, leaving him smiling back.

'Sorry, I won't mention it again. I'd say you're right, though. I can't see any other reason why they would feel the need to protect one of their clients to such a degree, unless they already knew they were involved.'

'Then you need to take a look inside that boatshed.'

Tanner nodded in agreement. 'We just need to find enough evidence to convince the local magistrate that it was where Gary Clayton had arranged to meet Nigel Harrison.'

'Excluding the address you found on his desk.'

'Correct again. Anyway, the plan at the moment is for me to head over there tomorrow morning, to see if anyone saw Harrison arriving there at the time in question.'

'What about CCTV?'

'There aren't any cameras in Coltishall, at least there never used to be.'

'There must be some. What about the pub? It's right next door.'

'I'm not sure. I'll have to ask them tomorrow.'

'Why don't we take a look now? It's only down the

road.'

Questioning lines of uncertainty rippled over Tanner's forehead.

'We can get something to eat at the same time,' Christine added.

'I assume you'd be driving?'

'I assume your car is still stuck in the garage?'

'They're awaiting parts, allegedly.'

'Come on then. I'll pay for the food.'

'I wouldn't hear of it!'

'No choice, I'm afraid. It's either that or I start paying you for bed and breakfast.'

- CHAPTER THIRTY FIVE -

'LOOK, THERE'S A camera up there,' said Christine, ducking her head to gesture up at the corner of the riverside pub as she steered her MX-5 into its gravel-lined carpark. 'It's facing this way. If Nigel Harrison was coming from Norwich, he would had to have driven past it in order to get to the Broadwater boatshed behind us.'

Tanner nodded thoughtfully. 'It's just a shame it's so far from the road. Probably too far to pick up a numberplate.'

'But if it had footage of his car, it's make and model at least, wouldn't that be enough?'

'I'm not sure, but either way, it's worth a look.'

Finding a place to park, they entered the pub to find it bustling with customers, forcing them to claw their way up to the bar.

'Hi Cheryl,' called Christine, catching the eye of one of the bar staff.

'Christine! I haven't seen you in here for a while.'

'Silly season, I'm afraid.'

The lady leaned over the bar. 'I know what you mean,' she whispered, adding a conspirational wink before glancing around at the pub's heaving clientele. 'Anyway, luv, what can I get you?'

'Any chance of a table for two?'

Stealing a glance over at Tanner, the lady pulled out a couple of menus from off the top of the bar. 'I doubt we've got anything in here, but there should be something outside. Are you two OK eating out by the river?'

'I think we'd prefer it,' Christine replied, taking the menus with an appreciative smile.

With the lady turning to leave, she called out, 'Before you go, I don't suppose you know if the CCTV cameras outside are working?'

'I know the one looking out over the river is.'

'How about the one facing the carpark?'

'It should be. I assume this is work related?'

'My friend here is a Detective Inspector for Norfolk Police.'

The lady's eyes turned to take Tanner in with more interest. 'Is it about what's been happening recently?'

'Possibly.'

'We all heard what happened to Martin,' the lady continued, returning her attention to Christine. 'Dreadful business.'

'I know. I still can't believe it.'

'And little Susie being taken. I don't suppose there's been any news?'

'Not yet.'

'And the others?'

'Again, no, but my friend here would be very interested in taking a look at any footage you have from the camera facing out towards the road.'

The lady turned to look Tanner up and down.

'I'll get my husband,' she eventually replied. 'He'll be able to show you what you need, but you better order first. At this rate, we're going to run out of food!'

About fifteen minutes later, Tanner found Christine sitting at a picnic table outside, tucking into one of two lasagnes laid out in front of her.

'How's it going?' he asked, taking a moment to

gaze out over the River Bure and the slowly setting sun beyond.

'Excellent, as always,' she replied, her mouth half-full of food. 'Sorry I didn't wait, but it was getting cold.'

'That's alright,' he replied, taking the seat next to hers.

'How'd you get on?'

'The camera only provides an oblique view of the road, and it's too far away to make out any numberplates. But it does show a silver Mercedes driving past at around the time in question, which look similar to the model Harrison owns.'

'Do you think it will be enough to be granted a search warrant?'

'Somehow I doubt it. There must be hundreds of silver Mercedes in and around the Broads.'

Leaving Tanner to start on his meal, Christine picked up her drink.

'I had another chat with Cheryl, after you left.'

'Uh-huh.'

'I asked her if she thought the Broadwater boatyard had any CCTV cameras.'

'What did she say?'

'She didn't know.'

More silence followed as Tanner continued tucking into his food.

'So anyway,' Christine eventually said, 'I was thinking that we may as well take a look before we go, to see if they do.'

'I think that would fall under the category of trespassing.'

'Not necessarily. Cheryl said you can see the main boatshed from the road, where the security fence is, so we wouldn't have to go inside.'

'OK, but I'm not sure there'd be any point. Even if

they did, we'd still need a search warrant to access the footage.'

'What if they use an external security company?'

Tanner stopped to gaze out over the horizon. 'You know what, that's not a bad idea. I'd have to ask Forrester, but I'd have thought it would be far easier to gain access if the footage was kept-offsite, by another company. There would certainly be a much lower burden of proof for a warrant.'

'Well, come on then!' Christine exclaimed, finishing her drink. 'Eat up, and we'll take a look.'

- CHAPTER THIRTY SIX -

WITH THEIR MEALS and drinks finished, they levered themselves out from the picnic table bench seat to make their way over towards where they'd left Christine's car. But instead of climbing inside, they continued past, onto the road to skirt around a thick line of shrubs and trees that separated the pub carpark from the Broadwater boatyard.

As they began creeping their way down a dark gravel entrance, overshadowed by the twisted branches of an ancient oak tree that creaked and groaned above their heads, Christine turned to whisper, 'Are you sure we should be doing this?'

'Er, I don't mean to be funny,' Tanner retorted, 'but I thought this was your idea.'

'Was it?' she queried, glancing around to present him with a playful look of questioning doubt.

'Well, it wasn't mine.'

'You're probably right. What was I thinking?'

'We can always go back.'

'We're here now,' she replied, as they both stepped up to a seven foot high security gate.

'Can you see anything?' she asked, joining Tanner in peering through the wire mesh, towards the boatshed they could see lurking in the shadows beyond.

'Not much. It's too dark. The wrong angle as well.'

Christine took a half-step back, staring up at the top of the gates to see a coil of barbed wire.

'You're not seriously thinking about climbing over?' he questioned, following her gaze.

'Well, I was,' she replied, looking down to consider the gap between the two gates. 'Do you think you could fit through there?'

'I'm not sure,' he replied, glancing down at himself. 'I probably couldn't have done two years ago. Fortunately, there's no need for me to find out.'

By the time he looked up, Christine was already forcing the gates apart to begin wriggling her way through.

'You know what you were asking earlier, about whether or not this was a good idea?'

'Uh-huh,' she replied, her body already halfway between them.

'Well, I really don't think this is.'

'We just need to see if there are any cameras,' she replied, making it through to the other side to hold the gates open for him.

With both of them through, Christine led the way around the side of a gravel courtyard to come to a halt underneath the shadow of a tree.

'There's a camera there,' she said, pointing up to the corner of the building. That should show if the lawyer's car was here. I can't see anything written on it, though. I'd have thought if it was owned by a security firm, it would have had their logo.'

'OK, well, I can probably find out tomorrow.'

'There are windows all the way down the side. We may as well take a look through one of them, whilst we're here.'

'I'm not sure.'

'If we should, or if there's any point?'

'I was thinking both, actually.'

'I can't see what harm it would do. Peering through windows could hardly be described as trespassing.'

'I think it can,' Tanner replied, 'being that we're already on private land.'

'But it's not a serious offence though, is it?'

'It's not a criminal offence, no; but...'

'Well, there we are then,' she concluded, leaving Tanner where he was to begin slinking her way over.

Shaking his head, Tanner took a furtive glance around the carpark before following after.

'Anything?' he questioned, seeing her lift herself up onto the balls of her feet to peer through the nearest window.

'About three hire boats, all up on stilts.'

'Anything else?'

'Not that I can see.'

'OK, good. Then we can head back to the car.'

Christine took a step back to glance over the building.

'What are you doing?'

'Trying to see if there's a way in.'

'You mean, before finding someone to ask if it's OK for us to have look around?'

'Look! The top of that window's been left open.'

'That's fascinating. Can we go now, please?'

'Don't you want to know what's inside?'

'You just told me. Three hire boats, all up on stilts.'

Christine paused for a moment before stepping forward. 'I'm going to take a look.'

'I'm sorry, but I can't let you do that.'

'Oh, please! Don't be so boring,' she scolded, taking hold of a pallet that had been left leaning up against the side of the building to drag it underneath the window.

'You do know that I'm a policeman, don't you?'

'I'm not,' she muttered, taking a moment to make sure that the edge of the pallet was digging into the gravel.

'You're talking about breaking and entering.'

'I'm not talking about it,' she replied, placing a foot onto the base of the pallet. 'Besides, I'm only going to enter. But if I do happen to break anything, I'll be sure to let you know.'

'Just so you that you're aware, you don't need to do both in order to qualify.'

'You mean; if I do I'll get a prize?'

'Does ten years count?'

Christine shrugged. 'I suppose it would depend where. An extended cruise in the Caribbean wouldn't be so bad.'

'I think you should be taking this a little more seriously.'

'Probably, but as long as I don't steal anything, or intend to cause either damage or harm, then surely it would just fall under the category of trespassing, which you've already said isn't a criminal offence.'

'Let me guess, you used to be a defence lawyer before you became a clinical psychologist?'

Christine smiled. 'But I'm right, though, aren't I?'

'Well, yes, but even if you did just happen to find something, we wouldn't be able to use it as evidence.'

'But if I did, it may help to convince your boss that you're on the right track.'

'Not if I was to tell him how I came about it.'

'Which is why you're staying there.'

Tanner let out an exasperated sigh as he watched Christine climb nimbly up the pallet to perch herself on its top, hooking her hands around the open windowsill.

'Christine! Please come down!' Tanner pleaded, but to no avail, as he was left to watch in helpless silence as she slipped through the narrow open window to disappearing from view.

'Shit,' he whispered, quietly to himself, glancing nervously around at the shadows growing steadily longer as the sun continued its inexorable descent towards the horizon beyond. It was only then that he saw a small rusty yellow sign, screwed into one of the planks of black treated wood, something that made his heart stop inside his chest.

The sign said, simply, "Guard dogs patrol this area!"

- CHAPTER THIRTY SEVEN -

PICTURING THE TWO vicious dogs he'd seen leaping out from the back of Frank Clayton's four-by-four, Tanner held his breath, tuning his ears for the slightest of sounds as his eyes scanned the shadows that seemed to be closing in around him.

Unable to see much of anything, with the only noise coming from the branches swaying gently in the breeze above, and the occasional shriek of laughter drifting over towards him from the pub next door, he stepped up to the base of the pallet Christine had used to climb up. If the dogs hadn't been left to patrol the grounds, there was every chance they were roaming around inside the boatshed.

Climbing up to balance himself on top of the pallet, Tanner peered through the half-open window, into the darkness beyond. Inside he could see the three boats Christine had described, but there was no sign of either her or the dogs.

Pushing his head through the gap, in a loud harsh whisper he called out, 'Christine!'

Scanning the large open space he listened again.

Still nothing.

He was about to call once more when he heard the ominous sound of scuffling coming from the furthest corner of the shed.

'Christine!' he cried, his voice lifting sharply in panicked desperation.

'All right! All right!' he finally heard her say, as he saw her clambering up onto the nearest boat. 'Tell everyone I'm here, why don't you.'

'Sorry, but you need to get out,' Tanner replied, extending one of his hands.

'So you keep saying.'

'Had I known there were dogs patrolling the grounds, I'd have never let you go inside.'

'Dogs!' she exclaimed, glancing madly down at the floor.

'I saw a sign outside, on the corner of the building.'

'Oh, I shouldn't worry about that. People are always sticking up signs warning of guard dogs. It would be a first if there actually were.'

'Maybe so, but did you see the ones that came out of Frank Clayton's monster truck?'

'Good point,' she replied, taking a firm hold of his still outstretched hand to climb quickly out the way she'd come in.

Once back through the open window, they jumped off the top of the pallet to the ground below.

'Did you find anything?' Tanner asked, keeping his voice low as they crept quickly back to the shadows provided by the over-hanging trees.

'I took a quick look around. There's a small office at the furthest end. I swear there was blood on the floor. It didn't even look like anyone had bothered to clean it up.'

'OK, but I'm afraid it doesn't help our cause much.'

'What if you knew it belonged to the dead lawyer?'

'Well, yes, but there's no way to know, not without being able to examine it, and we can't do that, as we don't have a search warrant.'

She caught his eye with a cheeky smile. 'And if we had a sample?'

'You collected some?'

'Of course!' she replied, fishing out a clear plastic bag to pass over to him.

Tanner held the bag up to what little light remained. 'What else is in there?' he asked, attempting to identify some of the objects he could see.

'Er...' she began, joining him in staring up at the bag. 'Basically, that's everything I can't fit into my purse.'

'But I can see three screws, an adjustable spanner, a GoPro mount, and what looks to be a radiator key.'

'I was wondering what that was.'

'But...why would you want to carry three screws, an adjustable spanner, a GoPro mount and a radiator key around in your purse?'

'I don't, obviously, which is why I keep them in there.'

'You do realise that makes absolutely no sense, don't you?'

'Does to me,' she shrugged. 'Anyway, you can see the dried-up blood at the bottom.'

'Well, at least the evidence hasn't been contaminated.'

'How d'you mean?'

'It doesn't matter,' Tanner replied, shaking his head. 'Dare I ask what you used to scrape it off with; one of the screws, the adjustable spanner, the GoPro mount or the radiator key?'

'My fingernail,' she replied, lifting it up to show him. 'Does it make a difference?' she asked, seeing the look on his face. 'You can still have the blood analysed, can't you?'

'I suppose,' he conceded. 'But even if it does belong to Nigel Harrison, I'm not sure how it's going to help our cause.'

'I thought you'd be able to use it to get a search warrant.'

'In an ideal world, but we won't be able to include it in the application, not without telling them how we got it. The moment we did, it would be considered inadmissible.'

'Oh, right. I didn't think of that.'

'Anyway, I'll run the idea by my boss, although I'm not sure what I'll say when he asks how I came by it.'

'Just tell him I found it,' she smiled.

'I see. So you think I should tell him that I helped you break into a Clayton family owned boatshed in order to collect evidence from what is potentially the scene of a murder?'

Christine thought for a moment. 'I know. Why don't you tell him that we were taking my dog for a walk when it slipped through the gate, climbed up the pallet and disappeared in through the half-open window.'

'I suppose it dragged the pallet there as well?'

'And then I caught the blood under my fingernail, when I was trying to cajole him out from underneath a desk.'

'Do you even own a dog?'

'Well, no, but that's hardly relevant, is it?'

- CHAPTER THIRTY EIGHT -

Thursday, 12th August

TOM PATTERSON HAD been awake for a good ten minutes. He was lying on his back facing the moulded plastic ceiling of the cheap hire boat he'd taken out a few days before, his mind busily fantasising about the previous night's events.

After months of trying, he'd finally been able to start having sex with Janice Franklyn, the girl he'd fancied ever since watching her stroll into the lecture hall during their first week at Norwich University, the very same girl who was now lying next to him, still fast asleep. That had been over a year ago. It had taken him a full nine months to work up the courage to ask her out. At first she'd refused, giving him the excuse that she wanted to stay focussed on her studies. It took him three attempts before she eventually agreed. But if it had been a challenge persuading her to go on a date, getting her into bed had proven to be mission impossible. She'd been happy enough for them to mess about, but when it came to going all the way, she'd point-blankly refused, her excuse remaining persistently the same; she was a virgin, waiting to meet the right man.

Despite her continued insistence that that was the case, Tom knew it wasn't true, at least not the part about her being a virgin. During the nine months it had taken him to build up the courage to ask her out, he'd heard of a least three guys who'd slept with her, at least that's what his mates had told him. It had been one of the same friends who'd given him the idea of asking her to go on holiday with him. The suggestion had been to whisk her off to one of the Greek Islands, but his financial situation left him looking for something closer to home, eventually forcing him to settle for a Broads boating holiday.

It had taken a little persuasion, but after three days of painting romantic descriptions for her, each one having them cruising through idyllic riverside villages before seeking quiet sheltered moorings to sit back and watch the sun set, she'd eventually agreed.

From first stepping on board the boat on Friday evening, it took exactly four hours and one bottle of wine for her to finally succumb to his inexhaustible charms. Once she had, his appetite had proven to be insatiable.

Tom lifted his arm to glance up at his watch, only to lower it down again in disgust. It had only just gone seven o'clock. There was no way he was going to be able to fall back to sleep, and the longer he lay there, thinking about what they'd been doing to each other the previous night, the more aroused he was becoming.

Turning onto his side to face the back of her head, he carefully moved a lock of her soft blonde hair away from her face. 'Janice. Are you awake?'

There was no response, just the continued rhythmic sound of her breathing.

'Hey, Janice,' he continued, sliding an arm under the covers, curling it over her slim naked waist to give her an eager hug. 'Are you awake?'

Immediately he felt her warm curvaceous body undulate under his touch as she reached over to pull his arm over her, as if it was the corner of a duvet.

'What time is it?' he heard her mutter, lifting her head.

'It's, er, getting late,' he lied.

'Give me five minutes,' came her muffled reply, only to bury her face back into the pillow.

A moment later he heard her take in a shallow breath, beginning to snore.

'Janice?'

'Huh?'

'You're not going back to sleep, are you?'

'Not at all.'

'You don't fancy...you know?' he asked, shifting over to press his already aroused-self against her.

'Not seriously?'

'Only if you want to.'

'But we only did it last night.'

'That was yesterday.'

'Er...I seem to remember it was one o'clock in the morning, so, technically speaking, it was today.'

'Maybe so, but still, that was over six hours ago.'

'Hold on,' Janice responded, rolling over so that she could look into Tom's face. 'You mean its only seven o'clock?'

'What makes you say that?' he replied, with an innocent smile.

'Because I did Further Maths for A Level,' she continued, taking hold of his wrist to stare down at his watch. 'You lying sack of shit! It *is* seven o'clock!'

'I never said it wasn't.'

'You said it was getting late.'

Tom shrugged. 'I suppose that depends on what you do for a living. If you're a prostitute, for example, it must be nearly bedtime.'

'Are you calling me a prostitute?' she demanded, a disparaging frown hiding a playful smirk.

'I don't mean to be rude, but I did pay for the boat.'

'Oh, I see. Then I suppose I'd better get back to work.'

With a mischievous smile, she was about to reach out to take hold of him when they heard something bump into the side of the boat.

They both stopped to stare over towards where the sound had come from, eyes wide, mouths hanging open.

'What was that?' Janice whispered.

'Not sure,' Tom replied, his voice equally as still. 'A log?'

As they continued to listen, a soft scuffling sound could be heard up near the front.

'That's no log,' stated Janice, hardly daring to breathe.

Without warning, the hire boat suddenly tilted violently to one side before rocking back to the other.

Janice pulled herself closer to Tom. 'Someone's trying to climb on board!'

Tom didn't reply. He was too busy listening.

'What are we going to do?' Janice continued.

'I'm – I'm n-not sure.'

'Can you see anything through the windows?'

'The curtains are closed.'

'Can't you open them?'

'But, if they see me, they'll know someone's onboard.'

'Don't we want them to know someone's onboard?'

'I don't know. Do we?'

The boat rocked again as they huddled together in silence, listening to the sound of someone, or something, hauling itself up the side.

'Do you think we should call the police?'

'What with? Our phones died two days ago. Besides, even if they hadn't, I'm not sure what we'd say. Someone's about to steal our boat, whilst we're still inside it?'

They continued to listen, as the noises coming from the boat's bow seemed to grow louder.

'Maybe we should just stay as quiet as possible, until whoever it is goes away?' Tom eventually proposed, his voice barely audible.

Janice glared over at him. 'Or maybe someone should go outside and tell them to get the fuck off our boat?'

'What; you mean me?'

'You don't expect me to go?'

'Shit,' Tom cursed, under his breath, scrabbling quietly around for his clothes.

Peeling them on, a loud thud of something heavy being dropped onto the boat's bow had them staring over at each other.

Tom turned to look at Janice. 'What the hell was that?'

'How should I know?'

They listened intently as the boat began rocking from side to side again, before they found themselves listening to nothing more ominous than the broad's water, lapping up against their hire boat's battered plastic hull.

'I think they've gone,' said Tom, crawling over to one of the windows.

'Anything?' asked Janice, watching him peel back one of the small flimsy curtains.

'Nothing, but I can't see the front.'

They remained silent for a moment longer, listening intently for the slightest noise, but there was nothing to be heard. Even the sound of the water, lapping up against the hull, was beginning to dissipate.

'I'm going to take a look,' Tom eventually

announced, dropping down onto the bed to pull on a pair of jeans.

'OK; but be careful.'

Crouching down, he cautiously eased open the cabin doors to curl his head over the top of the cabin's roof, peering out through the windscreen towards the front of the boat.

'There's nobody there,' he eventually whispered, directing his voice down into the cabin.

'Are you sure?'

'Well, I can't see anyone.'

He cast his eyes over the mist-covered broad they were moored in the middle of, bringing his gaze around to take in some of the various vessels moored up around them, each swinging on their anchors on a gradually shifting breeze.

'Then what was that all about?' Janice demanded, her cute makeup-free face appearing at the cabin door.

'I've no idea. Whatever it was, it looks like they've gone.'

'They must have been doing something. Have you checked the front?'

'Hold on. I'll take a look.'

Stepping out of the cockpit, he looked forward again, out through the windscreen. There, distorted by the morning's condensation, was what he first thought to be an old blanket, hanging over the railings at the very front.

'Can you see anything?' Janice demanded.

'I'm not sure,' he replied, stepping up onto the walkway.

Taking a firm hold of the handrail, he crept his way slowly forward, his eyes fixed ahead.

As soon as he was able to look past the windscreen's distorted image, he stopped.

Slumped up against the railings at the very front of the boat was the body of a man, his ashen grey face staring up towards a brightening sky, crimson blood flowing out from his neck to the floor where it meandered like a river, heading towards Tom's cold bare feet.

Following the trail of blood with his eyes, he saw Janice coming up to join him.

'I – I don't think you should look,' he said, his eyes returning to the body.

'Why, what is it?' she questioned, stepping lightly onto the walkway to look first down at the stream of bright red liquid, then up towards the bow.

It took a full second for her to realise what it was, her mouth widening to let out a horrified scream.

- CHAPTER THIRTY NINE -

WAKING UP STUCK out in the cockpit once again, this time with a hangover, Tanner spent a few moments recalling the events of the previous evening, and just how much he'd drunk with Christine after they'd got back. It wasn't until he was making the coffee, thinking about the day ahead, when he remembered that he was supposed to have organised a hire car for himself.

Forced to graciously accept another lift into work with Christine, he crept his way past the growing bank of journalists, eventually finding himself sitting behind his desk, staring once again at his computer screen, hoping nobody had noticed that he was over ten minutes late.

After checking his email, he'd only just finished arranging for the sample of blood Christine had found the night before to be sent over to forensics, when he saw Forrester's bald head emerge from his office to glower at him, beckoning him to come over.

Curious to know what he'd done this time, he pushed himself up from his chair to skulk his way towards the DCI's door.

'You wanted to see me, sir?'

'Close the door, Tanner, and take a seat.'

Doing as he was told, Tanner sank down into one of the chairs being offered.

'How're you doing?' Forrester asked, placing his

elbows firmly down on the desk to stare over at him.

'Er, fine, thank you, sir,' Tanner replied, unable to shake off a feeling of nervous trepidation. It was most unlike Forrester to invite him inside his office just to ask after his wellbeing.

'Did you get up to anything special last night?'

'Not much. Yourself?'

'You didn't find yourself taking a pleasant evening stroll through the village of Coltishall, by any chance?'

Tanner cleared his throat to shift uncomfortably in his seat, his mind racing to fathom how Forrester could have possibly known what he'd been up to. 'I went to the pub there; if that's what you mean?'

'I was actually thinking about the boatyard next door?'

Fighting the temptation to simply hold up his hands and admit to having trespassed on Clayton-owned property, Tanner found himself saying, 'I'm not sure what you mean.'

'Please don't treat me like an idiot.'

'Sorry, sir; I'm still not with you.'

'I've just received an email from Allen & Atkinson. I assume you remember who they are?'

'Yes, sir. Nigel Harrison's law firm.'

'Attached is a CCTV video showing two people breaking into the Broadwater boatshed in Coltishall,' Forrester continued, swivelling the screen around for Tanner to see, 'one of which they've pointed out looks remarkably like you.'

Tanner took a moment to watch the grainy footage as he tried to work out where the camera must have been.

'Well?' Forrester demanded.

'Well, sir, they're going to have a job proving it was me, if that's all they've got. I mean, it's hardly the clearest image.'

'Sorry, Tanner, wrong answer.'

'What answer were you looking for?'

'That it wasn't you!'

'I think the image clearly shows that it wasn't, being that I'm not the one climbing up through the window.'

'But it does show you doing nothing whatsoever to prevent the other person.'

'I may not have been *physically* trying to stop her, but I can assure you that I was doing everything in my power to do so verbally. It's just a shame the camera doesn't have a microphone, else you'd have heard me.'

'For God's sake, Tanner, you *have* to take this seriously!'

'To be honest, sir, I'm struggling to see why. All the video shows is a man watching someone climb in through the open window of a larger than average shed. And as I know nothing was taken, and no damage was done, the best the owners could hope for would be a conviction of trespassing, and they'd have to have some proof as to who it was, which they're not going to get if that video footage is all they've got.'

'You're completely missing the point, Tanner.'

'I am?'

'You're a member of CID, for Christ's sake! You can't be caught gaining illegal access to someone's private property, especially when that property belongs to a suspect in an on-going murder investigation.'

'Forgive me, sir, but as I said before, I wasn't the one gaining illegal entry.'

'Which brings be to my next question. Who the hell was that with you? Please God, tell me it wasn't Vicky.'

'Er, no sir, it wasn't.'

'Then who was it?'

'Just a friend of mine.'

'A "friend!"'

'Yes, sir.'

'You're telling me that you asked a friend of yours to break into one of the Clayton family's boatsheds on your behalf?'

'Not at all. She's the one who suggested it.'

'And why on God's good Earth would she have done that?'

'To help prove that Nigel Harrison was lured there by Gary Clayton in order to torture and murder him. She thinks as I do, sir, that whoever killed him and her colleague, Martin Longshore, is the same person who broke into her house and tied her to a chair, in preparation to do something remarkably similar.'

Forrester stopped to stare over at him.

'You mean to tell me that the woman in the video is Christine Halliday, the Broads Ranger who used to work with Martin Longshore?'

Tanner closed his mouth, furious with himself for having given her identity away so easily.

'What the hell are you doing hanging out with her?' Forrester continued.

'I said she could stay on board my boat for a few days, after she was attacked inside her home.'

'But...' began Forrester, his face the picture of incredulity, '...she's a suspect in what is now a double murder investigation!'

'Hardly a suspect.'

'You're telling me that she *wasn't* Martin Longshore's work colleague, and subsequently had never seen him before in her entire life?'

'Er, no, sir. I meant that she's hardly on our list of suspects.'

'I see. And that's according to who?'

'Well, me, sir.'

Forrester glowered over at him as a familiar purple vein began pulsating on his forehead.

'I'll be honest with you, Tanner, I'm becoming increasingly convinced that the whole idea of you coming back to work wasn't the great idea I first thought it was.'

'Do you honestly think you'd be better off with just DI Cooper?'

'At least he's not sleeping with one of the suspects, for Christ's sake.'

'Who the hell said I was sleeping with her?'

'Oh, come on, Tanner.'

'I invited her to stay on board my boat for a few days after her house was broken into. She's in the cabin, I'm in the cockpit. That's the full extent of our relationship.'

A sharp knock at the door was followed by Cooper's head.

'Sorry to disturb you, sir,' he began, without bothering to acknowledge Tanner, 'but another body's been found, dumped on the front of someone's boat.'

'For fuck's sake!' Forrester raged, crashing his fists down onto the top of his desk.

Tanner pushed himself up to his feet. 'I'll be heading back to my yacht then, shall I?'

'What?' Forrester demanded, staring up at him with a look of confused bewilderment.

'You said you didn't require my services.'

'I said no such thing, now shut up and sit down.'

'Yes, sir,' Tanner replied, returning to his seat whilst supressing a smirk.

'Where is it?' demanded Forrester, catching Cooper's eye.

'South Walsham Broad.'

'I don't suppose we know who it is yet?'

'Not yet. Forensics are on their way, as is Dr Johnstone.'

'OK, you'd better get yourself over there.'

Seeing him turn to leave, Forrester added, 'And take young DC Townsend with you. No doubt he could do with the experience.'

With Cooper closing the door on his way out, Forrester returned his attention to Tanner.

'I assume you've been able to pick up a hire car for yourself, in between bouts of breaking and entering?'

'Well, sir, I was going to, but...I...er...'

Forrester shook his head in despair. 'Then may I ask how you're going to get yourself down to the crime scene?'

'I thought I could ask Vicky to give me a lift.'

'Then I suppose you'd better go and ask her then, hadn't you!'

'Yes, sir,' Tanner replied, climbing to his feet.

'But if I hear so much as a whisper that you've been involved in any more illegal activities, even something as insignificant as picking up a parking ticket, then I'll have no choice but to terminate your services. Is that clear?'

'Crystal,' Tanner replied, 'although, saying that, I think it would be a little challenging for me to get a parking ticket, due to my current lack of transportation.'

'Which reminds me,' Forrester continued, scowling up at him. 'If you haven't sorted something out for yourself by tomorrow, feel free to consider yourself unemployed.'

'I'll – er – make sure to have a car by then, sir.'

'If you could. And close the door on your way out, there's a good chap.'

- CHAPTER FORTY -

'THIS LOOKS LIKE us,' commented Vicky, gazing up to the end of the narrow track they found themselves on.

Ahead was a cluster of emergency vehicles cluttering up each side of the lane, leaving just enough space for them to squeeze themselves past.

Parking the car behind a Police Forensics Services van, they climbed out to find themselves staring out over a purpose built mooring, pristine neatly trimmed grass verges hugging the edge of the wide expanse of water known as South Walsham Broad.

They didn't need to look far to find the boat the body had been found on. It had been tied to a mooring kept free for visitors, surrounded by an eclectic mix of both uniformed police and white overall-clad forensics officers.

Seeing Cooper standing idly on the grass beside DC Townsend, neither looking as if they were doing anything more productive than to stare vacantly at the hire boat to their right, Tanner and Vicky made their way over towards them.

'What've we got?' Vicky called out, raising a hand to help garner their attention.

'The body is at the front,' Cooper replied, guiding their eyes towards where they could see the broken heavily bruised body of a half-naked man, slumped up against the railing at the boat's bow, congealed blood matting the thick dark hair that covered his exposed barrel-like chest.

'Do we have an ID?'

'Not yet.'

'Cause of death?'

'Johnstone's still having a look. The couple who found it said they think someone dragged it up there when they were still in bed.'

'What time was that?'

'About seven this morning.'

Vicky checked the time on her watch. It was gone ten. 'Any idea why it took them so long to call it in?'

'They were moored up in the middle of the broad and said that their phones were dead. Then they couldn't get the engine started, so they were left stranded for a while, trying to get someone to give them a tow.'

'I don't suppose there's any chance they saw who left the body there?'

'They said they didn't.'

Tanner glanced around to see a young couple sitting in the back of an ambulance. 'I assume that's them?' he asked, gesturing over.

'It is,' Cooper nodded, following his gaze, 'but we've already taken a statement.'

'I'm sure it won't do any harm if we have a quick word,' Tanner replied, turning to lead Vicky over towards them.

'Excuse me,' Tanner called out, a few moments later, 'but was it you who found the body?'

'We've already spoken to someone,' came the young man's curt response, turning to help an attractive woman climb down to the ground.

'We were told you were inside the boat when you heard the body being dragged up onto the bow.'

'As per our statement,' the man replied, placing a protective arm around the woman's trembling shoulders.

'You didn't see who it was?'

'We were in bed.'

'Not asleep, though? I mean, whoever left it there must have made a hell of a racket.'

'We weren't asleep, but we weren't about to climb out to have a look, either.'

'What about when the person left?'

'I looked, but I didn't see anyone.'

'So, you don't even know how they got the body on board?'

'Well, we did hear something hit the side.'

'Hard or soft?'

'I'm sorry?'

'Was it a hard knock, like another boat, or more of a soft thud, like an inflatable dinghy?'

'It was loud, so it must've been another boat.'

'And was the noise high up the side, or down near the waterline?'

'Er...about halfway up the hull, I suppose,' the young man responded, glancing around at his girlfriend.

'But you didn't see anything?'

'We waited until whoever it was had gone.'

'Before you even thought to look out the window?' Tanner questioned.

The young man shrugged to stare down at the ground, leaving his girlfriend to reply.

'We had no idea who it was or what their intentions were. For all we knew, they were going to murder us in our bed, so no, Mr Whoever-you-are, we didn't look out the window. We didn't do anything until we knew they had definitely gone.'

'OK, fair enough. And how long was that,

approximately?'

'I don't know. Two minutes?'

'It wasn't much more than that,' the boyfriend agreed.

'And then?'

'Then Tom went out to take a look,' the young woman continued.

Tanner's focus returned to the man. 'What did you see?'

'Just the body.'

'You didn't see any boats nearby?'

'Only the ones moored up around us.'

'And you were in the middle of the broad.'

'That's right.'

'Did you see anyone on the other boats?'

The man shook his head.

'Did you hear anything?'

'Not then, no.'

'The sound of an engine? A sail flapping? The splash of water?'

'As I said, we didn't see or hear anything. Just the body. Nothing else.'

- CHAPTER FORTY ONE -

'IT SOUNDS LIKE whoever dumped the body must have used either a rowing boat or some sort of sailing dinghy,' said Tanner, making their way back to where the hire boat was tied to the hardstanding.

'But that doesn't explain how they could have disappeared so quickly,' Vicky said, stopping to stare out over the broad. 'Not if it's true that they only waited a couple of minutes before heading up on deck to take a look around; not without an engine.'

Tanner glanced up at the tops of the trees on the other side of the river.

'They could have sailed away. There's enough breeze, just about. The other option is that they rowed away; although I must admit, it doesn't seem very likely. You can't row a boat without making at least some noise, especially not if you're in a hurry. But to be honest, at this stage I'm more interested to know why whoever did it went to the trouble of leaving the body on the bow of a hire boat anchored out in the middle of a broad? And why take the risk of being seen? They must have known someone would have been on board. People don't typically anchor their boats up in the middle of a large body of water only to then abandon them for the night.'

'Could it be something to do with who owns the boat?' questioned Vicky.

'How d'you mean?'

'I don't know if you noticed, but it's got the Broadwater Boats logo on the hull.'

'I hadn't,' said Tanner, glancing over.

'Could it be that someone wanted to make sure that the Clayton's would definitely find out about it, in a similar way to how the body of Nigel Harrison was left on the edge of Frank Clayton's estate?'

'Which leaves me increasingly curious to find out who our new victim is,' Tanner continued, staring out into the middle of the broad. 'We really need to speak to the people on board all those boats. Someone must have seen something.'

The distinctive clatter of an anchor chain being hauled up the front of one of them had Tanner turning to add, 'Preferably before they all leave, as well. I assume Cooper has requested police boat support?'

'I'd have thought so. They're probably still on their way.'

'Well, if they don't get here soon, we're going to have lost the chance to ask them,' Tanner replied, reaching into his pocket to dig out his phone.

'Who are you calling?' questioned Vicky, with a curious expression.

Tanner held up a finger, turning his head away.

'Christine, hi, it's John. Listen, I don't suppose you're anywhere near South Walsham Broad, by any chance?'

- CHAPTER FORTY TWO -

'I THINK DR Johnstone's finished,' observed Vicky, hearing Tanner ending his call.

Putting his phone away, he followed her gaze to see their medical examiner step down from the boat to begin heading over towards where Cooper remained standing with the new DC.

'It's definitely murder, I'm afraid,' they heard him say, as they hurried over to join them.

'Is the method used the same as the previous two?' Cooper questioned.

'Assuming you're referring to Martin Longshore and Nigel Harrison, then I'd have to say yes, but there are more similarities with the latter than the former.'

'And those are?'

'The width of the blade would appear to be the same. I'd say he was also tortured before being killed. And again, it didn't take place here.'

'Time of death?'

'Probably no more than four or five hours ago.'

Tanner checked his watch whilst listening to Cooper continue.

'That would put it at sometime between five and six this morning, which means he couldn't have been killed far from where we are now.'

'Especially if he was carried out into the middle of the broad in a sailing dinghy,' noted Tanner.

Cooper gave him a disparaging look. 'What makes

you think they used one of those?'

'From what the couple who found the body said: that they heard something hard knock against the hull, about halfway up the side.'

'And that means it was a sailing dinghy, does it?'

'It means that it couldn't have been anything particularly large, like another motor cruiser, and the fact that they didn't hear the sound of an engine excludes the use of a small power boat.'

'You're suggesting they sailed away?'

'It's possible,' Tanner replied, his gaze drifting up to the tops of the trees. 'Assuming the breeze was similar to what it is now, coming from the south west, if they left the broad to head out towards the River Bure, it would have been downwind all the way.'

Cooper looked over Tanner's shoulder, in the opposite direction. 'In that scenario, they could have just as easily used the public slipway on the other side of the broad.'

'Well, yes, but then they would have had to have tacked up into the wind, which would've taken them three times as long. They'd also had to have lifted the boat out of the water.'

'Unless they simply decided to leave the boat here?' proposed DC Townsend.

Both Tanner and Cooper looked over at him.

'Or else he just kept himself hidden out of sight,' the young man continued, 'maybe behind one of those large motor cruisers anchored up in the middle of the broad, waiting for the right time to slip away, when nobody was looking.'

'That would probably make the most sense,' Tanner conceded, turning to catch Johnstone's eye. 'I don't suppose you have any idea who the victim is?'

'I can go one better than that,' he responded, delving into a pocket in his coat to produce a clear plastic evidence bag, inside which they could see a black leather wallet.

'This was in his back pocket. According to what we found inside, his name is Richard Oakley, a chartered accountant working for a small firm based in Horning.'

'Right then,' Cooper began. 'We'd better start by finding out all we can about our latest victim.'

'Don't we need to start asking everyone in the surrounding boats if they saw anything; before they all disappear?' Tanner proposed, glancing around behind him to see a gleaming white motor cruiser, slipping gracefully through the water towards them. 'Like that one, for example.'

Cooper scowled over at it. 'I did ask for boat support,' he muttered, looking down at his watch. 'I've got no idea what's taking them so long.'

'They're probably sticking to the 4mph speed limit,' commented Vicky.

The blast of a siren had them all craning their necks to look down the channel of water that connected the South Walsham Broad to the River Bure beyond.

'Well, anyway, it looks like they've arrived.'

'That's not a police boat,' said Townsend, his youthful eyes penetrating the distant haze of the steadily rising sun. 'It's a Broads Ranger.'

- CHAPTER FORTY THREE -

'AM I IN time?' Christine called out, easing off the throttle to let her patrol boat drift slowly in to where Tanner stood waiting.

'Well, you managed to get here before any of the police boats.'

'That's probably because they have to stick to the speed limit.'

'And you don't?'

'You said it was urgent,' she grinned.

He frowned back a response, placing one foot onto its narrow walkway to use the other to push the boat back out into the dyke. 'Can we start by flagging down that motor cruiser? We should then be able to stop the others as they start coming out.'

'No problem,' she replied, spinning the wheel to begin motoring towards the boat Tanner was gesturing at. 'What do you need to ask them?'

'Another body's been found,' Tanner replied, holding onto the wheelhouse roof as he made his way up to the boat's bow.

Christine paused before asking, 'Is it related to the others?'

'Looks like it. At least, he'd been killed in the same way. This time, whoever did it decided to drag the body up onto the bow of a hire boat, anchored up in the middle of the broad with a young couple staying on board.'

'Did they see anything?'

Tanner shook his head. 'I think they were too scared to look, which is fair enough. Probably a good thing too. I'd hate to think what would have happened if they had seen his face.'

'But I assume you're hoping someone else did?'

'They said they only waited inside the cabin for a couple of minutes after the person had left before stepping out to have a look around, by which time the person was nowhere to be seen, leaving us wondering how they could have left so quickly.'

'It shouldn't have been too difficult. I mean, South Walsham is hardly the largest broad.'

'Without an engine?'

'Ah.'

'Anyway, hopefully someone else saw something,' Tanner continued, holding up his police ID to the approaching boat.

'Is there a problem?' came a man's voice, drifting down from a flybridge at its very top. 'We weren't speeding, were we?'

Tanner stared up at the rotund sunburnt face of the balding middle-aged man staring down at them.

'I don't know if you're aware, but a body was found on the deck of one of the boats anchored up near you this morning.'

'Good God!' the man exclaimed, glancing around at the equally sunburnt face of the woman standing next to him. 'We were wondering what was going on.'

'It was found on the bow of that hire boat moored up over there,' Tanner continued, gesturing behind him. 'Do you recognise it? Was it anchored anywhere near you?'

'Right next to us,' the man nodded.

'I don't suppose either of you saw anything?'

'Anything, as in...?'

'The couple staying on board said they heard someone lift the body on board, at around seven o'clock this morning, possibly from a boat that pulled up alongside, but they didn't see who left it there.'

'I'm afraid this is the first we've heard about it.'

'You didn't see anything odd, or unusual?'

'I'm sorry, but my wife and I were still in bed,' the man replied, glancing over at her for confirmation.

'You did get up, though,' she replied, catching his eye, 'at around that time.'

'Yes, thank you darling, but I didn't see a dead man being dragged up onto the bow of a hire boat. I'm fairly sure that would have been something I'd have remembered, don't you think?'

'Did you see any other boats?' Tanner continued, smirking at the obvious tension between them. 'Something smaller, perhaps?'

'Well, there was a large wooden dinghy, but that was on the other side.'

Tanner glanced briefly around at Christine before returning his attention to the sunburnt couple.

'Was there anyone on board?'

'Just some old man.'

'Did you see his face?'

'Not really. He was wearing one of those old-fashioned peaked fishing caps, pulled down over his eyes. I was also looking down on him, which didn't help.'

'But you said he was old?'

The man thought for a moment. 'Well, he looked old. His shoulders were hunched over, and what with the hat, and the boat he was in. I suppose I just assumed he was.'

'And the boat?'

'As I said. It was a dinghy, at least I think it was.'

'Did it have an engine?'

'Not that I could see, just one of those old dark red sails, curled up at the bottom.'

- CHAPTER FORTY FOUR -

SEEING A POLICE patrol boat finally begin creeping its way up the dyke towards them, Tanner took the couple's contact details before waving them on.

Asking if Christine would be able to remain in the area for a while, to help prevent the other boats from leaving, she sped him to the shore where he found Vicky, waiting for him on the immaculate grass.

'Anything?' she asked, watching him step lightly down.

'Not much. They were anchored directly opposite the hire boat; but didn't know anything about a body being found. The husband did, however, see someone in a small open wooden boat, lurking on the other side, so it looks as if Townsend was right.'

'I don't suppose they saw his face?'

Tanner shook his head. 'Only that he had one of those peaked sailing caps on, pulled down over his eyes, and that he may have been in his senior years.'

'Nothing else?'

'There was a dark red sail stowed at the bottom of the boat.'

Vicky raised an eyebrow. 'Doesn't that mean the person murdering these men could be the same person who's been taking the children?'

Tanner shrugged. 'It could, but it's not exactly conclusive. As I think we all know by now, there are loads of old sailing dinghies around here with dark red sails.'

'Did they see where this person went?'

'The boat was gone by the time they got up, but hopefully someone onboard one of the other boats did.'

Seeing Cooper wandering over towards them, he leaned in to whisper. 'He doesn't look very happy.'

'Does he ever?'

'I've instructed that police patrol boat to interview everyone on board the other boats,' Cooper began, stopping in front of them to stare briefly over at it, before turning his attention to Tanner. 'There should be another one along any minute now, so you can tell that Broads Ranger girlfriend of yours that we won't be needing her services anymore.'

'She'll be delighted.'

'I assume you got a statement from the people on board that boat you spoke to?'

'We did, but they didn't know anything about the body, at least not until we told them. They did see someone in a small sailing dinghy on the opposite side, though.'

'Did they see a face?'

'Not enough for a description.'

'OK, well I think we're about done here. If you two haven't got anything better to do, it may be an idea for you to start going around the houses surrounding the broad to ask if anyone saw anything?'

'You mean, if they saw anything from all the way over there?' laughed Tanner, pointing over towards the far side of the broad.

'Sorry, do you two have some sort of romantic dinner engagement you need to get ready for?' Cooper asked, his eyes flickering between the two of them.

The sight of Vicky's face visibly darken made Tanner think back to when she'd asked him out, and if Cooper had somehow known she had.

'I meant,' Tanner began, struggling to maintain control of his own emotions, 'what would be the point? They must all be at least half a mile away from where the hire boat was anchored. How on God's good Earth could anyone have possibly seen anything?'

'I see. So we're just to assume that none of them did, are we?'

'Well, no, but...can't you send a couple of uniform around?'

'We can't spare the manpower.'

'But you can spare us?'

'It's your job.'

'Hardly.'

'Well, part of it,' Cooper sneered. 'You're also forgetting that its possible someone saw a body being carted onto the boat that took him out there. Whoever did it may have even stolen one of their dinghies to do so.'

'Then they'll no doubt report it as being missing.'

'Not if nobody was in at the time.'

'If nobody is in, knocking on their front door isn't going to make much difference.'

'Either way, I want you and Vicky to go around to find out.'

'May I ask what you're going to do, whilst Vicky and I spend the entire day going door to door, asking if anyone just happened to be staring out into the middle of South Walsham Broad with a pair of binoculars whilst their next door neighbour was having their dinghy stolen?'

'If you must know, I'm taking Townsend around to have a chat with the accountancy firm our victim apparently worked for. If the Claytons turn out to be clients of theirs, I'll be recommending to Forrester that we bring Gary in for questioning.'

- CHAPTER FORTY FIVE -

LATER THAT EVENING, Christine leaned up against her car to watch Tanner clamber his way out of an old pale blue Nissan Micra. 'What is *that?*' she asked, with a self-amused smirk.

'It's my new car!' Tanner announced, closing the creaking door to stand back and stare at it, his face a mixture of both uncertainty and heavy regret.

'Please don't tell me you bought it?'

'Oh, come on, it's not *that* bad.'

'If you say so,' she laughed.

'Anyway,' he continued, staring at the key fob as he tried to work out how to lock it, 'with the budget on offer, it's all I could afford.'

'You mean; you *did* buy it?'

'It's a rental.'

'Thank God for that!' she responded, clasping a hand to her chest as if she'd been about to have a heart attack.

'Hopefully, it will only be for a day or two,' Tanner continued, realising he had to use the key to lock it manually.

'Do you think it will last that long?'

Tanner sent a forced smile over at her, before stooping down to insert the key into the door.

'What about your car? Haven't you heard from the garage yet?'

With the Nissan Micra successfully locked, Tanner

gave her a look of exhausted relief. 'They're waiting on parts. It's a somewhat dated Jaguar, making them difficult to find, at least that's what the garage said. Anyway, how was your day?'

'After the excitement of the morning, the afternoon was remarkably uneventful. You?'

'I spent the afternoon going around all the houses surrounding South Walsham Broad, knocking on doors.'

'I'd have thought that sort of thing was a little below your pay grade.'

'Me too. But Cooper seemed to think it was a good idea.'

'And was it?'

'Not really. Hardly anyone was in. Those who were said they were still in bed at the time, which made sense, given that most of them seemed to be staying here on holiday.'

'And what did Cooper do, whilst you were going door-to-door?'

'Apparently, he went round to have a chat with the victim's employer, a firm of accountants based in Horning. He said that if he could find any evidence that they worked for the Claytons, he'd recommend Gary Clayton be brought in for questioning.'

'And did he?'

'I'd have heard by now if he had. To be honest, I can't imagine he'd push hard enough to find out, which will leave us hoping that either forensics, or our medical examiner, will find something to confirm what we have so far.'

'What about that blood sample I gave you?'

'Ah! About that...'

'You didn't lose it, did you?'

'Nothing like that. I sent if off. Hopefully we'll hear back from them tomorrow as to who it belongs to. It's just that I neglected to tell my boss that we found it.'

'Because I broke in?'

'Because we were caught on camera doing so.'

'Shit! Really?'

'There must have been one on the other side of the carpark we didn't see. Fortunately, for both our sakes, the quality of the footage wasn't all that great.'

'You can't see our faces?'

'Not really. I think the only reason they recognised me was because of my beard.'

'By "they", you mean the Claytons?'

'My boss received an email from their legal firm this morning. The CCTV footage was attached.'

'I don't suppose you know what the email said?'

'No doubt threatening to press charges, although I'm not sure what for. I made it abundantly clear that we didn't take anything, apart from the blood sample, of course, which was why I felt it probably wasn't the right time to mention it.'

Tanner stopped to watch as Christine tugged open the boot of her car to heave out an impressively large suitcase.

'Been shopping?' he enquired, with a curious smile.

'I stopped by my house after work to pick up a few more things.'

'I assume that means you're happy to stay with me for a little longer?'

'Sorry,' she replied, dropping the hefty-looking item onto the ground to tug out its extendable handle. 'I should have asked. It's OK, isn't it?'

'Of course. I'm just not sure how all three of us are going to fit.'

'The three of us?'

'You, me, and that rather large suitcase of yours.'

- CHAPTER FORTY SIX -

Friday, 13th August

DRIVING HIMSELF INTO work, Tanner arrived in good time to find an email from forensics, waiting for him in his inbox. With the only thing written in the subject being Sample 2953, he raised a curious eyebrow to sit down and open it.

The moment he realised it contained the results from the blood sample Christine had scraped off the boatshed floor, his heart picked up a beat.

Opening the attachment to scan through the results, a broad smile spread out over his face when he came to the part about who the sample belonged to, just as he saw Forrester's head emerge from his office to summon first Cooper, then himself over.

'You wanted to see me?' Tanner enquired, arriving first to find Forrester standing by his window.

'Just for a quick update. I see you managed to find yourself a car.'

'If you can call it that,' Tanner joked.

'Any news of that Jag of yours?'

'Not yet, but hopefully it won't be long.'

Forrester turned to see Cooper's head emerging through the half-open door.

'Take a seat, both of you.'

Doing so himself, Forrester dragged a notepad

over the desk towards him.

'I just wanted to get the two of you in here for a quick update on how you've been getting on since our meeting yesterday.'

'Yes, fine,' Cooper replied, giving Tanner an indignant glance.

'Oh, great! So, you've managed to catch the murderer and have found all those missing children?'

'Well, no sir. I didn't mean...'

'Then it's hardly fine then, is it!' Forrester stated, raising his voice.

'Sorry, I meant that I feel we're making good progress, sir.'

'Then you'd better tell me what that progress is,' Forrester continued, retrieving a pen from the top of the desk, 'because from where I'm sitting, I'm struggling to see it.'

Cooper cleared his throat. 'As you know, sir, we've already managed to identify the body found on board that boat yesterday.'

'You mean, your extraordinary detective skills enabled forensics to somehow discover his wallet, being that it was stuffed into the back pocket of his trousers?'

Cooper shifted uncomfortably in his chair. 'I actually meant that we've been able to confirm his identity, via his dental records.'

'Yes. And?'

'And, sir?'

Forrester paused to take in a calming breath.

'Who is he?'

'Sorry, I thought you knew. His name's Richard Oakley, an accountant for a small firm in Horning.'

'You're right, Cooper, I did know that,' Forrester said, staring over his desk at his senior investigating officer. 'I meant; who is he in relation to the investigation?'

'Er...' Cooper said, seemingly lost for an answer.

Forrester took a moment to calm himself down. 'Do we have any idea why he was murdered in what I've been told is the exact same way as one of the Claytons' dodgy lawyers and some seemingly innocent Broads Ranger?'

'At the moment, sir, we're not exactly sure.'

'You're not *exactly* sure, or you don't have a single bloody idea?'

Perhaps wisely, Cooper elected to remain silent.

After glowering over at him for a few moments, Forrester let out an exasperated sigh. 'Did you find anything out from your visit to the victim's accountancy firm?'

'Nothing yet, but we've put in a request for a court order to take a look into their accounts.'

'To look into the accountants' accounts?' Forrester queried, giving Cooper a questioning look.

'Er, yes, sir. To see if anything suspicious is going on.'

'I see. And once you're in receipt of them, you'll be able to tell, will you?'

'Well, not me personally, but our forensic accountants will.'

'I don't suppose you could have just asked them for a client list, I mean, surely all we need to know is if there's any connection between their deceased employee and the Clayton family?'

'I did, but they wouldn't tell me.'

'They - wouldn't - tell - me,' Forrester repeated, taking a moment to write the words down.

Seeing him do so, Tanner snorted, leaving Forrester raising his head to stare over at him.

'Sorry, for a minute I forgot you were there. Tell me, Tanner, what did you get up to yesterday?

Hopefully nothing involving either breaking and entering, or attempting to climb into bed with one of our suspects?'

'Not yesterday,' Tanner replied, his remark laced with bitter sarcasm.

'What *did* you do then?'

'Well, sir, after preventing the boats that were anchored up in the middle of South Walsham Broad from leaving, taking any potential witnesses with them, I set about following Detective Inspector Cooper's direct orders, sir.'

'And what were those?'

'To spend the entire day with DI Gilbert, visiting every single house surrounding South Walsham Broad, to ask if those inside just happened to be pointing a telescope in the direction of its centre at around seven o'clock in the morning, that being the only way they'd have been able to see a body being hauled up onto a hire boat anchored up in the middle of it.'

'He was also supposed to ask them if they'd seen anyone suspicious, lurking nearby, and if any had had a sailing dinghy stolen, that being the method we believe the body was transferred onto the hire boat.'

'And did anyone?' Forrester questioned, still looking at Tanner.

'No, sir, although in fairness, we were only able to speak to a handful of people. Nobody was inside the vast majority of them, which was hardly surprising, as most were holiday rentals, and their occupants were all out.'

Forrester shook his head from side to side, whilst slowly returning his attention back to Cooper.

'Why are you under the impression that the person used a sailing dinghy?'

'The couple on board at the time said they heard

something hard bump against the side, about halfway up the hull, so it must have been something quite small, but not inflatable. They also didn't hear it either approach or move away, leading us to believe that it couldn't have used either an engine or a set of oars.'

Tanner sent Cooper a wry smile but said nothing about how it had been his conversation with the couple in question which had led to that conclusion.

'We were also able to speak to the couple anchored next to them,' Cooper continued. 'Apparently, they saw an old man in a small sailing boat lurking nearby.'

'Did they see his face?'

'Only what he was wearing.'

'But they knew he was old?'

'I'm, er, not sure. It was actually Tanner who spoke to them.'

'Tanner?'

'I believe they made that assumption based on his posture, his clothes and the boat he was in. A peaked sailing cap and the angle of view prevented them from seeing his face.'

'From that I assume that they weren't even able to confirm if it was a man?'

'Again, they couldn't be sure.'

Forrester let out another heavy sigh. 'I don't suppose anyone else got a look at this person?' he continued, the question directed at Cooper.

'I'm afraid they were the only ones, sir.'

'Well, that's just great! Do either of you have any idea as to why the body was left on board a hire boat in the middle of South Walsham Broad?'

'I'm afraid we don't know that either, sir, at least not yet.'

'Vicky did point out that the hire boat was one of

the Claytons',' interjected Tanner.

'I'm not sure that's relevant, sir,' Cooper replied, his eyes shifting over towards him. 'Half the boats on the Broads are owned by the Claytons.'

Tanner sat forward in his chair. 'You're honestly trying to tell us that you don't think it's significant that whoever did this went to so much trouble to deliberately dump the body on the very front of a Clayton owned boat, in much the same way as the last body was left on the boundaries of Clayton owned land?'

'What about the victim before that; the Broads Ranger? There was no evidence linking that to the Claytons.'

'Apart from the method used to kill him, of course, and the fact that Gary Clayton has an unhealthy interest in small children.'

'I said that there was no *evidence*, Tanner. You do know what that word means, don't you, or should I get you a dictionary?'

'All right, you two.'

'My point is,' continued Tanner, 'that every time the name Clayton comes up, DI Cooper here seems to find some extraordinarily lame excuse as to why they can't possibly be involved.'

'That's because none of what Tanner says ever seems to make any sense. I mean, I can understand why they might want to have the Broads Ranger killed, but why on Earth would they decide to go about murdering people who work for them, to then leave their bodies lying about in places that would only seem to encourage us to investigate them? And I know Tanner's answer involves some sort of reverse psychology; that they left the bodies on Clayton owned property to make us think that it couldn't possibly have been them, but it's just utter bollocks, sir. Criminal organisations don't deliberately leave their victims in their own back gardens in the vague hope that it will derail suspicion. Personally, I think it's far more likely that someone is trying to send them a message, possibly someone from one of their rival gangs, or maybe someone else holding a grudge.'

'But that theory doesn't explain why the Broads Ranger was murdered,' stated Tanner, catching Forrester's eye.

'Then it must be separate,' Cooper continued.

'Despite the fact that the same method was used to kill all three?'

'Johnstone did make it clear that there were obvious differences, those being that the lawyer and accountant were tortured beforehand, and that he thought the blade used on the Broads Ranger was different.'

'But the method was still the same.'

Forrester sat back in his chair to steeple his fingers together. 'Do either of you have any suggestions as to how we move forward from here; Cooper?'

'I think we need to wait for the forensics and post-mortem reports for the body found on the boat.'

'And if nothing comes from that?'

'Then we need to start looking into who may be holding a grudge against the Claytons.'

'Jesus Christ!' Tanner laughed. 'If you're seriously going to try and pull up a list of people who are holding a grudge against the Claytons, you'll be there all bloody day.'

'I suppose you've got a better idea?'

Tanner turned to look at Forrester. 'I think we should bring Gary Clayton in for questioning, sir.'

'On what possible grounds?' Cooper continued. 'We've already established that we don't have a single piece of evidence to suggest that he's had anything to do with this.'

'What about the DNA we found on the lawyer's body?'

'Which was there because he was his client, not because he'd murdered him.'

'It would also give us the chance to search his house,' Tanner continued, 'and the Broadwater boatshed in Coltishall.'

'You mean, the one you just happened to accidentally break into the other night?' Forrester said, leaning back in his chair.

Cooper jumped in his seat to stare over at Forrester. 'Tanner broke into Gary Clayton's boatshed?'

'*Alleged* to have,' corrected Tanner. 'The quality of the CCTV footage was hardly conclusive.'

'Sorry, does that mean you did, or you didn't?'

'A friend of mine may have accidently found herself climbing in through a half-open window. I think she may have been looking for her dog.'

Cooper looked over to see Forrester rolling his eyes up to the ceiling.

'I think I need to mention that I did just happen to send what she found there over to forensics.'

Forrester glared over at him. 'You told me you didn't take anything!'

'Nothing they'd notice. She just happened to scrape a sample of dried blood off the floor in its office. Forensics came to me with the results this morning.'

'For fuck's sake, Tanner!'

'They confirmed it belongs to the lawyer, Nigel Harrison.'

The office fell into a sterile silence, as Forrester continued to glare over at him.

'We can't use it,' commented Cooper, folding his

arms over his chest with a particularly smug expression.

'I appreciate that,' Tanner replied, 'which is why I didn't mention it before, however, it does mean that we're on the right track. It also means that if we pull him in to conduct an official search, we'll know what we're likely to find.'

'Unless he's had it cleaned up.'

'If he hadn't done by the time we found it, I doubt he'd have bothered.'

'But if he has, we'll be right back to where we started, with just a single strand of hair his lawyers will easily be able to explain, given the nature of their relationship.'

'I'm sorry, Tanner, but Cooper's right. We just don't have enough.'

'OK, but what if it does turn out to be him, and he kills again, at which point the press finds out that we did nothing to try and stop him, despite having found his DNA on one of the previous victims?'

A knock at the door brought the conversation to a close, as the three of them turned to see DI Gilbert's head appear.

'Yes, Vicky, how can I help?'

'Sorry to bother you, sir. I just thought you should know that the forensics report from the body found on the boat has just come in.'

'Have you looked through it?'

'Only briefly.'

'And...?'

'It looks like Gary Clayton's DNA was found on the body again.'

- CHAPTER FORTY SEVEN -

'YOU'D BETTER COME in, Vicky,' said Forrester, sitting forward in his chair. 'And close the door.'

'I assume that means we can move forward with bringing him in for questioning?' posed Tanner.

Cooper shifted in his seat. 'I still don't think it's enough.'

'I'm afraid I'm going to have to go with Cooper,' agreed Forrester.

Tanner let out an exasperated sigh. 'I'm sorry, but how much more evidence do we need, exactly?'

'It's not enough for a conviction, Tanner. You know that.'

'But we only need an excuse to gain access to his boatshed.'

'If they've cleaned up the blood your friend said she found,' Forrester began, 'we'd be forced to let him go, leaving us needing a raft of new evidence if we were to arrest him again.'

'Unless we found something else?'

'Like what?'

'I've no idea.'

'Look, Tanner, if it was anyone else, I'd probably agree with you, but this is Frank Clayton's son we're talking about. We're going to need a water-tight case against him if we're to stand even the vaguest chance of a conviction.'

'Look, sir, we all know its him. The DNA found on Richard Oakley proves it. We just need to gain access to that boatshed.'

'I'm sorry, Tanner, but we're going to need to find something else.'

Tanner thought for a moment. 'How about we arrest him *for* something else?'

'How do you mean?'

'What if we brought him in on suspicion of abducting the children, instead of committing the murders?'

'But sir,' pleaded Cooper, 'we have even less evidence that he took the children!'

Tanner caught Forrester's eye. 'Maybe so, but if we did, we'd at least be able to gain access to his boatshed.'

'And if we don't find anything?'

'Then we'll release him with nothing lost. We'd still be in a position to arrest him again for the murders should something else turn up, without having to sacrifice the evidence we've already got.'

Forrester gazed over towards his window with a sagacious frown. 'We'd still need something to justify his arrest, else his lawyers would demand his immediate release. They'd also be able to obtain a court order to prevent us from accessing his property as well.'

'I'm sure that won't be a problem. The files we had on him down in London will be enough to justify our actions. I don't think it will matter too much if they relate to charges he's already been cleared of.'

Cooper caught Forrester's eye. 'You do realise that the minute his lawyers find out that their client has been arrested using evidence he's already been acquitted for, they'll come down on you like a ton of bricks; and that's before they tell his father what we're up to.'

'What's the worst that can happen?' Tanner continued. 'We don't find anything, forcing us to release him?'

'You're talking about publicly accusing Gary Clayton of being a predatory paedophile, with zero evidence that he actually is,' stated Cooper.

'So what?'

'Ok, but don't you think he's going to be just a little bit miffed?'

'With any luck,' Tanner replied, with a rueful smirk.

'Well, I'm sorry, sir, but I'm having nothing to do with it.'

'Why? Because it's vaguely unethical?'

'There's nothing vague about it!'

Forrester flattened his hands over his desk before glancing up at Vicky, still standing quietly in front of the door. 'What do you think?'

'Well, sir, I think it's too much of a coincidence for Gary Clayton's DNA to have been found on the bodies of both Nigel Harrison *and* Richard Oakley. I also think that we need to be seen to be doing something. If another child goes missing and the press finds out that we've been sitting on this much evidence, I don't think it will be Gary Clayton we'll need to be worried about.'

'I assume by that you agree with Tanner?'

'If it means being able to gain access to his boatshed, then yes, sir, I do.'

'No surprises there,' Cooper muttered, just loud enough for everyone to hear.

Vicky turned her head to glare down at him. 'And just what's that supposed to mean?'

'Nothing,' Cooper replied, offering her an innocent grin.

'There is another option,' said Tanner, catching Forrester's eye.

'Go on.'

'That we arrest him without stating a reason.'

'Er...' began Cooper, 'I think Detective Inspector Tanner has spent a little too long at sea, being that the act of doing so would in itself be illegal.'

'I'm fairly sure we don't have to,' Tanner continued, 'at least not immediately. From what I remember, our only legal obligation is to do so as soon as we reasonably can, which could be hours afterwards, giving us time to gain access to his boatshed. If we find the blood, then we can proceed on the basis of murder. If it's been cleaned up, then we'd be able to fall back on suspicion of child abduction, and just hope something else turns up.'

'I'm still not having anything to do with it,' Cooper muttered.

'Sod it!' stated Forrester, planting his fists firmly down on the desk. 'Tanner, I want you to contact London. Ask if they'd be willing to send over any information they have on file for him relating to the paedophile charge. Assuming they will, I want you to bring him in. Just try to put off telling him the reason why for as long as possible.'

'Thank you, sir,' said Tanner, pushing himself up from his chair.

'And the moment you have him in custody, I want his boatshed, house, car and anything else you can think of searched, preferably before his lawyers find out what we're up to.'

- CHAPTER FORTY EIGHT -

'WE MEET AGAIN,' said Tanner, forcing a smile into the piercing blue eyes of the immaculately dressed elderly man he could see waiting for him outside the door to one of the station's interview rooms. 'Mr Atkinson, wasn't it?'

'Of Allen & Atkinson,' he confirmed. 'I'm here to represent my client, Mr Gary Clayton.'

'Well, I suppose someone had to. Did you draw the short straw?'

'Most amusing. Sorry, I can't remember your name?'

'Detective Inspector Tanner,' he replied, glancing around to introduce the good-looking young man standing behind him, 'and my colleague, Detective Constable Townsend, who'll be sitting in with us.'

'I assume you are going to be telling my client *why* he's been detained, at some point?'

'All in good time, Mr Atkinson.'

'I'm afraid that wasn't the answer I was looking for.'

'I'm sorry about that, but we have a few questions to ask before doing so.'

'Then you should have asked him those questions before you arrested him, shouldn't you!'

'Perhaps, but the opportunity failed to present itself.'

'Look, inspector, the law is exceptionally clear on this. Anyone who is arrested *must* be given a reason.'

'I'm fully aware of that, thank you, Mr Atkinson, however, the law also states that we don't have to do so immediately.'

'But you do have to do so just as soon as you reasonably can, otherwise we're fully within our rights to claim that the arrest has been unlawful.'

'And we shall be. Now, shall we begin?' Tanner continued, gesturing at the door.

The solicitor glared at him for a full moment, before reluctantly standing to one side.

'Sorry to have kept you,' said Tanner, leading the way into the small windowless interview room to glance briefly over at Gary Clayton, sitting in one of the chairs.

'Can I go now?' Gary demanded, pushing himself up to stare over at his legal representative with a look of hopeful expectation.

'The police wish to ask you a few questions first.'

'But they haven't told me why I've been dragged in here yet!'

'They are aware that they need to.'

Gary exchanged a fretful glance between Tanner and Townsend, as he watched them take a seat opposite him. 'So...?'

'As your solicitor said,' began Tanner, 'we have a few questions to ask before we do.'

'I thought you said they have to tell me why I'm being detained,' Gary muttered, in a forced whisper, his eyes following the solicitor as he skirted around the back of his chair. 'And that if they didn't, I'd be able to go.'

'They've assured me that they will; haven't you, inspector?'

'Just as soon as we reasonably can,' Tanner replied, offering the solicitor a thin smile, as he reached over to turn on the recording device bolted to the wall.

'The time is half past eleven, on the morning of Friday, 13th August. Present in the room are Mr Paul Atkinson, Detective Constable Mark Townsend, myself, Detective Inspector John Tanner, and Mr Gary Clayton, who is currently helping us with our enquiries.'

'Inquiries into what? the solicitor questioned, making a point of glancing down at his watch.

'Just as a reminder,' Tanner continued, his eyes focussed on the suspect, 'you do not have to say anything, but it may harm your defence if you do not mention when questioned something which you later rely on in court, and anything you do say may be given in evidence.'

'You still haven't told us why he's here?'

'I can assure you that we'll be coming to that.'

'OK, I'll give you five minutes.'

'Mr Clayton,' Tanner began. 'May I call you Gary?'

'You can call me whatever you like.'

'Are you married, Mr Clayton?'

'What the hell's that got to do with anything?'

'Sorry, of course you are. It says so right here in your file. I don't know quite how I missed that.'

'Four minutes and fifty seconds, inspector.'

'Do you have any children, Mr Clayton?'

'No, I don't have any children.'

'Was that because you couldn't, or that you didn't want to?'

'Seriously?' Clayton queried, staring over at his solicitor.

'Inspector Tanner, I do hope that this is rapidly leading towards placing you in a position where you'll be able to inform my client as to what he is doing here?'

'I can assure you that I'm coming to that. In the meantime, it would be useful if your client could answer the question.'

The solicitor signalled for Clayton to go ahead.

'I've got absolutely no idea what it has to do with anything, but it was our choice.'

'But you do like them, though?'

'Ah, I get it now. You've dragged me in here desperately hoping that I'm the person who's been abducting all those children, but you don't have a single shred of evidence to back it up, which is why you're being so reluctant to say why you have. You do realise that the moment my solicitor here realises that his client has been arrested with zero evidence for having committed the crime, he'll be insisting I'm let go, shortly before he advises me to sue you for wrongful arrest.'

'Sorry, does that mean you do like children, or you don't?'

'Is that true, Mr Tanner?' demanded the solicitor.

'I don't know. Your client has yet to answer the question.'

'I meant, is it true that you've arrested my client under suspicion of child abduction, without any evidence of his involvement?'

'Not at all. We have the evidence. I'm just waiting to find out the answer to my last question; before we say officially why we've placed him under arrest.'

The solicitor narrowed his eyes at him.

'May I at least see this so-called evidence?'

'By all means.'

Tanner surreptitiously slid over a thick folder to him, before sitting back to watch as the man put on a pair of glasses to begin leafing quickly through it.

'But...this is all from the Metropolitan Police.'

'Uh-huh,' Tanner confirmed.

'Dated over five years ago.'

'Correct again.'

'Relating to a charge that's already been ruled against. How can this possibly be considered evidence?'

'With four children having gone missing in as many months, we're speaking to everyone in the area who has even the vaguest history of paedophilia.'

'You mean you *have* arrested my client of suspicion of child abduction?'

'I think that depends on how he intends to answer the question.'

'Sorry, which question was that?'

'Does he like children?' Tanner repeated, glaring over the table at Gary Clayton.

'This is ridiculous,' Clayton muttered, bristling in his seat.

'On that I'd have to agree,' his solicitor commented, removing his glasses to push the folder back over the table.

Tanner took a moment to glance down at his watch. 'Tell you what, I just need to pop out to make a very quick call. Maybe you could discuss your answer together, whilst I'm gone.'

Without waiting for a reply, he leaned over to talk directly into the recording device. 'Interview suspended at eleven forty, with the expectation that it will re-commence within the next five minutes, give or take the odd second or two.'

- CHAPTER FORTY NINE -

TANNER LED TOWNSEND out of the interview room to dig out his phone.

'Vicky, hi, it's Tanner. How's it going?'

'We've managed to gain entry; and have begun working through the boatshed.'

'Have you found the blood?'

'Not yet.'

'Did you look in the office?'

'I'm there now.'

'And...?'

'I'm sorry. There's nothing here. To be honest, the whole place looks as if it's only just been deep-cleaned. Everything smells of bleach. Some sections of the floor are even still wet. It's almost as if they were expecting us.'

Tanner cursed quietly to himself. 'Have you found anything? Anything at all?'

'We found a laptop, which was a little odd.'

'Why odd?'

'It was locked inside the filing cabinet. I've no idea what it was doing in there, but I've asked forensics to make it a priority.'

'Was there a serial number on it?'

'I've already sent it over to Sally. Hopefully she'll be able to find out who it's been registered to.'

'OK, I'd better have a word with her.'

Tanner was about to end the call when Vicky's

voice came back over the line.

'How've you been getting on with Gary Clayton?'

'I've been stalling for time, hoping you'd find the blood.'

Vicky paused before responding, her voice dropping to a whisper. 'Maybe it's time for us to use that insurance policy we discussed earlier.'

'You'd be willing to do that?'

'I'll admit that I was reluctant when you first suggested it, but as it looks like someone's tipped them off, I think we should.'

'Are you sure? I don't want you to do anything you're not comfortable with.'

'If that roll of knives could mysteriously go missing, I only think it's fair to do something to help redress the balance.'

'OK, well, you've got the sample. I'll leave it with you.'

Ending the call, Tanner glanced up to find DC Sally Beech beside his desk, batting her eyelids at him, as she had a tendency to do. Anxious to know how long she'd been standing there, and more importantly, how much of his conversation she'd overheard, he gave her a broad innocent smile. 'Hey, Sally. How can I help?'

'I've found out something about the accountant, Richard Oakley. I was going to tell Cooper, but I can't find him.'

'OK. Go on.'

'I've discovered he had another email account. It hasn't been used much. It looks like he kept it for one particular purpose.'

'Which was?'

'To stay in contact with the Clayton family. From what I can make out, he'd been acting as their personal accountant for over twenty years.'

'Excellent work, Sally!'

'Thank you, sir.'

'I don't suppose you saw anything that might be a sign of them disagreeing, or falling out over anything?'

'Nothing that I've found. It's all just boring accounting stuff.'

'Nothing about him knowing anything about Gary's unnatural interest in children?'

'Again, nothing, but I've only just started going through it.'

'OK, well, keep plugging away, and let me know if you find anything.'

'There are a couple more things as well, sir,' Sally continued, as Tanner stood up from his desk. 'Vicky gave me a laptop serial number, telling me to chase forensics for anything they could tell us about it.'

'Of course. I meant to ask you about that. Have you found out who it belongs to?'

'I have,' she replied, her eyes twinkling.

'And?' Tanner urged, with a hint of impatience.

'It's registered to the Broads Ranger, Mr Martin Longshore. And I've just got off the phone with forensics. They've found Gary Clayton's prints all over it.'

- CHAPTER FIFTY -

ASKING SALLY TO update Forrester on his behalf, Tanner led Townsend back into the interview room.

'Sorry about that,' he apologised, glancing over to see the solicitor push his chair back to stand up, encouraging Gary Clayton to do the same.

'Unfortunately, Mr Tanner, you're too late,' the solicitor began. 'We'll be making a formal charge for wrongful arrest. Subsequently, we're leaving.'

'I shouldn't bother if I were you.'

'I beg your pardon?'

'You'll only find yourself having to come all the way back again.'

'And what makes you say that?'

Tanner smiled, first at the solicitor, then at the man standing beside him.

'Mr Gary Clayton, I am arresting you on suspicion of murder.'

'What?' the solicitor replied, his mouth falling open.

'Once again, you do not have to say anything,' Tanner continued, 'but it may harm your defence if you do not mention when questioned something you later rely on in court.'

'You said this was about the child abduction.'

'Anything you do say may be given in evidence.'

'You better have some actual evidence this time,

inspector, or we'll be adding police harassment to the charge of unlawful arrest.'

'Do you understand the charge being brought against you?' Tanner continued, his attention remaining on the suspect.

'But – I – I thought I could go.'

'I'll take that as a yes,' Tanner replied, gesturing down at the chairs. 'If we could begin?'

Waiting for them to reluctantly re-take their seats, Tanner and Townsend did the same.

With the interview formally re-started, Tanner began by opening the file he'd brought in with him to slide out an A4 sized photograph.

'Mr Clayton, do you recognise this man?'

Clayton glanced down to see the close-up image of a man's head, lying face up on a section of freshly turned earth, rivers of congealed blood crossing his pale narrow neck.

'Not that I know of, but in fairness, it's not every day I'm forced to look at the face of someone who looks decidedly dead.'

'If I said the name Nigel Harrison, would that help?'

Clayton looked again at the picture, tilting his head. 'It could be, I suppose, but to be honest, it's been a while since we saw each other. We'd normally communicate via email.'

'But he was your lawyer, though?'

'I don't know, was he?' Clayton asked, glancing around at the man sitting beside him.

'Mr Harrison was a partner of our firm,' Atkinson replied, with narrowing eyes, 'but I'm fairly sure Mr Tanner already knew that.'

'You say you mainly communicated via email?'

'That's correct.'

'Can you remember the last time you actually met,

face to face?'

Clayton glanced briefly over at his solicitor. Seeing him return a cautionary nod, he turned back to say, 'I couldn't give you a date.'

'Roughly?'

'It was when I first moved up here.'

'So, what, about twelve months ago?'

'About then.'

'And you're sure you've not met since.'

'One hundred percent.'

'I see. So how do you think it was possible for our forensics department to find a sample of your DNA on his body?'

The solicitor cleared his throat. 'I think my client is simply miss-remembering the last time they must have sat down for a meeting. If he was given a chance to review his movements over the past few days, I'm sure he'd be able to recall a far more recent occasion. Isn't that right?' he added, placing a hand gently down on his client's arm.

Clayton nodded back in response. 'Now that I've been given a chance to think about it, I remember we did meet quite recently.'

'Oh my, that *is* convenient!' Tanner replied. 'And where abouts was this, may I ask?'

'It was in our offices in Norwich,' the solicitor responded. 'We had a joint meeting together. Nigel only took part at the very end, which is probably why my client was initially unable to remember.'

'And when was this so-called meeting that your client seemed to have completely forgotten about, until just a second ago?'

'I'd have to check my diary.'

'Would you be able to do that now?'

'Unfortunately, I don't have it with me, but I'll be sure to send over both the date and time as soon as

I'm able, together with a list of other people in the room who'll be able to testify to the fact that my late colleague, Mr Harrison, also took part.'

'Well, thank God for that. For a minute there I thought the reason why Mr Clayton's DNA was found on the body of your former colleague was because he'd murdered him!' Tanner stated, offering both Clayton and his solicitor a grimace of mock relief.

'Was that it?' the solicitor queried.

'Sorry, was that what?'

'Was that the extent of your "evidence"?'

'Hold on, let me check,' Tanner replied, running his fingers through his beard as he returned his attention back to the file. 'Oh yes, that's right, I nearly forgot. I don't suppose you know this person, by any chance?' he continued, taking out another printed-out photograph to slide over the table.

Clayton took a moment to stare down at the image, this one featuring another man's face, his large fat head leaning back against the rusted dented railings of what appeared to be some sort of a boat.

'I'm...not sure,' came his hesitant response.

'He's an accountant; if that helps.'

'Well, to be honest, I've met a number of them over the years.'

'Recently?'

'I'd have to check my diary.'

'You'd have to check your diary to see if you've recently met with an accountant?' Tanner questioned, with a curious look.

Clayton shrugged back a response.

'Don't you at least want to know who he is before you do?'

'Not really, but no doubt you're going to tell me.'

'His name's Richard Oakley. His body was seen being dumped on board a boat anchored in the middle of South Walsham Broad yesterday morning. Are you sure you don't know him?'

'I never said that I didn't.'

'But you're sure you haven't met him recently.'

'Er, no. I said I'd have to check my diary.'

'To find out if you've had a meeting with someone who you're not sure you even know.'

'Mr Tanner,' Clayton's solicitor interrupted, 'is there any chance you could get to the point?'

'I was endeavouring to find out if your client either knew or indeed has ever met with Mr Oakley, being that, once again, our forensics department has found a sample of his DNA on the body.'

'If my client says he neither knew the man, nor had he knowingly met him before, then they must have brushed past each other somewhere, maybe at a restaurant, or out walking in the street. Finding a person's DNA on somebody is hardly evidence of murder, now is it.'

'Maybe not, but when the same DNA is found on the bodies of two separate individuals, each one killed in the same way, using what would appear to be the exact same weapon, then it would certainly raise a few eyebrows, don't you think?'

'If you say so, but it's circumstantial at best. Hardly enough for someone to be charged with murder, let alone convicted of it. And there's something else you're missing as well, something which I think you'll find to be equally as problematic.'

'Oh yes, and what's that?'

'Motive, inspector! What possible reason would my client have for murdering not only one of his lawyers, someone whose job it is to help defend him from people like you, but also some accountant he's not even sure he knows?'

'Another valid point,' Tanner remarked, returning

his attention back to his file. 'How about this one?' he continued, drawing out another photograph.

Both Clayton and Atkinson looked down to find the image of yet another man's head, also facing up, again with dark dried up blood covering his exposed neck.

'Detective Inspector Tanner,' Atkinson began, making a point of glancing down at his watch, 'is this all you're going to be doing for the next twenty-three hours and thirty-six minutes; showing my client a seemingly never-ending series of photographs to ask if he's able to recognise any of the people featured in them, a task made harder by the fact that they all appear to be dead?'

'That's the last one, I promise.'

The solicitor let out a lengthy sigh of world-weary capitulation. 'Very well, but you're the one who's on the clock. Mr Clayton, you may answer the inspector.'

'Again, I've no idea,' Clayton replied, his eyes meeting Tanner's with growing confidence, 'but I'd have to say, he really doesn't look very well.'

'He was a Broads Ranger by the name of Martin Longshore. You may remember we spoke to you about him a few days ago?'

'Vaguely. I suppose you're now going to say that you found my DNA on him as well?'

'Not that I'm aware of, but we have found this, though,' Tanner continued, slipping out another picture from his file.

'It's a laptop.'

'Correct!'

'Let me guess, the battery died under suspicious circumstances, and you think I had something to do with it?'

Tanner met the man's antagonistic grin with one of his own.

'You'll never guess where we found it?'

'Lying in a gutter outside PC World?'

'Someone had hidden it at the back of a locked filing cabinet inside the Broadwater boatshed, with your fingerprints plastered all over it.'

Clayton's face darkened, his eyes shifting between Tanner's.

'And how the hell do you know that?' he demanded, whipping his head around to face his solicitor. 'Don't they need some sort of a search warrant before they're allowed to go traipsing through someone's private property?'

'As I'm sure Mr Atkinson knows,' Tanner continued, 'section 18 of the Police and Criminal Evidence Act 1984 gives us the right to search any premises owned by someone who is currently being detained for a serious offence, as is the case with murder.'

Seeing the solicitor give his client a reluctant nod, Tanner pressed ahead with his advantage.

'So, again, Mr Clayton, do you have any idea what it was doing there?'

'Not a clue. Sorry.'

'But you do know who it belongs to?'

'It's probably one of my old ones. They never seem to last very long.'

'It's actually registered to someone who you said, less than one minute ago, you didn't know, that being the murdered Broads Ranger, Mr Martin Longshore.'

Clayton was about to answer when the solicitor cleared his throat once again. 'I think you'll find that my client must have found it somewhere and brought it back to his office, hoping someone might come along to claim it. And when nobody did, he must have decided to lock it inside his filing cabinet for safe keeping.'

Tanner drew in an impatient breath. 'Mr Atkinson, I'm sure we all appreciate your input, but we're here to interview Mr Clayton, *not you!*'

The solicitor shrugged. 'My position here is to act on behalf of my client.'

'I understand that, but if you could give him the chance to respond before you do, it would be most greatly appreciated.'

'I'll do the best I can, but as I'm sure you must have realised by now, all the so-called evidence you've managed to collect still remains purely circumstantial. Nothing you have can directly link my client to the deaths of any of the victims.'

'When treated separately, you could be right, but not when you add them all together. With your client's DNA on the bodies of both Nigel Harrison and Richard Oakley, Martin Longshore's laptop found hidden inside a filing cabinet with his fingerprints all over it, together with the fact that all three victims were killed using the exact same method, we're confident we'll be able to see this through to a conviction.'

'Then you must have a better understanding of the way our legal system works than I do. There isn't a jury on Planet Earth that would convict someone of murder based solely on what are nothing more than a string of unfortunate coincidences. And there isn't a judge in the land who'd guide them towards such a verdict, either.'

'Then I suppose it's a good job we have something that could be considered to be a little more compelling.'

'This should be interesting,' muttered the solicitor, leaning back in his chair to fold his arms over his sumptuous dark grey suit.

'I must admit,' Tanner began, glancing down at his

folder, 'we were a little surprised to find that the boatshed had been deep-cleaned, just before our arrival, as if we'd somehow been expected, however, it would appear that whoever did so must have missed a bit.'

Tanner lifted his eyes to look first at the solicitor, then the client he was representing.

'A blood sample was found on the floor inside the boatshed's office.'

Out of the corner of his eye he saw DC Townsend turn his head slightly to glance over at him, before casting his eyes down to the file to shift uncomfortably in his seat.

'Admittedly,' Tanner continued, ignoring his colleague's somewhat surprised reaction to focus his attention on the suspect's narrowing eyes, 'it wasn't a particularly large sample, but it was enough for our forensics department to determine who it belonged to; Allen & Atkinson's former partner, Nigel Harrison.'

Seeing the solicitor open his mouth, Tanner held a hand up to his face.

'And before you start spinning some highly imaginative story that provides an innocent explanation to this as well, no doubt something about how your deceased colleague must have been the one to find Martin Longshore's laptop, on his way to a meeting with your client inside his boatshed, where he just happened to slice his finger open on a particularly dangerous looking Post-it Note, let me take a moment to share with you what I believe to be a more likely story.'

'As I said before, Mr Tanner, you're the one who's on the clock,' the solicitor replied, tapping a finger against his watch.

'It's my belief that your client took the laptop when

he went to pay a visit to Martin Longshore on board his boat, the night he was killed.'

'That's nice, but with zero evidence to prove that he was anywhere near either him or his boat, it is as you said; nothing more than your belief.'

'The question is,' Tanner continued, casting his eyes up to the ceiling, 'why would he have wanted to meet with a Broads Ranger, of all people, and why he felt it necessary to leave with the man's laptop after inserting a knife into his brain? It couldn't have been because he was in the process of robbing the place, and the man just happened to get in his way. If it was, then he'd have taken the wallet which we found lying in plain sight beside his bed.'

'I know,' said the solicitor, half raising his hand. 'Because he was nowhere near the place and just happened to find the laptop whilst out for a walk one day.'

'I think it's more likely,' Tanner continued, happy to ignore the alternative suggestion, 'that he took the laptop because of what he feared someone might find on it, were it to have been left behind, which brings me back to the reason why he was there in the first place.'

'You do realise that this is all pure conjecture, don't you, Mr Tanner?'

'The most obvious reason is that the Broads Ranger had found out something about your client, and not realising who he was; the son of Frank Clayton, head of the infamous Camden Crime Syndicate, he made the mistake of trying to blackmail him. What he discovered is, I believe, fairly obvious, especially in light of your client previously being charged with the sale and distribution of child pornography, and for being a predatory paedophile.'

'Both of which he was acquitted,' interjected the

solicitor.

'But when you take into account the abduction of Martin's five-year-old daughter, either because she'd witnessed your client murdering her father, or simply because he just fancied the look of her, I'd say your defence is beginning to show significant signs of weakness, wouldn't you say?'

'As fascinating as all that was, it still doesn't provide even the vaguest idea as to why my client would have felt the need to murder one of his lawyers, together with some accountant he didn't even know.'

'I suspect it was for the same reason.'

'Oh, I see. They were all trying to blackmail him?' Atkinson laughed.

'I was referring more to your client's alleged carnal interest in children. I've no doubt that there are large numbers of lawyers and accountants who are more than used to turning a blind eye to the more criminal goings on of their clients. There may even be some who encourage it, but I suspect they'd draw the line at child abduction and molestation, present company excepted, of course.'

'But again, Mr Tanner, my client has already told you that he didn't know the accountant you keep referring to.'

'Er, as I understood it, he said he wasn't sure.'

'Then I suggest you ask him again.'

'That won't be necessary.'

'Uh-huh. And why's that, may I ask?'

'Because we've already found out that Richard Oakley was working for the Clayton family; and had been doing so for over a decade.'

- CHAPTER FIFTY ONE -

WITH THE SOLICITOR requesting time to consult with his client, Tanner was happy enough to suspend the interview.

Once back out in the main office, he asked Townsend to grab him a coffee, leaving him to hurry over to where Sally was sitting.

'Any news?' he asked, glancing at her computer screen, only to realise she was doing nothing more productive than staring vacantly at The Norfolk Herald's website.

Jumping in her chair, she quickly closed the page.

'Sorry, sir, I - I haven't been able to find out anything else.'

'Nothing to suggest the accountant knew anything about Gary Clayton's interest in children?' he asked, disappointed, although not altogether surprised to have caught her skiving-off at such a critical time.

'Not yet, but I've only just finished going through his emails. I haven't started on his social media accounts yet.'

Tanner took a moment to glance around the office. 'I don't suppose there's been any news from Vicky?'

'I think she's still down at the boatshed.'

'She hasn't called in?'

'Not that I know of.'

'And Cooper?'

'I haven't seen him for ages.'

'OK, keep plugging away.'

Desperate to speak to Vicky, to confirm that she'd been able to plant the evidence of Nigel Harrison's blood, Tanner was about to head outside to see if he could get hold of her on the phone when he heard Sally call out behind him.

'Before you go, sir, I think you'd better see this.'

'See what?' he asked, turning back.

'It's what I was looking at when you came over,' she continued, pulling up the web page he'd seen her close down so quickly. 'It's The Norfolk Herald. They're reporting that we've arrested Gary Clayton.'

Tanner leaned over her shoulder to take a look.

'No great surprises there. They must have recognised him when we brought him in.'

'Yes, but they're saying we arrested him for the abduction of all those children, without having any evidence.'

'What?'

'They're also saying that we only did so to gain access to his private property, as we didn't think we had enough evidence to be legally granted a search warrant.'

'But how the hell did they...?'

'It gets worse, I'm afraid. The article goes on to accuse you, personally, of having broken into the Broadwater boatshed at Coltishall to plant evidence that he also murdered Martin Longshore, Nigel Harrison and Richard Oakley.'

'Jesus Christ!'

'Excuse me, Tanner,' came the sound of Forrester's voice, calling over to him from the door to his office. 'Might I have a quick word?'

Cursing under his breath, he turned around to give the DCI a look of mystified nonchalance. 'I was just about to continue with Clayton's interview, sir.'

'This won't take long.'

'Good luck,' he heard Sally whisper, as he saw Forrester duck back inside, leaving his door hanging open for him.

- CHAPTER FIFTY TWO -

'I ASSUME YOU'VE seen what the newspapers are saying?' said Forrester, as Tanner stepped inside to close the door behind him.

'Only The Norfolk Herald.'

'Then it probably won't surprise you to learn that I've had Superintendent Whitaker on the phone.'

'I hope you told him it wasn't true.'

'Which part?'

Tanner had to think for a moment. 'Well, sir, the part about me planting evidence.'

Forrester leant back in his chair.

'Fortunately for us, at the moment the story's only come out in the one paper nobody ever pays much attention to, else I suspect we'd both be facing a disciplinary enquiry.'

'Which would unearth nothing more than what I've already told you,' Tanner lied, his mind busily regretting what he'd asked Vicky to do.

'To be honest, Tanner, at this stage I'm more concerned about how they got hold of the story, being that the vast amount of it *is* true. I sincerely hope you haven't been discussing the case with that Broads Ranger girlfriend of yours.'

'As I've said before, sir,' Tanner replied, shifting his weight from one foot to the other, 'we're not going out with each other.'

'That doesn't answer my question.'

'It didn't?'

'Have you been discussing the investigation with her?' Forrester demanded.

'Er, well, a little, perhaps.'

'Please, God, tell me you're joking.'

'In my defence, sir, it's been a little difficult not to when she's been so actively involved in the investigation. I mean, if it wasn't for her, we'd probably still be waiting to get over the water at Brayden Marsh to examine Nigel Harrison's body. We'd also have been unable to speak to any of those onboard the boats surrounding the one Richard Oakley was dumped on. They'd have all left their anchorages a long time before our patrol boats got anywhere near the place.'

'None of which alters the fact that the first person found dead was her long-time work colleague. She *has* to remain a suspect, Tanner. You shouldn't be within ten feet of her, let alone sleeping on board the same boat. And under absolutely no circumstances should you be discussing the investigation with her whilst doing so.'

'I appreciate that, sir, really I do, but it doesn't alter the fact that she's proven to be so helpful.'

'Like the time when she decided to break into Gary Clayton's boatshed, where she just happened to find a sample of Nigel Harrison's blood?'

Tanner took a half-step away from Forrester's desk. He knew what he was about to accuse her of, and was beginning to feel sick to the stomach that he'd not considered the possibility himself.

'For God's sake, Tanner. How do you even know she found the blood there?'

'Well, I – I...'

'You said yourself that she went in alone. For all we know, she could have had the sample in her pocket all the time.'

'I think that's highly unlikely, sir,' Tanner responded, recalling the plastic bag she'd presented the sample to him in, along with the other objects that had been inside. 'For a start, she'd had to have collected a sample of his blood from somewhere.'

'Who was first to arrive at the scene after the lawyer's body was found?'

Remembering it was Christine, Tanner stuttered, 'I – I know, but I just can't believe she would do something like that.'

'You can't believe she would do something like that?' Forrester repeated, glaring over at Tanner with a look of un-hinged incredulity.

'But – what could she possibly have to gain?'

'I've no idea, Tanner, but it's our job to assume everyone is guilty, not to assume someone isn't just because you've fallen in love with them.'

'Oh, c'mon sir, I've hardly fallen in love with her.'

'You're saying you *don't* find her physically attractive, despite all accounts that she is?'

'But that's just...'

'And since you met, you seem to have spent the entirety of your free time hanging out together?'

'As she's currently staying on board my boat, sir, it's a little difficult not to.'

'Just the fact that she *is* staying on board your boat, Tanner, seems to prove my point, don't you think?'

'I'm sorry, but I fail to see how any of this is relevant,' he replied. 'There's no motive for her to have killed any of the victims, and she's certainly not some sort of predatory paedophile who's been going around nabbing children off the ends of boats in order to have her wicked way with them.'

'And yet she lost her own child in a motorway pile-up?'

Tanner stopped to stare over at the DCI. 'How do you know about that?'

'Because, Tanner, in the absence of anyone around here seemingly able to do their jobs properly, I felt obliged to do some digging of my own. Did you know she quit her former profession as a clinical psychologist to become a Broads Ranger?'

'Yes of course. She told me.'

'But did you know that she spent the first year after the accident inside a psychological institution, and that she's still receiving treatment to this day?'

Tanner's eyes dived between Forrester's; his mind refusing to listen to what he was being told.

'You know, Tanner, when I first took up this position, I read through the file on Miss Susan Follett.'

The sound of the name made Tanner's head jolt backwards.

'A seemingly harmless receptionist,' Forrester continued, 'who set about cutting un-born children from the wombs of her victims to keep their tiny rotting corpses inside some dilapidated windmill.'

'You're not seriously comparing Christine Halliday to that psycho nut-job, I hope.'

'My point is, Tanner, we don't know anything about her. And why? Because nobody's bothered to look! And yet there you are, shacked up together in the same boat, whilst giving her regular updates on everything that's been going on. You must realise just how dangerous that could be?'

'If she had anything to do with it, then yes, but she didn't. Don't forget that she's a victim as well, thanks to whoever broke into her house. And we know that for a fact because we were there.'

'You mean, *you* were there.'

'Well, I'm fairly sure it wasn't Miss Halliday who shoved me out the way whilst making a run for the front door, being that she was tied to one of her own kitchen chairs. The guy who attacked her even left his roll of knives behind as if to prove it.'

'Which promptly went missing.'

'Which had nothing to do with me. If anyone, you can thank Cooper for that. You may also want to talk to him about how the press found out about that story. Apart from you and Vicky, he's the only one who knew about our plans to arrest Gary Clayton on the pretence that he was responsible for all the child abductions.'

'You didn't tell Ms Halliday?'

'How could I have done? We only came up with the idea a few hours ago.'

Forrester thought for a moment. 'I don't suppose it could have been Vicky, talking to the press?'

'I think it's far more likely to have been Cooper, sir, probably to get back at me for turning up out of the blue to start stomping all over his investigation.'

Forrester took a moment to think about that as he leant back in his chair to stare out through the partition window. 'I must admit, his behaviour has been a little erratic recently, not helped by the fact that he's just called in sick.'

'Really?' Tanner queried, with a dubious frown.

Forrester nodded slowly back, gazing over at his empty desk. 'He said he must have eaten something for lunch that didn't agree with him. Not great timing, I must admit.'

- CHAPTER FIFTY THREE -

AS FORRESTER CONTINUED to stare out, the sound of incoherent shouting could be heard drifting over towards them.

'What the hell's going on out there?' he muttered, pushing himself up from his chair.

With the commotion becoming increasingly audible, Tanner stood up, tugging open the door to send everyone in the open-plan office beyond a questioning frown. But nobody was looking back. They all had their eyes firmly set on the double doors that led out to reception.

'We'd better take a look,' said Forrester, pushing past to lead Tanner through the main office, heading for what appeared to be the source of the commotion.

Bursting through the doors at the end they saw none other than Frank Clayton, shaking with vehement rage at the duty sergeant and two other uniformed officers, their faces pale, fraught with anxiety.

'If you don't release my son NOW,' the old man raged, spittle flying out from his twisted mouth, 'I'm going to tear this place apart with my bare fucking hands.'

'I think you're going to have to calm down,' stated Forrester, raising his arms in a bid to placate him.

'Ah, just the man I wanted to see,' Clayton continued, his eyes drilling into the DCI's. 'I sincerely hope you've come out here to tell me that there's been a massive mistake and you're about to release my son. If not, then I'm going to fetch my shotgun from the back of my car, come back in here and blow your fucking head off!'

'Your son is currently under arrest for the murder of Martin Longshore, Nigel Harrison and Richard Oakley.'

'For which the only evidence you have was planted there by one of your police officers!'

'I suggest, Mr Clayton, you should be a little more careful with which newspaper you choose to get your information from.'

'I didn't get it from a newspaper, I got it from the TV!'

'Then whichever channel you were watching should make sure to verify their sources before they start spreading malicious and wholly inaccurate miss-information.'

'You're telling me that the story isn't true; that you didn't arrest him under the baseless accusation that he's responsible for all those child abductions, for the sole purpose of gaining access to his private property to find the evidence you'd already had someone plant there?'

'I can assure you that nobody working at this station would stoop to the level of planting evidence.'

'I see. Then who was it I saw CCTV footage of, climbing through a window of the boatshed over at Coltishall?'

'I have no idea, but I can assure you that it was nobody working under me. Furthermore, if I believed, even for a second, that they *had* planted evidence,' Forrester continued, his eyes resting on Tanner for the briefest of moments, 'your son wouldn't be the only one to find himself under arrest.'

'Then I suggest you'd better start telling me what evidence you do have?'

'Unfortunately, I'm unable to do that.'

'Because you don't have any!'

'Because, Mr Clayton, I'm not at liberty to discuss the details of an investigation with a member of the public, even if that person is the suspect's father.'

'And I'm not supposed to go around shooting high-ranking police officers in the head, but today I just might make an exception.'

Forrester let out an exasperated sigh.

'We found your son's DNA on the bodies of both Nigel Harrison and Richard Oakley, both of whom had spent a significant number of years working for your family's business, each one having been murdered using a method favoured by a certain London-based criminal organisation.'

'Is that it?'

'And during an on-going and completely legal search of the Broadwater boatshed at Coltishall, despite having arrived to discover the whole place had been scrubbed clean just minutes before our arrival, our forensics department were able to find a blood sample from one of the victims. Last, but by no means least, they also found a laptop registered to Martin Longshore, the Broads Ranger murdered by the exact same method, on which your son's fingerprints were found. So, as you can see, we have more than enough evidence to have arrested him on suspicion of murder. Whether or not we have enough to charge him, we'll have to wait and see, but as I've no doubt you already know, we have the legal right to detain him for up to twenty-four hours before having to make a decision as to how best to proceed. If at that point we feel the evidence would not withstand the scrutiny of a Crown Court trial, we'll be able to let him go. Until then, I suggest you go home and turn that TV of yours off, else you could find yourself facing a charge of violent disorder.'

The reception fell into a deathly silence as Clayton continued to glare at the DCI, his eyes like the barrels of the shotgun he'd been threatening to fetch from outside.

'So what's it to be,' Forrester continued, 'a formal charge followed by an uncomfortable night in a holding cell, or a trip back home for tea and cake?'

'This isn't over,' Clayton snarled, turning to storm out. 'Not by a long way.'

- CHAPTER FIFTY FOUR -

WAITING FOR FRANK Clayton to stomp his way out, Tanner was finally able to return to the interview room, only to find the man's son sitting behind the table; his arms folded, his mouth firmly closed.

With their prime suspect refusing to answer any more questions, and with their senior investigating officer apparently in bed with a bout of food poisoning, Forrester instructed him to play it safe by applying to the local magistrate for a thirty-six hour holding extension.

Doing so, he spent what remained of the day re-reading medical and forensic reports before eventually heading for home.

'How was your day?' asked Christine, glancing over at him from behind a book, her feet up in the cockpit.

'Oh, you know. About average.'

'I saw the news on my phone.'

'You and just about everyone else, it would seem.'

'I hope your boss doesn't think that *I* planted the blood sample?'

'Only a little,' he replied, offering her a sanguine smile. 'But don't worry, we're confident that we have our man.'

'Are you sure? The news said you arrested him without evidence.'

'Yes, well. I suspect the person who told them that had an ulterior motive.'

'Which was?'

'To make me look like an idiot? Something like that. Anyway, we should have enough to hold him for a few days before having to formally charge him.'

Christine pushed herself up to put her book away.

'I was sitting around with nothing much to do, so I thought I'd make you something to eat. I hope that's OK?'

'I suppose that depends what it is?' Tanner replied, cautiously eying a large pot on the stove, its contents hidden by a lid.

'There's no need to look quite so worried. Cooking is a hobby of mine.'

'Is that good or bad?'

Standing up, she sent him a chastising frown.

'Dare I ask what it is?'

'Rat-au-van!' she announced, with a triumphant expression.

Tanner gave her a curious look.

'At least, that's what I've decided to call it,' she continued. 'You see, I found this dead rat lying outside the boat when I got back, and as it looked like it had been runover by a van...'

'I think you've been watching too many Blackadder re-runs, at least I hope you have.'

'Would you be happier if I said it was Cock-au-van?'

Tanner winced as he watched her remove the lid. 'What is it really?' he asked, realising it both looked and smelled delicious.

'I just told you.'

'Someone's cock, runover by a van?'

'Close enough.'

'Nobody's I know, I hope?'

'It's a chicken casserole.'

'Oh, right. Sorry. Of course.'

'I assume you'd like some?'

'Yes please!'

'OK, let me heat it up for you.'

'Can I get you a drink?' he offered, climbing inside the cockpit to make a beeline for the bottle of rum he kept under the starboard side locker.

'Go on then, but only one. I've got to get up early tomorrow.'

'For any particular reason?' he asked, placing two glass tumblers down on the table.

'I volunteered to spend the day putting up some barbed-wire fencing.'

Filling each to the half-way mark, he offered her a curious look.

'Why on Earth would you do that?'

'To volunteer, or to put up some fencing?'

'Well, both, really.'

'Land management is all part of the job. Admittedly, it never used to be. Back in the day there were two types of rangers, Countryside and Navigation, but government cutbacks forced them to eventually merge.'

Tanner downed his glass to immediately pour himself another. 'Did you know you'd be out fixing fences when you took the job?'

'As long as I'm outside, I really don't mind. It's the time I have to spend stuck inside the office in some boring planning meeting that I object to.'

'I know what you mean,' he replied, taking a moment to stare out at the fast-setting sun, the rum already having its desired effect.

'OK, I reckon this is ready. Where do you want to eat?'

'Here's fine,' he replied, glancing down.

DAVID BLAKE

Watching her ladle out some of the steaming casserole, he finished his second drink and slid his legs under the table.

'You'd better slow up with that rum of yours,' Christine commented, 'else you'll have passed out before being able to sample my culinary delights.'

'I didn't know we were so well acquainted,' he joked, beginning to feel increasingly relaxed.

'I think that's up to you,' she replied, catching his eye with a flirtatious smile.

Finding himself feeling suddenly both uncomfortable and a little embarrassed, in need of a distraction he cleared his throat to begin searching for his phone.

'Shit,' he soon muttered, unable to find it.

Christine placed a bowl down in front of him. 'What's up?'

'My phone. I must have left it at work.'

'Do you need it?'

'Well, no, but I've got a probable serial killer in custody and there are four children still missing. I won't be able to sleep without it.'

She watched as he shunted himself out from under the cockpit's table. 'Can't you eat something first?'

'I'd rather get it now,' he replied, standing up only to feel his head spin.

'How much have you drunk?' she asked, watching him place a steadying hand onto the side of the cabin.

Tanner glanced down at the table, first at his empty glass, then over at the half-empty bottle of rum standing innocently by its side. 'Probably more than I should've.'

'Well, you can't drive. Not in that state.'

'It's only down the road.'

'And you call yourself a policeman?'

'Well, yes, but I'm on a short-term contract. I'm

250

not sure it counts.'

Christine glared over at him, clearly unamused.

'OK, then I'll have to walk.'

'I'm not sure you'd even be able to do that, not without falling into the river. Let me grab my keys. I'll drive you in.'

- CHAPTER FIFTY FIVE -

PASSING THE NEWS vans flanking the road outside Wroxham Police Station, Christine pulled her MX-5 into the dark, virtually empty carpark.

Stepping out amidst a light smattering of flash photography, they hurried over to the entrance.

'You'd better wait in reception,' said Tanner, pulling the door open to guide her inside.

Giving a bleary-eyed duty sergeant a quick nod, Tanner headed over towards the doors leading through to the main office, only to be met by none other than DI Cooper, charging out the other way.

'What are *you* doing here?' Cooper questioned, coming to a sudden halt, his eyes dancing erratically between Tanner's.

'I could ask you the same thing. The last thing I heard you had your head stuck down a toilet.'

'Yes, well, I got better.'

'So you thought you'd come in at, what...nearly eleven o'clock on a Friday night,' Tanner said, glancing down at his watch, 'to do a little catching up?'

'That's because I'm a dedicated professional, unlike some people I could mention.'

Tanner snorted back a response.

'Anyway, what about you?' Cooper continued, pulling himself up straight. 'Judging by the fumes, I'd say you were halfway through a pub crawl and took a wrong turn.'

'I left something behind.' Tanner replied, glancing over his shoulder at the main office behind him.

Cooper stepped to one side. 'Please; don't let me stop you.'

Shoving past, Tanner was about to push his way through the doors when they heard the jarring sound of the station's rear exit buzzer.

'Who the hell's that?' he queried, turning his head towards the duty sergeant, only to see him staring back at him with a similar blank expression.

'Don't worry, I'll get it,' Cooper replied, spinning around to make his way over towards the small corridor leading to the carpark at the back.

Seeing Christine glance over at him from the notice board she was looking at, above a row of plastic chairs, Tanner shrugged his shoulders at her before turning to make his way inside the dark deserted main office. Once there, he'd only just started scrabbling around for his phone when the muffled sound of voices could be heard drifting out from reception.

Assuming it to be some homeless drunk, he continued his search, until the piercing sound of a woman's scream had him spinning around to sprint back out to find himself face-to-face with a giant of a man, a black ski-mask pulled down over his wide round face.

'What the...!'

'GET DOWN ON THE FLOOR!' the man shouted, shoving him back with something long and heavy held in his black gloved hands.

Managing to stay on his feet, Tanner darted his eyes about. Behind the reception desk's security screen was the duty sergeant, standing with his mouth hanging open. Next to the door leading out to the back of the building stood another masked man; and over in the corner, crouched on the floor with her hands held on top of her head, was Christine.

It was only when he realised that each of the intruders was brandishing sawn-off shotguns, one drifting between the duty sergeant and the top of Christine's head, that his heart began thundering deep inside his chest.

'I SAID, GET DOWN!' the gorilla-sized man beside him yelled.

Tanner took to a knee to continue scanning the room, searching for Cooper. Unable to see him, he stared up into the eyes of the masked man above.

'You do know that we don't keep any money here, don't you?'

'SHUT UP!'

'I mean, this isn't a corner shop.'

'I SAID, SHUT THE FUCK UP!'

The appearance of a third man, his ski-masked head emerging from around the door leading out to the back of the building, allowed Tanner to finally realise what was going on.

'We've got 'im,' he heard the man say.

'Got who?' Tanner demanded, knowing full well who they must have meant.

'Someone you 'ad no right taking in the first place,' replied the one closest, the shotgun's twin barrels staring down into his face.

'I hope you're not contemplating the idea of taking Gary Clayton.'

'Too late, mate,' the man continued, edging his way back.

'I reckon we should take the girl as well,' said the one standing next to Christine, 'for insurance purposes, like.'

'Don't even think about it,' Tanner muttered, glancing over to find her staring at him, her eyes pleading for his help.

'You know what,' continued the one with his gun still trained on his head, 'I think that's an excellent idea.'

Before Tanner had a chance to say anything, Christine screamed as she began being dragged over the floor by her hair.

Without thinking, he launched himself towards her, when an explosion slammed into his side, spinning him around to leave him lying face-down on the floor.

As white-hot pain tore itself along the nerves of his arm, face and neck, an all-too familiar noise drilled itself down into his brain, obliterating everything but the sound of his heart, until that too began drifting away to leave nothing but a hollow chasm of all-consuming darkness.

- CHAPTER FIFTY SIX -

Saturday, 14th August

TANNER'S EYELIDS FLICKERED slowly open. He was lying on his back inside a small dimly lit room, one arm bandaged over his chest, the other underneath a crisp white bedsheet. He didn't need to look around to know where he was. He'd been there often enough, certainly during the days, hours and minutes that had eventually led to the news of his fiancée's death.

The harrowing memory forced his eyes closed, only for them to be re-opened by the sound of something moving over to his right.

'You're awake,' came a softly spoken woman's voice, drifting over towards him from the corner of the room.

For one tortured second, Tanner's mind clutched at the idea that it was Jenny's voice, that she'd somehow managed to slip through the impenetrable veil that separates the land of the living from that of the dead.

But of course, neither was true.

Turning his head, he saw Christine's sparkling green eyes resting on his, a fragile smile tugging at the corners of her mouth.

'How're you feeling?'

'I'm – I'm not sure,' came his honest reply to send

a mental probe down the length of his body. 'A bit numb, I suppose. How do I look?'

'Actually, not bad, all things considered, but only because it looks like someone has had the good sense to shave that ridiculous beard of yours off.'

'What?' Tanner said, dragging a hand out from under the covers to reach for what he found to be nothing but a raw, stubble-covered chin.

'To be honest,' Christine continued, 'I'd no idea just how devilishly handsome you were.'

'Aren't they supposed to ask my permission before taking quite such drastic action?'

'I'm not sure they had much choice, unless you wanted half a dozen shotgun pellets to remain buried inside your face.'

Finding what felt like surgical dressing covering half of one side, he let his hand fall back to begin recalling the events of the night before.

'How about you?' he asked, staring over at her. 'Are you OK?'

'Oh, I'm fine.'

'They didn't take you away?'

'Fortunately for me, they decided to shoot you instead.'

Tanner smiled over at her. 'What happened then?'

Christine shrugged. 'I suppose they must have panicked and made a run for it.'

Tanner reached for his heavily bandaged arm.

'What time is it?'

'Er...' Christine replied, glancing down at her watch, '...about half-eight in the morning. You've been out cold most of the night.'

'Don't tell me you've been here all this time?'

'Er, no, sorry. I dropped in on my way in to work. Speaking of which, I'd better be off. I'm supposed to be over at Brayden Marsh, working on that barbed-wire fencing job.'

'Isn't that where we were the other day; on Frank Clayton's estate?'

'Near to it.'

'But not actually on it, though?'

'Don't worry, I'll be down the other end of the dyke,' she replied, standing up from her chair.

'Are you going now?'

'I should have been there two hours ago.'

Tanner pushed himself up from his pillow, wincing in pain as he did. 'OK, hold on. You can drop me off at the station on the way.'

'I'm sorry?'

'If you don't mind?'

'I don't mind, of course, but...I think the staff here might object.'

'Don't worry, I think they know me well enough by now to know not to bother, besides, I still need to get my phone. If you can give me five minutes to find my clothes, I'll meet you out in reception.'

- CHAPTER FIFTY SEVEN -

WITH CHRISTINE DROPPING him off just past the news vans, still cluttering up the road outside, Tanner crept into the station to find it resembling something more akin to a crime scene than a place of work.

Nudging his way past a couple of overall-clad forensic officers, he pushed through the doors to the main office to begin glancing about. He was looking for Vicky, but the only person he could see from CID was DC Sally Beech, busily chatting to someone on the phone whilst staring at her monitor.

After finally being able to recover his phone from off the top of his desk, he stared down at the screen for any missed messages. An email from Vicky, sent to him earlier that morning, had him stopping to take a look. It contained photographs forensics had found on Martin Longshore's laptop. Expecting to find a series of disturbing images depicting Gary Clayton doing something utterly disgusting to some poor child, he braced himself before opening up the first. But the image was nothing more innocuous than a photograph of Norfolk's coast, featuring people walking their dogs along a windswept beach; a pretty white yacht in the distance being tossed about by a turbulent sea.

Shaking his head in frustration, he put the phone away to stroll over to Forrester's office.

'Ah, Tanner!' the DCI exclaimed, glancing up from a file. 'So, the rumours are true. You're *not* dead.'

'I just thought I'd drop by to see how everything's going?'

'As well as can be expected, under the circumstances,' Forrester replied, taking a moment to look Tanner up and down. 'How about yourself? I see being shot at point-blank range by a sawn-off shotgun finally persuaded you to shave that horrendous beard of yours off.'

Tanner once again reached a hand up to massage the still unfamiliar stubble. 'It was removed without my consent.'

'At least it wasn't your arm,' Forrester commented, taking in the pale blue NHS sling hooked around Tanner's neck.

'I assume they did take Gary Clayton?'

'I'm afraid so. At the moment, I'm just grateful nobody was hurt in the process.'

'Er...' began Tanner, glancing down at himself.

'Sorry, I meant none of our full-time members of staff.'

'Oh, I get it now. You're joking.'

'Not really,' Forrester smirked.

'I take it everyone's out searching for him?'

'Just about. Vicky's taking a look at the car they used.'

'You found it already?'

'It wasn't difficult. The journalists camped outside caught their escape on camera, so we had a numberplate to go on. Then they were kind enough to set fire to it, which made it even easier to find.

'I don't suppose you'd be able to add anything to the statements already given by Cooper, Taylor and that Broads Ranger friend of yours?' he continued, reaching over his desk for a notepad.

'That would probably depend on what they said,' Tanner replied, curious to know himself, especially with regards to Cooper's.

'That three masked men entered the building through the rear entrance brandishing sawn-off shotguns, leaving five minutes later with our prisoner in tow.'

'Apart from the fact that one of them shot me, not much.'

'You didn't recognise any of them?'

'Well, no, but only because I don't know anyone who spends their life walking around wearing a black ski-mask.'

'I meant by their voices.'

Tanner shook his head. 'I can't say that I did. They weren't local, I know that much. At a guess, I'd say they were from London.'

'You don't think one of them could have been Frank Clayton?'

'None of them sounded much like him, but I assume we're proceeding on the basis that he was behind it, presumably to save his son from being banged-up for murder?'

'I'd have thought it was probably more to stop him from telling us everything he knows about his family's criminal organisation. Either way, we were granted a warrant to search Frank Clayton's house this morning.'

'Anything?'

'Cooper's on his way over there now.'

Tanner caught Forrester's eye. 'And you trust him?'

'Who, Cooper?'

'You said yourself that he's been acting a little erratically recently.'

Forrester gave him a cautionary look. 'I've no idea

where you're going with this, Tanner.'

'It's just that he seems to have been constantly going out of his way to prove that neither Gary Clayton, nor his father, had anything to do with either the murders or the child abductions.'

'You could say the exact opposite about yourself, Tanner.'

'I've only been following the evidence. Cooper, on the other hand, seems to be making it mysteriously disappear.'

'Seriously?'

'The roll of knives left at Ms. Halliday's house.'

'OK, but that's hardly the first time evidence has gone missing; and was far more likely to have been forensics fault than anyone else's.'

'He was first on the scene as well, and only a few minutes after I called it in. How he got there so quickly, I've no idea.'

'Are you suggesting he was tipped off?'

'Whoever attacked Ms. Halliday would have known they'd left the knives behind, which I'm sure would have had some traces of DNA on them. Knowing that, they'd have been desperate to make the evidence disappear. Then there was the story appearing in the newspaper, saying how we'd intentionally arrested Gary Clayton, knowing that we didn't have any evidence. The boatshed as well; how it had been scrubbed clean, minutes before forensics arrived. Then there's how he refused to take part in having anything to do with Clayton's arrest, and how he disappeared shortly after we did, citing having eaten a dodgy sandwich for lunch, only to appear a few hours later, just in time to let three masked men waltz into the back of the building to lead Clayton straight out the same way they'd come in.'

Forrester leant back in his chair to stare over at

Tanner through steepled fingers.

'What would Cooper's motive be?'

'Something the Clayton's have on him? They could have even bribed him, or maybe he owes them money? I've no idea, but you know as well as I do the methods used by criminal organisations to apply leverage.'

A sudden knock at the door brought the conversation to a rapid close.

'Come in,' called Forrester, staring over to see Sally's head appear.

'Sorry to bother you,' she began, exchanging furtive glances between her uncle and Tanner. 'I just thought you should know that I've had forensics on the phone.'

'Any news?'

'They've identified a hair sample found at the Broadwater boatshed at Coltishall. They said it belongs to Thomas Longshore, the father of Martin, the Broads Ranger found dead on his boat.'

- CHAPTER FIFTY EIGHT -

SILENCE FELL OVER the office as Forrester's gaze turned from his niece over towards Tanner.
'Any idea what Martin Longshore's father would have been doing sneaking around inside Gary Clayton's boatshed?'

'I'm not sure,' Tanner replied, sinking down into one of the chairs.

'Could he have been trying to frame Gary for the murder of his son?' the DCI continued.

'If that had been his intention, I'd have thought he'd have left evidence of his son's DNA, not a dried up pool of Nigel Harrison's blood.'

'Maybe he snuck in to hide the laptop?' proposed Sally, still standing beside the door.

Tanner's eyes drifted slowly up towards the ceiling. 'It's possible, but we found it covered with Gary Clayton's fingerprints, not Thomas Longshore's. We also found it hidden inside a locked filing cabinet.'

He paused for a moment. 'I don't suppose there's any chance that he was the one who killed the lawyer? Maybe the accountant as well?'

'Of course it's possible,' Forrester replied, 'but for what reason?'

'To frame Gary Clayton for their murders, as a way of getting back at him for murdering his son,' Tanner proposed, as much to himself as anyone else. 'Although, if that had been his intention,' he continued, deep in thought, 'it would still have made more sense for him to leave his son's DNA inside the boatshed, not the lawyer's. There isn't even any reason for him to have known that one of the victim's was the Clayton family's lawyer and the other was their private accountant. I mean, it took us long enough to find out. Then there's the method used to kill them, that being the same as how his son was murdered.'

It was Forrester's turn to lean back in his chair.

'It would at least explain what Dr Johnstone said about the weapon used to kill Martin Longshore, that it was different to the one used on Harrison and Oakley.'

'But not why they'd been tortured before being killed. If he'd killed them simply to frame Gary Clayton, again, why bother?'

'Sorry to interrupt,' came Sally's voice, 'but aren't you forgetting about the little girl who was taken?'

'How d'you mean?' Forrester asked, glancing over.

'That she isn't only Martin Longshore's daughter, she's Thomas Longshore's granddaughter as well. I'd have thought he'd have been tearing his hair out trying to find out where she was. Maybe he thought that either the lawyer or the accountant would know. Or maybe he was simply trying to get them to tell him if it had been Gary Clayton who'd taken her?'

Forrester sat forward to plant his elbows on the desk.

'It's not a bad idea, although he'd still have had to know who they were in relation to the Clayton family.'

'How do we know he doesn't?'

'Of course, there is one more possibility,' began Tanner, crossing one leg over the other. 'That he doesn't have anything to do with either attempting to frame Gary Clayton, or for the torture and killing of the other two. He could have simply gone into the boatshed to do nothing more nefarious than hire one of their boats.'

Forrester pushed himself up from his desk to wander over to the window. Clasping his hands firmly behind his back, he turned slowly around to face the room. 'OK, here's what I want us to do. Sally, see what you can find out about Thomas Longshore. Does he know either Nigel Harrison or Richard Oakley, and more importantly, their connection to the Clayton family?'

With a nod, Sally spun around to totter back to her desk.

'Tanner, I want you to head down to that pub of his to have another chat with him. See what he has to say about his DNA being found inside Gary Clayton's boatshed. Also ask him about his whereabouts at the times the lawyer and accountant were killed. And whilst you're there, ask him if he owns a dinghy like the one reported hiding behind that boat on South Walsham Broad, the morning Richard Oakley's body was found.'

Standing up, Tanner took a moment to glance down at his arm.

'Er...there is one slight problem, sir.'

'What's that? Please don't tell me you have a prior engagement.'

'Er, no, sir. It's just that I think I might struggle behind the wheel of a car.'

'Fair enough. I'll give Vicky a call. She'll have to come back to give you a lift.'

- CHAPTER FIFTY NINE -

'I THOUGHT YOU'D still be at the medical centre?' said Vicky, staring at Tanner's arm as he levered himself down into the passenger seat of her car.

'Yes, well, I've never been much for lounging about in bed.'

'Not even after being shot at point-blank range?'

'It was only a sawn-off shotgun. Had it been a bazooka, I'd have probably stayed till after lunch.'

'You know, you should be grateful that you came out in one piece.'

'Er...I'm not sure grateful is the word I'd have used.'

'Maybe not, but at least some good came from it.'

'What's that?'

'Your beard's gone.'

Tanner narrowed his eyes at her.

'Anyway,' Vicky smirked, 'where are we going again?'

'The Anchor Inn. Thomas Longshore's pub over at Potter Heigham. Forensics found a sample of his DNA inside Gary Clayton's boatshed.'

'I assume Forrester's thinking that he may have had something to do with what happened to Nigel Harrison?'

'Sally is trying to find out if there was any way Longshore could have known that Harrison was working for the Clayton family.'

'If he did have a hand, what would have been his motivation for wanting him dead?'

'That depends if Longshore thought Harrison knew anything about either the death of his son or the abduction of his granddaughter.'

'OK, say he did murder the lawyer,' Vicky began, 'why would he have chosen to do so inside Gary Clayton's boatshed?'

'Possibly to make it look like Gary was responsible.'

'And what about the accountant, Richard Oakley?'

'Maybe for the same reason, again trying to make it look like Gary Clayton had killed him.'

'But none of that really explains why he'd go to all the trouble of dumping one body on Frank Clayton's land and the other on the front of one of their hire boats.'

The car continued along in silence for a while.

'I don't suppose it could have anything to do with those pictures I sent you this morning?' she eventually continued.

'Which pictures were those?' Tanner replied, staring absently out of the window.

'The photographs found on Martin Longshore's laptop.'

'You mean, the ones featuring people enjoying a pleasant walk along the beach?' he queried, turning his head to stare over at her.

'Didn't you read what I said about them?'

'Er...I think I just went straight to the attachment.'

'They were sent in an email from Martin Longshore to Gary Clayton, three days before he turned up dead.'

'What did the email say?' Tanner asked, scrambling around for his phone.

'Not much, but I think it was fairly obvious what he was implying.'

With Vicky's email open, he read aloud from the screen. 'I think we need to meet.'

'As has already been suggested,' Vicky continued, 'he must have been trying to blackmail him, without realising who he was.'

'Or more to the point, who his father is,' added Tanner, re-opening the attached photographs to begin examining each with more focussed attention.

'I still can't see what's so incriminating about them,' he eventually continued. 'They're all the same; just some people taking an early morning stroll along a beach. We can't even see who any of them are.'

'If they're the reason Martin Longshore was killed, then they must be evidence of something.'

Tanner tucked the phone away as he sucked in a lungful of air. 'Well, let's just hope Martin Longshore's father is able to shed some light on this. To be honest, at the moment I'm not sure I've got a single idea what's going on.'

- CHAPTER SIXTY -

STOP/STARTING THEIR way through the Broads' heavy seasonal traffic, they eventually arrived at Potter Heigham to find it heaving with tourists.

Unable to find a parking space, Vicky eventually gave up, leaving her car parked awkwardly on the edge of the grass bank that led down to the River Thurne.

Making their way inside the burgeoning Anchor Inn, they elbowed their way to the bar where Tanner attracted the attention of the same woman he'd spoken to before, her face glistening with sweat.

'Yes, sir, what can I get you?' she called out over the cacophony of noise.

'We're looking for Mr Longshore.'

'He's not around. Can anyone else help?'

'We were here a few days ago,' Tanner continued, holding up his formal ID. 'Norfolk Police.'

The lady finished serving a customer to hurry over, staring at Tanner with unfamiliar eyes.

'I used to have a beard,' he prompted, 'instead of the surgical dressing.'

'Of course, sorry. I didn't recognise you.'

'Don't worry. You're not the first. Is it alright if we come round to the back to have a word with him?'

'Sorry, luv, but as I said, he's not here.'

'Oh, right. Do you know where he is?'

'He said he was going away for a few days, shortly after you left. Hardly a surprise, though; not after what happened to Martin, and with little Susie being taken. I don't suppose there's been any news of her?'

'Not yet,' Tanner replied, glancing around the bar. 'I don't suppose he told you where he was going?'

'Where he always goes when the place gets too much for him.'

'And where's that?'

'Sailing.'

'What, you mean at sea?'

'Oh, I doubt it,' she laughed. 'I don't think he's got the right sort of boat for that sort of thing.'

'What sort of boat has he got?'

'It's an old wooden dinghy with a tatty red sail. Hardly suitable for crossing an ocean.'

- CHAPTER SIXTY ONE -

BURSTING OUT INTO the brightness of the day, Tanner didn't wait to speak to Vicky before pulling out his phone.

'Forrester, sir, it's Tanner.'

'I was just this second about to give you a call,' the DCI replied.

'We've discovered something rather interesting about Thomas Longshore.'

'As have we!'

Tanner stopped to offer Vicky a quizzical frown.

'OK, well...you first.'

'Sally's just found out that Longshore isn't his real name,' Forrester began, 'at least it wasn't the one he was born with. He took it from his mother, Alison Longshore.'

'So...who's his father?'

'Someone we both know rather better than we'd probably like to.'

'Not Frank Clayton?'

'The one and only.'

'Jesus Christ! I'd no idea!'

'Thomas was Frank's firstborn.'

'Making Gary his younger brother.'

'Correct.'

'Any idea what happened to make him want to change his name?'

'That's where it gets interesting. About twenty-five

years ago, his brother accused him of trying to assassinate his father, in an attempt to take over the family business.'

'That must have been before my time. I assume nothing came of it?'

'The case never went to court, but the tabloids were happy enough to run with the story. They'd already chalked Thomas up as being some sort of psycho nut-job, and that his father used him primarily for intimidation purposes, probably murder as well. I think they were happy enough to conclude that the story must have been true. Anyway, it ended up with Frank disinheriting Thomas, kicking him and his wife off the family estate, which must have been why he decided to change his name to end up buying a pub in the middle of Norfolk.'

'I suppose that means that there isn't a huge amount of love lost between the two brothers,' mused Tanner.

'Well, I doubt they send each other Christmas cards every year, if that's what you mean. What did he have to say for himself?'

'He wasn't there. According to the woman behind the bar, he hasn't been since we told him what happened to his son and granddaughter.'

'I don't suppose she has any idea where he went?'

'Apparently, he owns an old wooden dinghy with a little red sail, one which he uses to go sailing around the Broads.'

'So, it's him then,' came Forrester's sullen response.

'I think it has to be, at least for the murder of Nigel Harrison and Richard Oakley. If he spent the first half of his life working under his father, he'd have known about the family's business relationship with them. He'd have also known about his brother's unnatural interest in children, and the family's preferred method of assassination, leading him to presume that it was his brother who took the life of his son, abducting his granddaughter at the same time.'

'And now he's out trying to track her down.'

'Whilst attempting to frame his brother for murder. You know, I think he might also be trying to convince his father that Gary's making moves to take over the family business, just like Gary had done to him. That would explain why he went to the trouble of dumping one body on his father's land and the other on the end of one of their hire boats, as if trying to make Frank think Gary was sending him a message.'

'That's all well and good, but all it means is that we now have two murder suspects instead of one, both who are now missing, and we still don't know why one of them would have killed the other's son, nor do we have a single bloody idea as to where all the missing children are.'

'I think if we can find the younger of the two brothers, I doubt the other will be far away, which should then lead to the children. Has there been any news from Cooper?'

'He called in earlier, from Frank Clayton's house. Apparently, there's no sign of Gary, at least none that he's found.'

'I'm sorry, sir, but he must be there. Either Cooper has been deliberately looking in all the wrong places, or he's not telling us the truth.'

'Then I suggest you and Vicky head over there to give him a hand. I'll give him a call to expect you.'

'If you don't mind, sir, in this particular instance, it may be more useful if we were able to surprise him.'

274

- CHAPTER SIXTY TWO -

ENDING THE CALL, Tanner turned to look at Vicky.

'Did you get any of that?'

'Just about. Any idea if there was anything to the story; that Thomas Longshore had made an attempt on his father's life?'

'I've no idea, but as Gary was the younger of the two, he probably just made the whole thing up as a simple solution to get rid of his older brother.'

'Did he say anything about Thomas owning a wooden dinghy with a dark red sail?'

'Not much. He knows it matches the one seen lurking around South Walsham Broad, after Richard Oakley's body was found on board that hire boat.'

'What about the fact that it's the same as all the witnesses say they saw, shortly after each of the children disappeared, yourself included?'

'You're suggesting Thomas Longshore is the person who's been taking all the children; Norfolk Herald's so-called Wherryman?'

'Why not? If it's true that Gary Clayton always had a thing for children, wouldn't it be possible for his brother to share a similar interest?'

Tanner raised an eyebrow. 'And it could also be that their father knows,' he added. 'Maybe he always has. Either way, Forrester's told us to head over to Frank's house to help Cooper look for him. It's the most logical place for Gary to be hiding. If he is there, then I don't think his brother will be too far away.'

Making their way back to the car, Vicky was about to skirt around to the driver's side when she stopped to stare over at Tanner.

'Hold on. If Frank's there, won't that mean his dogs will be as well?'

'Probably, but don't worry. It won't be like last time.'

'It won't?'

'Well, there'll be other officers on site, for a start.'

'There were other officers on site last time.'

Tanner glanced over to see the petrified look on her face. 'Tell you what, if we arrive to find them roaming around the estate, you can always stay in the car.'

'I'm sorry,' she apologised, with an embarrassed guilty look, 'I don't normally have a thing about dogs, but those Rottweilers scared the absolute crap out of me.'

It was Tanner's turn to stare over at her.

'What?' she demanded. 'I'm fairly sure I'm not the only person on the planet to have a thing about Rottweilers.'

Tanner looked away to dig out his phone. 'It's not that. It's those pictures you sent me this morning; the ones Martin Longshore emailed to Gary Clayton.'

'What about them?'

'They're of Frank and his gang,' Tanner continued, opening up the first.

Vicky joined Tanner in staring down at them. 'How can you tell? You said yourself, you can't see anyone's faces.'

'Maybe not, but I know a Rottweiler when I see one,' he replied, pointing down at the corner of the image before scrolling through the rest. 'There's something else as well. That sailing boat in the distance. Its sails are up, but it's not going anywhere. It's in the same position in each of the photographs. With the wind kicking the sea up like that, it should be motoring along. If I was to hazard a guess, I'd say it was hove-to.'

'I see,' said Vicky, nodding sagaciously.

Tanner gave her a spurious look. 'You don't know what hove-to means, do you?'

'Not a clue. Sorry.'

'It's when a boat's sails are set in such a way as to stop it from going either forwards or backwards. It's normally used as a temporary measure, to give the crew a break from sailing when the wind picks up.'

'OK, but so what?'

'And you see that, there?'

'That, where?' she queried, peering with some intensity at a seemingly unremarkable patch of darkened water that Tanner was pointing at.

'I reckon it's a tender.'

'A tender what?'

Tanner shook his head. 'A tender is a small boat used to transport either people or goods to and from a larger one.'

'Oh, you mean a dinghy?'

'What I mean,' Tanner continued, happy to ignore Vicky's nautical ignorance, 'is that I'm fairly sure I know what Martin Longshore had managed to un-earth, and why the Claytons would have been so keen to have him silenced. I think it also goes a long way to explain their real reason for wanting to re-locate up to Norfolk.'

- CHAPTER SIXTY THREE -

CLAMBERING INTO THE car, Tanner put another quick call through to Forrester, leaving Vicky to begin speeding them over Potter Heigham's Medieval bridge, heading for West Somerton and Frank Clayton's estate beyond.

Arriving at an ostentatious pair of black wrought iron gates, an oblique view of a red-bricked farmhouse to the left, they stared about, looking for some sort of intercom device.

With nothing in sight but a couple of security cameras facing down at them, Tanner volunteered to step out to take a closer look.

Levering himself out, grimacing in pain as he did, he'd only just stepped up to the gate when he heard a loud click, closely followed by the sound of a low mechanical whir as the gates began to open.

With a quick shrug of his shoulders directed over at Vicky, peering out at him from behind the wheel, he was about to head back to join her when a familiar car appeared around the corner ahead.

Stopping where he was, he watched as the car came to a halt on the gravel, leaving just enough room for the gates to continue peeling themselves back.

'What the hell are you doing here?' came DI Cooper's voice, climbing out of his immaculate bullet-grey Audi A5 to glare at first Tanner, then Vicky.

'Forrester suggested we come over to give you a

hand,' Tanner replied, offering the senior investigating officer a thin smile.

'Did he? Well, you may as well turn around and head back to whichever hospital bed it was that you crawled out of. I've already had a good look around. Gary Clayton isn't here. Neither are the missing children.'

'Forrester's keen for us to take a look anyway.'

Cooper paused for the briefest of moments, his head tilting slightly as if searching his mind for a suitable response.

'OK...' he eventually continued, 'but, unfortunately, I've already informed the owner that the search has been completed. So, if you do want to have a look around, you'll have to apply for another warrant. But I can't imagine why it would be granted, being that my official report will say there's no sign of the suspect, missing children, or anything else that could be considered even vaguely suspicious.'

Tanner drew in a calming breath. 'Sorry, Cooper, but I think the time has come for me to ask you what's going on?'

'Nothing's going on!' he stated, his shoulders rising with his voice.

'Look, whatever the Claytons think they have on you, you have to tell us. You can't continue down this road. There's nothing good at the end of it, I promise you.'

Cooper shot an anxious glance up at one of the cameras, before returning to stare over at Tanner.

'As I said, there's nothing going on. Now, I suggest you ask Vicky to move her car, so I can get past.'

'Sorry, but we still need to have a look around.'

'I've just told you that you can't, not without applying for another search warrant.'

'As you should know, the official search of a

property isn't over until the last police officer has left the site. Assuming this gate marks the boundary, that means you're still on it.'

Cooper's face darkened with rage.

'Then I suppose I'd better be off then, hadn't I,' he spat, turning sharply on his heel to dive back into his car.

Watching him slam his door closed to re-start the engine, Tanner crossed the property's threshold to take up a defiant stance, directly in the path of his car.

As Cooper leaned on his horn, nudging his Audi forward until its bumper was just inches from his legs, Tanner remained where he was, watching the gap slowly begin to close.

'If you so much as touch me with that car of yours, Cooper, I'll be filing an assault charge against you.'

The young DI wound his window down to lean his head out. 'Can you please stop being such a dick and get the fuck out of my way?'

Tanner gave him a generous smile, before stepping slowly to one side. 'No problem, but I'm officially on the property now, so it looks like there won't be a need for a new search warrant.'

'Fine!' Cooper stated, wrestling with the gear lever, 'but you're wasting your time. You're never going to find him.'

Tanner leapt back as the car careered away, its wheels spinning on the gravel, leaving him standing in a cloud of gathering dust.

Taking a moment to watch the car tear off down the road, Tanner caught Vicky's attention to wave her through the open gates that had already begun to close.

'Did he say what I thought he said?' she asked, pulling up beside him to push open the passenger-side door. 'That we'll never be able to find him?'

Tanner nodded, levering himself down into the seat. 'I'm afraid so. The Claytons must have something on him. There's no other reason for him to be acting in such a belligerent way.'

- CHAPTER SIXTY FOUR -

PULLING UP BESIDE Frank Clayton's familiar mud-splattered four-by-four, they climbed out to make their way over to the farmhouse entrance, only to find the door had been left wide open.

'Looks like someone's expecting us,' commented Tanner, offering Vicky a curious glance.

But she wasn't looking back. She'd stopped where she was, her eyes fixed on the shadows beyond the open door, blood fast draining from her lightly freckled face.

Tanner came to a standstill to follow her gaze. Just inside the doorway were two pairs of luminous almond-shaped eyes, inching their way through the darkness towards them.

'Don't move,' he whispered, raising a protective arm in front of her.

'I wasn't planning on,' she replied, her voice nothing more than an icy whisper.

Remaining completely still, they continued to watch as the eyes began to narrow, revealing two pairs of teeth, strands of saliva clinging to each.

'What do we do?'

'Let's see if we can edge our way back to the car.'

Seeing her nod from the corner of his eye, Tanner dared take a half-step back, but his movement was only met by ominous growls as the already bared teeth seemed to elongate before their very eyes.

'Shit,' he muttered, beads of sweat erupting over his forehead. 'Change of plan. When I say run, *run!*'

'You're not serious?'

'You only need to make it back to the car.'

'And what about you?'

'I'll stay here and distract them.'

'I see. And just how, exactly, are you going to do that? Throw a stick for them?'

'That's not a bad idea. I don't suppose you've got one?'

'Er...not on me, no.'

'Joking aside, are you ready?

Vicky turned her head slightly to see how far the car was. The moment she did, the muscle-bound Rottweilers leapt out from the shadows, jaws wide as the sight of their bone-white teeth surged up from the ground, reaching for the flesh of their unprotected throats.

- CHAPTER SIXTY FIVE -

'GET DOWN, BOYS!' came the distinctive voice of Frank Clayton, stepping out from the doorway; shirt sleeves rolled up, his face dripping with sweat.

Dropping instantly to the ground, the dogs' heads turned to stare obediently around at their master; tongues dangling out from the corners of their mouths.

'You two are lucky to be alive!' the estate's owner stated, watching with a self-amused smirk as Tanner turned to help Vicky pick herself up from the dusty gravel drive she found herself lying on.

Bursting out from the doorway behind them came a vast heavy-set man, about as wide as he was tall, the elongated barrel of a shotgun hanging from a pair of thick, slab-like hands.

'You alright, boss?' he asked, coming to a halt to cast an ominously familiar pair of eyes over at Tanner.

'Perfectly, thank you. You can head back inside now.'

'Are you sure?'

'You seem to forget, Fred, I have Tiberius and Caligula to look after me, don't I boys?'

Hearing their names, the two dogs tilted their heads to stare up at their master, each offering him a doleful expression of loyal curiosity, as if desperate to be given another command.

Tanner waited for the man to disappear before continuing. 'You know, I could have sworn I'd seen that gorilla-like friend of yours before, quite recently in fact. I hope he's got a licence for that gun of his.'

'It's my gun, actually, and yes, I do.'

'I don't suppose any of them have had their barrels sawn off, by any chance?'

'Not that I can remember, but I do have quite a few, so I'd have to check.'

Taking another moment to make sure Vicky was alright, Tanner turned back to meet Clayton's gaze.

'I believe I mentioned to you before, Mr Clayton, that it's your responsibility to keep your animals under control, and I don't just mean your dogs.'

'What's wrong? They didn't bite you, did they?' Clayton replied, taking a moment to roll down the sleeves of his shirt.

As he did, Tanner couldn't help but notice the knuckles of his hands, both of which were red and visibly swollen.

'In the eyes of the law,' he continued, also noting the beads of sweat running down each side of his face, 'they don't have to bite to be considered dangerous.'

'That's a new one,' Clayton laughed.

'I suppose it is, relatively speaking. It was one of the amendments made to the Dangerous Dogs Act which came into effect in 2014. I made the effort to look it up after our last encounter. The changes also mean that it's your responsibility to ensure the safety of visitors attending your property.'

'But you're not visitors though, are you? You're trespassers. Very much unwelcome ones, at that.'

'Welcome or not, we're here to continue the search of your property.'

'I'm afraid that ship sailed, my friends. One of your

colleagues has already been and gone.'

'Detective Inspector Cooper, yes. We saw him on the way out. He's the person we're taking over from.'

Clayton's eyes shifted between Tanner's and Vicky's.'

'Your colleague informed me that the search had been officially completed, which I've been reliably informed means that you'll need to go fishing for another warrant.'

'I'm not sure who told you that,' Tanner replied, supressing a grin. 'The search is only over when the last remaining police officer has left the property in question. DI Cooper was still on your land when we arrived.'

'You're a sneaky little bastard, aren't you?' the man growled, much like one of the dogs sitting patiently by his feet.

'Right, well, anyway,' Tanner continued, glancing down at his watch, 'if you could make sure your dogs are suitably restrained, we'd better push on.'

'And if I don't?'

'Then we'd be left with little choice but to call for an armed response unit, have your dogs put-down, and have you carted-away for obstruction.'

Clayton folded his arms over his chest. 'I know, why don't you tell me what you're looking for. Maybe I can help?'

'You know what we're looking for, or should I say who. Your youngest son, Gary Clayton.'

The old man stopped to stare over at Tanner. 'My *younger* son?'

'OK, I must admit, we're looking for the older one as well; Thomas, isn't it? But first things first.'

'Well, I can assure you that neither of them are here. As I explained to your colleague, the last thing I heard – from your own DCI no less – was that Gary was being held inside Wroxham Police Station under some totally trumped-up and probably illegal charge. As for my other son, I've not seen him for decades, literally, not since I kicked him and that conniving bitch of a wife of his off my estate.'

'So I heard. Something about him attempting to have you assassinated in order to take over the family business.'

'Something like that.'

'And that was according to who?'

'I'm sorry?'

'Who told you that he tried to have you assassinated? It wasn't Gary, by any chance?'

Clayton shook his head, as if freeing it from unwanted memories. 'Forgive me, but what the hell has Thomas got to do with any of this?'

'Do you know where he went, after you kicked him out?'

'Not a clue.'

'You never tried to make contact?'

'Why on God's good Earth would I have wanted to do that?'

'No matter. I'm sure you'll be delighted to learn that he moved up here, to Norfolk.'

'Well, good for him!'

'He bought the Anchor Inn, the one over at Potter Heigham. You may have heard of it?'

'I can't say I have, but I've never been much of a pub goer.'

'You may be interested to hear that he had a son.'

'Really? That's nice.'

'His name's Martin, or at least it was. He grew up to become a Broads Ranger, shortly after having a daughter by the name of Susie.'

Clayton's stance changed ever-so slightly; his eyes dancing between Tanner's.

'Susie Longshore? You may have read about her in the news. She'd only just turned five and was about to start school when she went missing, shortly after her father was found murdered on board his boat.'

Tanner watched as the colour drained from the old man's face, leaving it pale and brittle, like the skin of a dried up rattle snake.

'Unfortunately, we've yet to find her. Neither have we been able to work out who murdered her father, at least not *exactly* who. But we're fairly sure we know why he was killed. Apparently, he was a keen photographer, often setting off before dawn to take pictures of the Norfolk coast. On one such trip he took a series of photographs featuring a group of people watching a tender being motored ashore from a passing yacht. At some point, either then or later, he must have worked out who those people were, more importantly, what they'd been doing there; using the quiet Norfolk coast to smuggle drugs into the UK, before hiding them inside a fleet of hire boats for unwitting tourist to help distribute them inland. I must admit; that last part is pure conjecture, at least for now, but I've requested a forensics unit to take a look at some of the hire boats in question. Anyway, having worked all that out, Martin Longshore then made the mistake of emailing the photographs over to your younger son, Gary, asking to meet. What he probably didn't realise was just exactly who Gary was, or more importantly, that you were his father, the founder and head of the notorious Camden Crime Syndicate. He certainly could never have known what the reaction would have been to the news that someone was trying to blackmail them. My only question is, was it you who murdered your grandson, or was that particular job left for Gary?'

Tanner watched as Frank Clayton's natural

intimidating demeanour all but disappeared, leaving in its place nothing but the dried-up husk of a tired old man, his eyes glazed; tears creeping towards the corners of each.

'And now your eldest son, the *legitimate* heir to your criminal empire, tricked out of his rightful inheritance some twenty-five years ago by your other more treacherous son, is seeking his bloody retribution for the murder of his own, torturing your most faithful employees to find out if it was you, or Gary who'd killed him, and just what one of you has done with his granddaughter.'

Clayton eyes fell to look down at his hands, turning them slowly over to show the swollen red knuckles lining the backs of each.

'And there's you thinking that it was Gary out murdering your most loyal associates, in what you probably thought was his own bid to take over your business, just as you'd been led to believe Thomas had attempted to do, all those years ago. Oh dear. I do hope you weren't too hard on him.'

A sudden explosion from inside the house had the three of them turning to face the doorway.

Jumping to their feet, the two Rottweilers charged around their owner's legs, barking with rabid fury as they hurled themselves through the still open front door, disappearing into the blackness beyond.

- CHAPTER SIXTY SIX -

TANNER AND VICKY watched in silence as Frank spun around to launch himself after the dogs, shouting incoherently as he did.

The briefest glance at Vicky had Tanner charging inside, through a dark wood-panelled hallway, the sound of Vicky hard on his heels.

Bursting out into a large open kitchen, they found him down on his knees, the blood-soaked head of his gorilla-sized security guard cradled in his hands.

'Fred? Fred?' they heard Frank mutter, staring down into the man's ashen coloured face.

'Sorry boss,' came an eventual response, blood from his mouth splattering onto Frank's sweat-drenched shirt. 'He got my gun. Cartridges as well. Then he took Gary. I tried to stop 'im. Guess I fucked up.'

'Who took him?' Frank demanded, squeezing the dying man's head between his hands.

The man opened his mouth to answer, only for his eyes to roll back inside his head; an empty whisper sliding out from his collapsed blood-filled lungs.

They watched in silence as Frank rested the man's head gently down onto the cold tiled floor.

'He must have meant your other son,' Tanner muttered, taking a tentative step towards them.

The distant sound of barking had him staring over to the back of the kitchen, where an old door with green flaking paint swung listlessly in the thick summer's air.

'Where does that lead?' he asked, stepping around the body, and the old man kneeling beside it.

Frank lifted his head to stare over at the door. 'The old boathouse, down by the river.'

Realising that meant whoever had taken Gary Clayton must have been planning an escape by boat, Tanner threw himself at it to begin charging down a unkept narrow path, a high crumbling wall on one side, trees and shrubs on the other.

Hearing Vicky following behind, he continued along, chasing the sound of the dogs barking with frenzied fury up ahead.

Another blast from a gun drove them on, around a corner, out into a barren patch of ground surrounded by the twisted branches of overhanging trees. Up ahead stood the boatshed, a rotting wooden structure with a crooked tiled roof. Lurking within its shadows Tanner could see two men. The largest of them was dragging the other one back, one arm locked around his neck. The other was hooked under the open hinge of a double-barrelled shotgun, a crooked finger clawing at the tops of two spent cartridges, tendrils of smoke drifting out from each.

But the sight of the gun wasn't what brought Tanner and Vicky skidding to a halt. It was the two Rottweilers they could see just a few feet away, one lying on the ground, a bloody stump where its head used to be. The other was down on his haunches, his teeth bared at the man who he must have seen butcher his canine brother, just moments before.

Desperate for a weapon of his own, Tanner corralled Vicky behind him before remaining just as still as possible. He knew who the two men were, even though the larger one's face was part-hidden by an old sailing cap pulled down over his eyes. The other's face was a virtually unrecognisable mess of blood and tears; snot dribbling down from a shattered nose.

'Thomas Longshore,' Tanner called out, 'you're going to have to let your brother go.'

A sterile silence followed, marred only by the ominous sound of growling from the remaining dog, and the whining sobs spluttering out from what was left of Gary Clayton's broken face.

Tanner continued to watch as Thomas Longshore fumbled with the cartridges as he attempted to re-load the gun. But with one arm clamped around his younger brother's neck, it was proving to be an impossible task.

Cursing in panicked frustration, he glared up at Tanner.

'You wouldn't be asking me that if you had any idea what he's done.'

'We know he killed your son, Mr Longshore, but this isn't going to bring him back.'

'You don't understand. This weasel-faced shit of a brother of mine has ruined my entire fucking life. Not only did he steal my inheritance, leaving me without a single fucking penny to my name, he then follows me to Norfolk, murders my only son and abducts my five-year-old granddaughter, dragging her off to wherever he's been keeping the others to have his disgusting way with her. So you'll forgive me if I don't comply with your request, at least not until he tells me where she is. Even then, I'm going to need some persuasion not to rip his fucking head off.'

'B-but I-I keep t-t-telling you,' his brother spluttered, tears cascading down his face, his hands tugging desperately at his brother's forearm, 'I didn't take her! I promise I didn't!'

'You're lying!' Longshore insisted, squeezing

Gary's neck to the point that blood started to ooze out from his snot-filled shattered nose.

The sound of footsteps thundering down the path behind them had Tanner turning to see Frank Clayton, running out into the clearing to stare about, sweat pouring down his weathered reddened face.

'Oh, look who it isn't,' Longshore spat, glaring over at him. 'Good of you to join us. You know, I'm surprised you're still alive; although, judging by the colour of your face, I doubt you will be for long.'

'Thomas?' Frank questioned, dragging his eyes up from the body of the decapitated dog, what was left of its body twitching spasmodically on the ground.

'Yes, dad, it's me! To be honest, I'm surprised you even remembered.'

'But – what have you done?' Frank continued, his attention drifting back to what was left of his dog.

'What, you mean apart from killing your little canine friend? Not much – unlike my fucked-up little brother. Did you hear he murdered my son? The child-molesting little shit took my granddaughter as well.'

'But – he didn't!'

'He didn't what? Murder my son, or take my granddaughter?'

'He didn't take your granddaughter!'

'I see. And how do you know that? Let me guess, he told you he didn't, so you believed him.'

'I know because I was there. I'm sorry, but it was me who told him to kill the Broads Ranger. I had no choice. The guy was trying to blackmail us, but I didn't know he was your son. I'd have never allowed a finger to be placed on him had I have known, I promise!'

Longshore laughed hysterically. 'What, you mean like how you never laid a finger on us when we were growing up? That's hilarious, Dad, really it is. I assume you've seen Gary's face, being that I reckon it was you made him look like that.'

'Yes – but – I – I thought *he* killed my lawyer and accountant. But it wasn't him, was it. It was you!'

'I must admit, the plan had been to make you think it was Gary, but that wasn't my main objective. I was endeavouring to find out what they knew about my murdered son and missing granddaughter; where she was, and if it was Gary here who was responsible. Unfortunately, my patience expired before they did, but I'm confident I'll have more luck with the actual culprit.'

'But I've already told you. Gary didn't take her. She was still on board when we left the boat.'

'LIAR!' Longshore screamed.

'He's t-telling the truth,' Gary gasped, straining his eyes to try and stare up into his brother's face.

'She's dead, isn't she?' Longshore demanded, tightening the grip around his brother's neck.

'I - keep - telling - you,' Gary gasped, his voice a faltering whisper, 'I - didn't - take - her.'

'Bollocks!' Longshore continued, increasing his vice-like grip, making his brother's eyes bulge as his face turned from red to puce. 'You've murdered her. That's why you won't tell me where she is, because there's nothing left but a rotting corpse, buried in a ditch with all the others.'

'Stop it, Thomas!' Frank shouted, his body shaking with furious rage. 'You're killing him!'

But his demand came too late. Gary's fingers had already begun slipping from his brother's forearm, his eyes glazing over as they did.

Seeing his arms fall down to his side like a discarded doll, the remaining dog took a deliberate step forward, saliva dripping from its glistening teeth.

It must have sensed that his master's friend was dead, leaving the vile-smelling human sheltering behind him vulnerable and exposed.

As the dog's hind legs crouched down to the ground, layers of sinuous muscle writhing beneath its lustrous black fur, Longshore must have known what was about to happen. His defensive shield had gone. All he had to keep him from being ripped apart by the raging animal in front of him was the shotgun, crooked helplessly over his arm.

Holding the dog's eyes, he eased the grip around his dead brother's neck to carefully pluck out the two spent cartridge cases. Discarding them onto the floor, he watched as the dog took another step forward, as he tried reaching down to his pocket, and the cartridges that could be seen bulging out from its corners. But he couldn't quite reach, not when his arm was still wrapped around Gary's limp broken neck.

'Fuck it,' he eventually muttered, letting his brother's body fall to plunge a hand deep into the pocket of his coat.

With the human's body now fully exposed, the giant dog lept at him in one swift movement, jaws open, teeth bared.

Falling backwards, Longshore cried out, the gun slipping through his fingers as he tried desperately to fight off the dog.

Tanner and Vicky stood helplessly by, as Frank Clayton charged forward, shouting furiously at the dog, desperate to rescue his last remaining son.

But this time the dog took no notice. Having tasted human blood, it didn't look like he was about to stop, not until he'd had his fill.

As its jaws clamped around Thomas's throat, Clayton lunged for the shotgun, fetching it off the ground to start scrabbling around for the cartridges.

With blood pouring over the dog's face as it gorged itself on what was left of his son's neck, Clayton fought to control his trembling hands. Finally able to insert a cartridge, he snapped the barrels closed, held the stock against his shoulder and fired.

- CHAPTER SIXTY SEVEN -

A NUMBING SILENCE followed as the smell of cordite drifted restlessly in the hot summer's air. At Frank Clayton's feet was what was left of the dog he'd shot at point-blank range, an unfeeling nerve making one of its paws spasm against the ground. Lying underneath the dog, his head hanging loosely from the end of a gouged-open neck, was his estranged older son, his body as still as the trees hanging above them.

Staring down into his son's unseeing eyes, Clayton fell to the ground to bury his face into the palms of his still trembling hands.

Tanner asked Vicky to call for an ambulance, before inching his way forward, curious to know if there was anything that could be done for the man's younger son. But before he'd even reached his body, he knew that he too was gone.

'It's my fault,' he heard Frank mutter, peeling his hands away to stare vacantly down at the ground. 'If I hadn't turned my back on Thomas, none of this would have happened.'

Tanner crouched down quietly beside him. 'Do you know where the missing children are?' he asked, his voice respectfully low.

'The missing children?' questioned Frank, his head lifting to meet Tanner's gaze. 'What about *my* fucking children?'

'Do you know where they are?' Tanner demanded, his voice strained with exhausted emotion.

'Jesus fucking Christ! How many more times! My son's not a paedophile! He didn't take that girl off the boat. It was that mental fucking retard.'

'What "mental retard"?' Tanner repeated, throwing his gaze over towards Vicky.

'The reed cutter. The one who works on my land. I saw him – as we motored away. He's the one who took the girl, not my son.'

'The girl, as in Susie; your son's granddaughter?'

Frank stared down at the ground again, nodding slowly as tears began falling from his screwed-up eyes.

Tanner glared at the side of his head with furious rage. 'You've known that all this time, but you never once thought to tell anyone?'

'Why should I care?'

'But – she was your great granddaughter!'

'Yes – but – I didn't know.'

'If you'd only told us,' Tanner began, 'your sons, the lawyer, and that accountant of yours; even your dogs – they'd all still be alive!'

Frank cast a confused pair of eyes into Tanner's.

'Thomas would have assumed it had been the reed cutter who murdered his son,' Tanner continued. 'He'd have had no reason to go after Gary.'

The faintest sound of a siren had Tanner shaking his head as he pushed himself up to his feet, leaving Frank Clayton's eyes to drift over the bodies that lay scattered on the ground around him.

Tanner turned to face Vicky. 'Did you tell the station?'

'I spoke to Forrester,' she nodded. 'Forensics has found traces of heroin in every Broadwater boat they've looked at so far.'

Tanner glanced back to see Frank Clayton reaching out for one of Thomas's lifeless hands. 'No surprises there. Did you hear what he said about who took the girl?'

'The reed cutter, yes.'

Tanner dug around inside his coat to pull out his notebook. 'I'm assuming he means the one who found the body of the lawyer,' he continued, rifling through its pages. 'What the hell was his name?'

With the sound of sirens drawing near, another much closer sound had Tanner glancing up towards the boathouse, and what he could see of the water beyond.

'I don't suppose that could be a police boat?' he queried, craning his neck.

'If it was, it would be some sort of record.'

As the dull white bow of a Broads Ranger's patrol boat drifted into view, a familiar woman's voice could be heard echoing out from the other side. 'Hello, is anyone there?'

'Christine?' Tanner called out, stepping over to the inky-black wooden structure to peer through to the other side.

'John? Is that you?' he heard the voice say, just as her messy head of curly greying blonde hair appeared through the gap.

'It is. What are you doing here?'

'I was downriver, working on that barbed wire fencing job, remember?'

'Of course. I'd forgotten about that.'

'I heard gunshots. Has anyone been hurt?'

Tanner deliberately avoided the question. 'You know that reed cutter we met a few days ago,' he began, ducking inside the boathouse to make his way over towards her, 'the one who used to be a client of yours?'

'You mean, Bill Thornton?'
'That's the one.'
'What about him?'
'I don't suppose you know where he lives, by any chance?'

- CHAPTER SIXTY EIGHT -

LEAVING VICKY TO manage the incoming emergency services, Tanner stepped on board the patrol boat, pushing it out as he did for Christine to begin motoring them further up the narrow meandering waterway.

'How far?' he asked, staring ahead to see the blades of Dunford Windmill, rising above a corn yellow blanket of gently undulating reeds.

'Only about ten minutes. It's a remote cottage at the end of the channel.'

With the boat falling back into silence, Christine angled her head to catch Tanner's eye. 'Are you going to tell me why I'm taking you to Bill Thornton's place?'

Tanner paused before answering. 'Gary Clayton's dead. His brother, too.'

'His brother?'

'Thomas Longshore.'

'You mean...Martin Longshore's father was Gary Clayton's brother?'

Tanner offered her a solemn nod. 'He was out for revenge for the murder of his son, whilst also trying to find out what happened to his granddaughter.'

'Jesus Christ. But – what's that got to do with Bill Thornton?'

'Frank Clayton saw him take Susie off Martin's boat.'

'You're telling me that Bill's the one who's been abducting all these children?'

'Looks like it.'

'No, I'm sorry,' Christine stated. 'I don't believe it. Bill's harmless. He wouldn't hurt a fly. Especially not children.'

'How can you be so sure?'

'Because I met with him for an hour every week for over fifteen years. There's no way he'd lay a hand on a child, not after what happened to his.'

Tanner tore his eyes from the horizon to look at Christine as she stood behind the wheel, her focus fixed on the water ahead. 'What happened to his children?'

Christine paused to draw in a breath. 'He found them when he came back from work one day. His wife had... She'd killed them with a kitchen knife, leaving their bodies floating down the river.'

A cold hard silence followed.

'She had a long history of mental illness,' Christine continued, 'but nobody ever thought she'd do such a thing.'

'How did you know it was her? Couldn't it have been the husband?'

Christine shook her head. 'It was definitely the wife. Apart from finding her prints on the knife she used, her clothes were drenched in their blood.'

'Did she actually confess?'

'She didn't have much of a chance.'

'How come?'

'Bill dealt out his own form of justice. He cut open her throat with the same knife she'd killed his children with.'

Tanner stared over at her with his mouth hanging open.

'But – you just said he wouldn't hurt a fly?'

'It was concluded the trauma of finding his children triggered a psychotic episode.'

'You mean, he wouldn't hurt a fly, apart from his wife.'

'It was an isolated incident.'

'According to who?'

'Me!' she stated, glaring over at him. 'And the jury agreed. It was a clear case of temporary insanity, very common in such horrific situations.'

Tanner returned his attention to the windmill. 'I assume he did time?'

'Ten years in Broadmoor.'

'Was it you who gave him the all-clear?'

'Not just me. The hospital's board of directors had to reach the same conclusion.'

'And then he was released?'

'On the condition that he continued to meet with me for an hour every week, until such a time as I felt he was well enough to continue without my help.'

'And when was that?'

Christine thought for a minute. 'It must have been a few months before...before I stopped practicing.'

'So how do you know something hasn't happened since then, to make him slip into a more permanent state of psychosis.'

'Well, I don't, but...'

'The constant sight of seeing people playing happy families together, up and down the Broads, for example? Isn't it true that people covet what they see around them; even more so if they're being continuously reminded of something they know they can never have? I'd have thought the sight of families enjoying endless holidays together could easily have sent him spiralling down into the depths of depression, eventually leaving him convinced that if he couldn't have children, why should anyone else.'

Christine shook her head with violent consternation.

'No! I'm sorry, John, but it's just not possible.'

'For the sake of the children, and all their families, I sincerely hope you're right.'

- CHAPTER SIXTY NINE -

THE BOAT FELL back into a sombre silence as they continued motoring along the narrow channel, the windmill looming ever-larger over the seemingly endless expanse of dry whispering reeds.

'It's up here somewhere,' said Christine, lifting herself up onto the balls of her feet to peer over the top of the wheelhouse roof. 'From what I remember, there should be a small pontoon on the right.'

'I think I can see it,' Tanner commented, his voice falling to a portentous whisper, 'or at least what's been tied to it.'

Jutting out from the bank ahead was the stern of a small wooden boat, a folded dark-red sail hanging off the end. 'You didn't tell me he had one of those.'

Christine shrugged, steering towards the short lopsided jetty they could see just past the boat. 'Doesn't everyone around here?'

Nudging the patrol boat between the old wooden dinghy and the time-blackened jetty, Tanner stepped carefully out, the wood beneath his feet creaking in protest as the entire structure leaned precariously over to one side.

With a mooring line held in his remaining good hand, he looped its end around a rusting chain, passing it back to Christine before helping her to step down.

Spying a gap in the reeds ahead, he led the way through, emerging moments later into an overgrown garden, a tired-looking cottage lurking at the end.

As they began picking their way over a weed-infested path, heading for the back of the house, a feeling of dread began turning over in his stomach. With a series of harrowing images dragging him back to the God-forsaken windmill he'd crept inside with Jenny, all those years before, he stopped where he was to stare over at a crooked set of steps that led up to a rotting door above.

Coming to a halt beside him, Christine glanced into his glazed-over eyes.

'Are you OK?'

'This place,' Tanner replied, his eyes remaining fixed on the door. 'It – it reminds me of something, that's all.'

She took a step forward. 'I can go in on my own; if you like?'

'No!' he replied, grabbing hold of her arm as she turned back to look at him. He'd grown fond of her over the last few days, but it was only then, staring down into her mesmerising green eyes, that he knew it had become something more. 'We can go in together,' he continued, pulling her gently back to climb the steps up to the veranda above.

Knocking hard on the door, he let it rattle on its rusty hinges to take a half-step back. As his eyes wandered over the house, up to the top, where a single dormer window jutted out from its grey thatched roof, for the briefest of moments he thought he saw a face, staring down into his. Blinking, he looked again, only to see that it wasn't a face, just the curved edge of a vase standing behind a pane of glass, smeared black with decades of dust and grime.

'Mr Thornton?' he called out, still checking the

house for signs of life. 'It's DI Tanner, Norfolk Police. Are you in there?'

The sound of a floorboard being trodden on, the other side of door they were standing beside had him jumping with a start.

'What do you want?' came the muffled unwelcoming voice of a man from the other side.

'We'd just like to have a quick word with you. That's all.'

There was no response.

'I have Christine Halliday with me,' Tanner thought to add, glancing around at her with a nod.

More silence followed, before the sound of a chain could be heard sliding off a metal latch.

As the door creaked open, a hooded pair of cold grey eyes peered out through the gap.

'May we come in?' Tanner enquired, offering the occupant an engaging smile.

'Why?' the man asked. 'I haven't done anything wrong.'

'We just want to come in for a chat, that's all.'

'Can't you ask me from out there?'

Tanner glanced over at Christine, inviting her to speak.

'Hi Bill,' she smiled, stepping forward. 'How've you been?'

'Well enough, I suppose,' he replied, his eyes resting on hers.

'We just wanted to ask you about the children; the ones who've been going missing recently. Maybe you've heard about them on the news?'

The man didn't reply.

'We were wondering,' she continued, with a nervous smile, 'we were wondering if you'd maybe seen any of them?'

'Why would I have seen them?'

'No reason. It's just that someone said they thought they might have seen you talking to one of them, onboard the boat she was taken from.'

The man's eyes shifted briefly over at Tanner before slowly returning to Christine.

'The only children I've seen are my own.'

'Your *own?*' she questioned, a look of confused uncertainty creasing her brow.

'Of course. You know I have children.'

'Yes, but Bill, that was a long time ago. Before your wife...'

'Before my wife...what? Ran off with that bastard brother of mine, dragging them along with her? Fortunately, for both their sakes, she came to her senses.'

'She "came to her senses",' Christine repeated, shooting Tanner a look of rising alarm. 'But – Bill – your wife. She's dead.'

'Don't be stupid!'

'Sorry, of course. My fault. That was silly of me. You should have told me she was back. Is it alright if we come in, to say hello? I haven't seen her in ages.'

The man narrowed his eyes. 'She's resting upstairs, with the children.'

'Just quickly. We won't be long.'

With his gaze shifting slowly to Tanner, the man eventually stepped back into the darkness behind, pulling the door open as he did.

Seeing her about to step forward, Tanner took hold of her arm to whisper, 'I don't like this.'

'Don't worry,' she replied, offering him a becalming smile. 'It's just a delusion he's having, nothing more. Once we show him that his wife isn't here, he'll be OK.'

'You don't think he's dangerous?'

'I really don't.'

'OK, but you'd better let me go first.'

'After you,' she smiled, gesturing ahead.

Taking a fortifying breath, Tanner lifted a foot to step cautiously inside, his eyes focussed on the cold grey eyes of the man staring at him from behind the door.

'Where did you say she was again?' Christine asked, nudging past Tanner.

'In the bedroom upstairs,' came Thornton's sullen response, lurching out of the darkness to begin guiding them towards the base of a dusty wooden staircase, one that didn't look like it had been used in years.

Following him slowly up to a landing above, the man stopped to rattle a key in the lock of a small dark wooden door.

'Sarah,' he whispered, nudging it open to take a half-step inside. 'There are some people here to see you.'

The cottage slipped into a heavy oppressive silence, broken moments later by the croak of what sounded like a woman's voice, drifting out from the inky blackness.

'But I told you, my dear, I'm resting.'

Tanner's head rotated slowly around, until he was staring directly into Christine's eyes.

'I think you've rested enough,' came the reed-cutter's chiding response.

Pulling his head out, he turned to face his two uninvited guests. 'You'll have to forgive her. She hasn't been well recently.'

Christine cast a reproachful eye over the man's dark weather-beaten face.

'Who've you got in there, Bill?'

'I've already told you.'

'Your wife is dead. You killed her, after she

murdered your children.'

'I can assure you that my wife is very much alive. Please, see for yourself.'

Christine's eyes darted over at Tanner, before she turned sharply on her heel to disappear into the darkness of the room beyond.

- CHAPTER SEVENTY -

DESPERATE NOT TO let her out of his sight, Tanner hurried in after to begin staring blindly about, his eyes straining to penetrate the darkness of the low ceilinged room in which he found himself stooping.

In what little light there was, he could just about make out an iron-framed double bed, pushed up against the wall to the left. It took him a full moment to realise that the bed wasn't empty. Lying inside, propped up against a large yellow-stained pillow, was a woman, a tangled mop of platinum blonde hair hanging down over a rake-thin skeletal face. But she wasn't alive. Far from it. Her body was nothing more than a desiccated corpse, its skin the colour of walnut, the lopsided hair a cheap synthetic wig.

The sound of shuffling from the opposite side of the room had Tanner and Christine lurching around. There, huddled in a shadow as black as the depths of hell, were the dirt covered faces of four tiny children, staring out at them like a discarded collection of porcelain dolls.

For one agonising minute, Tanner thought they too were dead, until one of them opened their delicate tiny pink mouths.

'Mummy? Daddy? Is that you?'

As a tidal wave of relief surged through Tanner's veins, he watched Christine drop to her knees, beaming a smile at them which overflowed with an abundance of love.

'I'm sorry, little one, we're not your mummy and daddy. Tell me, what's your name?'

'Alice,' the small girl replied.

'Alice! How lovely,' Christine replied. 'And who are your friends, Alice?'

The girl nudged her head around to take in the three children nestled in around her, their faces streaked with salt from long dried-up tears.

'This is Sam, and this is Charlie. The littlest one is Susie.'

'Well, it certainly is nice to meet you all. Tell me; would you like to come outside? Maybe we could get you all an ice cream. Then we can find your mummies and daddies. Would you like that?'

Each of the four children gave her a nervous nod, their petrified eyes never leaving hers.

'OK, just stay there for one moment. I'm going to have a very quick chat with your Uncle Bill.'

Rising to her feet, she turned slowly around to face their captor, a castigating scowl creasing her brow.

'The children you're keeping here, Bill; you know they're not yours.'

The giant of a man drew in a deep shuddering breath.

'I found them crying,' he eventually replied. 'Their parents weren't with them,' he continued, his sultry grey eyes glistening like slate left out in the rain. 'They couldn't have loved them, not nearly as much as I knew we could. So I brought them here to be with us, so we could start over.'

'But Bill, their parents *do* love them. They love them so very much. You can't take them away. It's not right. You know it's not.'

'But we can give them a good home here, filled

with laughter and love. I know we can. We just need to be given a second chance.'

'But Bill, your wife...!' Christine continued, her head turning to take in the body propped up inside the bed.

By the time she'd looked back, the reed-cutter's countenance had changed, the hue of his eyes morphing from a soft shimmering grey to something more akin to the colour of a steel-clad battleship.

'Anyway,' he said, lifting his head to pull his shoulders back. 'They're staying. And now that the two of you have so kindly decided to join me, you can remain here with us too.'

- CHAPTER SEVENTY ONE -

TANNER AND CHRISTINE looked on as Bill Thornton stepped back through the door, onto the landing behind.

Seeing him take hold of the handle, ready to pull the door closed, Tanner jumped forward, jamming his foot onto the frame.

Slamming the door against it, the reed-cutter cursed, pushing it open to try again.

Before he had the chance, Tanner threw himself through the gap, charging into his body with all his force.

Stumbling back, Thornton fell hard against the landing's rotting wooden banisters. As they first splintered, then gave way, he teetered on the edge, his body falling steadily backwards, like an ancient pine being forced down into a gorge by an unrelenting gale.

Seeing him disappear from view, Tanner was about to plunge over himself, when he felt a hand grab hold of his coat to heave him back.

Breathing hard, he turned to see Christine's head appear by his side.

Offering her a nod filled with both gratitude and relief, he watched as she edged her way towards the banister's splintered stumps, and the gaping precipice beyond.

With the floorboards creaking under her weight,

she leaned forward to stare down, leaving the house to fall into a stunned, mollified silence.

'Is he dead?' she eventually asked, her voice as brittle as an ancient corpse.

Tanner joined her to see Bill Thornton's body crumpled on the floor, his neck twisted and bent, blood as black as the night draining from a cracked open skull.

'I'd say he was,' came his eventual response.

A shuffling noise from behind had them both turning to find the children, peering out from the room they'd been imprisoned inside for so long.

'Is it all right if we come out now?' the tallest of them asked, her pleading eyes staring up into Christine's.

'Of course you can,' she replied, her face breaking into a smile as she crouched down to the floor.

Tanner turned away, searching his coat for his phone. 'I'm going to call the station,' he said, 'to let them know we've found them. Then I suggest re-uniting them with their parents.'

'But – I promised them ice cream,' Christine responded, glancing up as the children began to slowly emerge.

'Of course,' he replied, smiling down, 'I'd almost forgotten. Don't worry. We'll just have to find some for them on the way.'

- EPILOGUE -

'ARE YOU SURE you're happy, moving back into your house?' asked Tanner, the light from the setting sun catching Christine's hair as he watched her pile her clothes back into her suitcase. 'You don't want to wait for a few more days?'

'What, you mean in case Gary Clayton comes back to life?'

'Well, no, but – we don't know that it was definitely him who broke into your house. It could have been someone who worked for him, or maybe even his father.'

'Who you've just arrested for smuggling heroin into the country.'

'A charge which is unlikely to stick, being that we've yet to find any evidence linking him directly to it.'

Christine stopped what she was doing to stare up at him, sitting out in the cockpit. 'But I thought he owns all the hire boats they were using to ferry it inland?'

'It's his business which owns the boats, not him personally. We're all fairly sure that he's just going to say that he didn't know anything about it, and that it was all down to his younger son.'

'Even so,' she continued, 'there's no reason for him, or anyone else for that matter, to break into my house, tie me to a chair and start torturing me, just to find out if I know anything about their heroin import business, being that everyone already knows about it.'

Returning to her packing, she made a rather obvious attempt at changing the subject. 'Any news of that car of yours?'

Tanner cast his eyes down to the River Bure, slipping gracefully past the heavily varnished hull of his Broads cabin cruiser. 'It's all done. I just need to find the money to cover the cost.'

'How long till you get paid?'

'It's normally at the beginning of the month.'

'Will it be enough?'

'Probably not.'

'I suppose I could lend you some?'

'It's OK. I've still got a credit card I can use. There is another slight problem, though.'

'What's that?' she asked, her eyes searching the cabin for anything she may have missed.

'My arm,' Tanner laughed. 'Even if I could afford to pay for the work, I doubt I'd be able to drive it.'

'Would it help if I brought it back for you?'

'Possibly,' he began, taking a moment to stare down at his arm, opening and closing the fingers of the still bandaged hand, 'but with any luck, it shouldn't be too long before I can start using it again. Also, the car's an automatic, which will help.'

Finding a stray sock, she stuffed it into the corner of her suitcase.

'How about your job?' she asked, closing the lid to begin pressing down; tugging at the zip as she did.

'What about it?'

'Are you going to stay?'

'I've already been asked.'

'And...?'

Tanner shrugged. 'Well, I still need the money, so I will for now, at least. They're also not sure what's going to happen with Cooper. It's fairly obvious that he'd been working to protect the Clayton family, which could easily see him being kicked off the Force. If that happens, then I suspect Forrester will be begging me to stay.'

'Wouldn't it depend on what his motives were; if he was being blackmailed, for example?'

'I'm not sure. We'll have to wait to see what Professional Standards has to say.'

Seeing Christine finish closing the suitcase to begin dragging it out of the cabin, Tanner stood up, ready to offer her a hand.

'Are you sure you can't stay? I get the feeling I'm going to miss not having you around.'

'I'm only down the road.'

'You know what I mean.'

Hauling the suitcase up onto the cabin's bench seat, she turned to stare into Tanner's eyes.

'Look, John, I wouldn't have minded staying, but not when your fiancée used to live here. It just doesn't seem right.'

'No, of course,' Tanner replied, his eyes falling away.

'But it doesn't mean we have to stop seeing each other. I mean, you haven't even asked me out on a date, yet.'

Tanner lifted his gaze to stare into her translucent green eyes. 'Would you like to – go on a date with me?'

'I don't know,' she replied, offering him a flirtatious smile. 'As I said, you haven't asked me yet.'

*DI John Tanner
will return in
Storm Force*

- A LETTER FROM DAVID -

Dear Reader,

I just wanted to say a huge thank you for deciding to read *The Wherryman*. If you enjoyed it, I'd be really grateful if you could leave a review on Amazon, or mention it to your friends and family. Word-of-mouth recommendations are just so important to an author's success, and doing so will help new readers discover my work.

It would be great to hear from you as well, either on Facebook, Twitter, Goodreads or via my website. There are plenty more books to come, so I sincerely hope you'll be able to join me for what I promise will be an exciting adventure!

All the very best,

David

- ABOUT THE AUTHOR -

David Blake is an international bestselling author who lives in North London. At time of going to print he has written nineteen books, along with a collection of short stories. When not writing, David likes to spend his time mucking about in boats, often in the Norfolk Broads, where his crime fiction books are based.